USA TODAY BEST.

RACHAEL
BLOOME

THE
UNCOMPLICATED
CAFÉ

a
Blessings Bay
N o v e l

Series Reading Order

BLESSINGS ON STATE STREET

THE UNEXPECTED INN

THE UNBOUND BOOKSHOP

THE UNCOMPLICATED CAFÉ

THE UNINTENTIONAL TEAHOUSE

This series will forever be dedicated to Gwenn, the woman who inspired me with her God-given capacity to love without ceasing

Special Bonus Offer

AS A SPECIAL THANK YOU FOR READING, I've created an exclusive (and completely FREE) members-only area of my website called the Secret Garden Club. When you join, you'll receive access to a wealth of bonus content, including exclusive bonus scenes and more.

Oh, and did I mention FREE BOOKS?

Adding to the fun, the content is regularly updated, so you never know what goodies you'll find.

By joining, you'll also receive exclusive emails with writing updates, sneak peeks, sales, freebies, and giveaways.

I'd love to stay in touch! You can join here: www.rachael bloome.com/pages/secret-garden-club.

Read this book and more for free!

Chapter One

CECE

CeCe Dupree sprinkled cinnamon over the creamy coconut milk latte, keeping an eye on the mysterious man at the corner table. He'd frequented her café every morning for the last five days, soaking up the summer sun that filtered through the ample front window. Always alone, he barely spoke a word, except to place his beverage order. He requested something different each day, ranging from a strong black coffee to a frothy cappuccino. Now, he'd moved on to the fancier drinks.

As a fellow introvert, CeCe wouldn't normally mind a man of few words who kept to himself. But there was something about this particular patron—who had yet to reveal his name—that piqued her curiosity. And, honestly, her concern. His muddied brown eyes bore a sadness so deep, one glance made her chest tighten.

"Here you go." She slid the cheery lemon-yellow mug onto the table with her friendliest smile. "One coconut milk latte, extra hot."

"Thank you." Without meeting her gaze, he dug a hand into the pocket of his worn Levi's. A rough hand with deep grooves and dark freckles. A hand befitting a day laborer who worked long hours in the hot sun, not the gaunt, rail-thin man seated before her. She guessed him to be about forty, maybe younger, but his pallid appearance made it difficult to pinpoint an age.

"Can I get you anything else?" She wanted to feed him half the pastries in her shop. His thin shoulders filled out the faded gray T-shirt about as well as a metal coat hanger.

"No, thank you." He set a small irregular-shaped stone on the table, freeing both hands to cradle the oversize cup. The smooth sliver of sea glass gleamed in the sun, enhancing its soft aqua sheen.

CeCe had noticed the trinket before but never had the courage to mention it. Until today. "It's beautiful." She nodded toward the stone. "Aqua is my favorite color of sea glass. According to legend, it's the color most coveted by mermaids and is thought to bring good luck."

"Not this one," he muttered under his breath. The melancholy words mingled with the steam wafting from his mug, but any further explanation was silenced by his first sip.

Should she ask him what he meant by his mumbled statement? Or leave well enough alone? Before she could decide, the bell above the front door jangled.

Abigail Preston, one of her dearest friends, waved as she stepped inside.

"Excuse me." CeCe left Mystery Man to welcome her friend with a hug.

Abby's shoulder-length brown waves felt warm against her cheek and smelled of sunshine and salty sea air. When she pulled back, her expressive hazel eyes shone with all the joyful radiance of a woman in love. "Is there anything more beautiful than summer in Blessings Bay?"

CeCe laughed at her friend's blissful exuberance. Abby

had moved to the small Northern California town in early December, making this summer her first taste of the season. While CeCe couldn't deny her hometown's quintessential charm, she had a feeling Abby's euphoric mood could be attributed to more than the idyllic weather. "Only two weeks left until the big day! How are the wedding plans coming along?"

"The biggest task left is the cake."

"I think I can help you with that." CeCe led the way to the long counter lined with spotless glass display cases. Nearly every pastry imaginable, from classic cupcakes and eclairs to more unexpected offerings like plantain tarts and Jamaican rum cake, filled the shelves.

Abby settled at one of the tall barstools while CeCe ducked into the kitchen and returned with a tray of three miniature cakes, each one a delightfully different flavor.

"He's here again?" Abby whispered, nodding over her shoulder at Mystery Man, who stared blankly out the window, sipping his latte. Only a few tables away, he could probably overhear their conversation if they didn't take care to lower their voices.

"Five days in a row," CeCe whispered back.

"It looks like he's waiting for someone," Abby observed with a sympathetic frown.

"It does. But no one ever shows up."

"How sad. Do you think I should introduce myself? See if he's new in town?"

CeCe smiled. That was so like her magnanimous friend. Abby owned the only bed-and-breakfast in Blessings Bay, which she ran with her characteristic hospitality. "You could try. You might have better luck than I've had. But first, let's decide on your wedding cake. Is Logan coming?" As business partners who ran the inn together, as well as a newly engaged couple planning a wedding in a short time frame, the pair didn't do much apart these days.

"No, he couldn't make it. He said I could decide without him. As long as it doesn't include pineapple."

"I've got you covered. Not a shred of pineapple to be found." CeCe nudged the tray closer to her friend, her heartbeat fluttering as Abby surveyed the three one-of-a-kind offerings. Abby had specifically asked for an untraditional selection. Instead of the more common rich and sugary cakes with layers of thick fondant icing, she wanted something subtly sweet and unexpected. CeCe had relished the challenge.

"They all look incredible," Abby gushed. "I don't know where to start."

"Try this one first." CeCe handed her a fork, gesturing toward the third cake with its golden coconut flakes and artfully drizzled glaze. Her personal favorite. Why save the best for last? She wiped a smudge of flour from her wire-rimmed glasses, not wanting to miss a nuance of Abby's expression when she sampled her first bite.

Ever since she was a little girl, mirroring her mother as they made their family's traditional Caribbean recipes, she'd loved creating culinary magic. They'd tie their wayward black curls into messy buns but wouldn't bother with aprons. Or, heaven forbid, gloves. They'd meticulously wash their hands, of course, but according to her mother, food should be touched—it should be felt all the way from the fingertips to the depths of a person's soul.

CeCe smiled at the mental image of her mother, elbow deep in a bowl of boiled sweet potato. While she mashed, she'd smear a dollop of the burnt orange paste onto each cheek, claiming it kept her skin youthful. Considering her mother's smooth, dark complexion had hardly a wrinkle, even in her sixties, CeCe was inclined to believe the beauty hack worked.

When they'd finally savored the sweet potato pudding, the fruits of their labor always tasted better than any store-bought brand. CeCe suspected it had something to do with the time they'd spent together, laughing, talking, and making memories.

"Food is the universal love language," her mother regularly reminded her. Not that all the five-star gastronomic master-pieces in the world could keep her globe-trotting father around. As an archeologist for hire, he preferred traveling the world excavating private dig sites in exotic and exciting locales to dinners at home with his wife and daughter. Tonight would be an exception, and he'd finally join them for a family meal.

"Now this, *this* is heavenly," Abby murmured, dragging CeCe's thoughts from her father's long-anticipated homecoming. "What is it?"

"It's my own twist on a Toto."

"Toto?" Abby cocked her head, trying to place the unfamiliar word.

"Caribbean coconut cake."

"Yes! That's what I'm tasting. Toasted coconut. And—?"

"A zesty lime glaze to complement the sweetness."

"Okay, this is it. This is the one I want. I don't even need to try the other flavors. It'll match our beach wedding vibe, and Logan and Max will love it. Max devours anything with coconut."

"Perfect." CeCe adored the way Abby lit up with a special motherly glow whenever she spoke about her foster son, Max. Her voice grew louder and more animated, too, as if she couldn't contain her happiness. "I'll box up the rest of the coconut cake, along with the other two samples, for you and Logan to enjoy later." She grabbed a pastry box from underneath the counter. "When does Max get back from summer camp?"

"In a few days. I can't wait. I've missed him like crazy.

Although, between Max being gone and Logan and I deciding not to book any more guests at the inn until after the wedding, I've been able to knock out the to-do list pretty quickly. I'm heading over to see Bonnie at Sweet Blessings next, to finalize the favors. We're bundling an assortment of saltwater taffy into cute little gift bags."

"Feel free to put a few extra in mine," CeCe teased.

"I'll see what I can do." Abby grinned as she slid off the stool.

CeCe arranged the sample cakes inside the box, then had an idea. Lifting the white chocolate amaretto flavor, she nodded toward Mystery Man. "Mind if I—?"

Abby followed her gaze, her eyes glinting with understanding. "Of course! That's a lovely idea. It's not like I need the extra calories two weeks before my wedding anyway," she said with a laugh.

CeCe set the cake off to the side, hoping she could convince the man to accept the gesture under the guise that it would go to waste otherwise.

Abby turned to go, the pastry box tucked under one arm, then hesitated briefly before asking, "Speaking of the wedding, have you decided if you're bringing a plus-one?"

CeCe grimaced. "No, I haven't. I'm sorry. But I promise to let you know soon. By tomorrow," she rushed to add, feeling guilty even though Abby assured her it wasn't a big deal.

As CeCe watched Abby step back into the bright summer sunshine, she resolved to make a decision once and for all. Go solo or succumb to another friend's persistent setup attempt? According to Sage Harper, her boyfriend's old college roommate was a total catch, despite his East Coast zip code. Never mind the fact that CeCe needed a long-distance relationship about as badly as food poisoning.

The only person she actually *wanted* to invite to Abby's

wedding was currently halfway across the world in the arms of another woman, which she should count as lucky. In the realm of bad decisions, dating her childhood best friend ranked higher than eating a batch of questionable shrimp, no matter how tantalizing.

Chapter Two

JAYCE

JAYCE HUNT gently cupped the side of his co-star's face with his palm, gathering a bolstering breath. *Okay, let's get this over with.*

Stacey Sawyer gazed up at him with her enormous brown eyes as the warm Bali breeze tossed her long shimmering blond hair around her bare shoulders. She looked every inch the A-list star in her ethereal white gauzy dress. No wonder the camera loved her.

She tilted her chin, simultaneously parting her lips and fluttering her eyelids closed. The woman could fake eternal love better than anyone in the business. He should take notes.

Sliding an arm around her waist, he drew her closer, just like they'd practiced a thousand times before, and shut his eyes. Her tanned skin smelled like fresh coconut. *Perfect.* The familiar scent would make it easier to imagine the woman he actually *wanted* to be holding on the beautiful white sand beach as the sun glittered across the water behind them.

Picturing his secret dream girl, he lowered his lips toward Stacey's, pausing the second he felt her gentle breath. He tilted his head, expertly angling his jawline to give the camera the appearance of a deep, undying kiss, without actually making contact.

They held the pose until the director shouted, "Cut! That's a wrap!" and then immediately snapped out of character.

"You had a poppy seed muffin right before filming, didn't you?" The twinkle in Stacey's eyes belied her accusatory tone.

"Smells better than fish taco breath, right? I'm making progress," he teased. "I don't have any seeds in my teeth, do I?"

"No, thankfully. Goodness knows we don't want to reshoot, since Harry is already in a foul mood thanks to you."

"Yeah, sorry about that." Jayce felt slightly guilty that the no-kissing clause he had written into every contract irritated the director, but not enough to change his mind. When he kissed a woman, he wanted it to mean something.

"Hey, don't apologize. Rob loves the clause. He says I should only film movies with you from now on." She laughed but kept her voice low enough to not be overheard by the film crew.

"Too bad you couldn't sneak him onto our flight. Bali would make the perfect honeymoon destination." He'd only met her fiancé once, but he'd instantly liked his easy, down-to-earth demeanor. The guy's only flaw—if it could even be called a flaw—was that he couldn't stand anything to do with Hollywood. According to Stacey, their relationship had only survived because she'd managed to keep it a secret from everyone except for family and a few close friends. He considered it an honor to be included in the tight-knit, clandestine circle. Not that he'd shared his own secret with her. At least, not yet.

"I know. We talked about it but decided it wasn't worth the risk. We're eloping after the RCAs in a few weeks," she said, referring to a prestigious award ceremony honoring achievements specific to the romantic comedy genre held in Hollywood each year. "And honestly, if we weren't each nominated in multiple categories, I'd skip the ceremony altogether. That's how excited I am!" She beamed as if the mere thought of her impending marriage lit her up from the inside.

"I'm happy for you two." He tried his best to sound sincere.

"You know, for one of Hollywood's most beloved actors, you're not very convincing," she said with a lighthearted smile.

"Sorry. It's not you guys. It's—"

"I know, I know," she groaned, hinting he may have shared his philosophy one too many times. "You don't believe in love. Which is ironic since *People Magazine* just named you the Swooniest Star on Screen."

"I believe in love. I'm just not convinced it lasts. At least, not for most people." And definitely not for his parents, who went from blissfully married to bitterly divorced by the time he hit puberty. As if dealing with razor burn and body odor wasn't bad enough.

"'Tis better to have loved and lost than to never have loved at all." Stacey recited Tennyson's old adage with exaggerated theatrics.

Jayce chuckled at her melodramatics, holding up his hands in mock defeat, although he still wasn't convinced. But hey, if other people wanted to risk the kind of soul-crushing pain caused by an inevitable breakup, who was he to stop them?

"You two were fabulous!" Gretchen Schroeder stumbled across the sand in her ridiculous high heels. Would it kill the woman to wear a pair of flip-flops?

He exchanged an amused glance with Stacey. They'd shared the same agent for years, and her absurd antics—like wearing a black Prada pantsuit on the pristine white beaches of Bali—no longer fazed them.

"Another blockbuster on the books." Gretchen wiped a damp strand of overly bleached hair off her forehead. "Ugh. I can't wait to get out of this wretched humidity."

She teetered on the uneven ground, and Jayce reached out a hand to steady her. He knew better than to remind Gretchen she could've stayed in Los Angeles. *Good ol' Gretch.* For better or worse, their agent slash publicist believed in being hands-on. While they occasionally found her dedication annoying—and Stacey struggled to keep her relationship with Rob a secret—they couldn't deny the woman's results. Their careers had soared ever since they'd signed with her, save for one tiny speed bump.

"This film is going to put you back on top after our momentary blip," Gretchen declared with inflated confidence. Ever since their romantic comedy *Tacos and Tango* didn't do as well as they'd hoped, she'd refused to mention it by name. She'd sidestep around the title with terms like *blip*, *hitch*, and *fluke*. "And I have just the strategy to catapult you beyond the stratosphere of stardom."

Jayce bit back a groan. By "strategy" she meant a publicity stunt. What would it be this time? For *Tacos and Tango*, she'd arranged for them to help teach tango lessons at a rec center in an underserved community. He was pretty sure they would've preferred free tacos instead, but when Gretchen got an idea into her head, she ran with it. And it usually worked. The operative word being *usually*.

"What is it?" Stacey asked warily. "I'll do anything as long as it doesn't prolong the press tour." They'd agreed to a two-pronged promotional attack—one tour after filming and another shortly before the film's release. Unfortunately, when it came to being an actor, the actual *acting* only accounted for half the job.

"Don't you worry your pretty little head. The schedule won't change. But I'll need you both on board with my plan." Gretchen shot a pointed glance between them. "I'm talking full cooperation."

Would she cut to the chase already? "What's your brilliant ploy this time?"

"Not a ploy. It's a tried-and-true tactic. It's worked for countless actors before, and it'll work for you two. If you do exactly as I say."

Good grief. At this rate, the movie would be done with post-production by the time she finished her pitch. "What's the plan, Gretch? We've never said no to one of your schemes before."

"Again. Not a *scheme.* A strategy." She fanned herself with the edge of her Hermès scarf. "It's no secret you two make the perfect couple. It's why you'll win a BOCA this year," she said, mentioning their nomination for the Best On-Screen Couple Award for the millionth time that month. "With Stacey's big Bambi eyes and her ability to pull off the sultry ingénue paradox, and Jayce, with your dark Italian good looks and a charm that's both roguish and boyish, you've been America's favorite sweethearts for years. And it's time we give the fans what they want."

Uh-oh. He didn't like where this was headed...

"By the time you two land back in LA we'll have *accidentally*"—she punctuated the word with air quotes—"leaked your off-screen romance."

His heart slammed into his stomach.

"And not just your boring, run-of-the-mill boyfriend-girlfriend situation," Gretchen continued. "You two are *engaged*." Her lips curled into a devious smile, reminding Jayce of a cartoon villain. "Your fans will eat it up."

And you know who won't? Jayce thought. *Stacey's actual fiancé, Rob.* He turned to gauge her reaction.

She met his gaze, her face pale. Her pleading glance said everything he needed to know.

"Sorry, Gretchen," he said crisply. "No can do."

"Excuse me?" Her green eyes narrowed. She wasn't used to hearing *no*.

"I know we agreed to let you call the shots, but we're going to have to pass this time. Why don't we come up with something else?"

"Why don't we come up with something else?" Gretchen repeated, her tone incredulous with a touch of *do-you-know-who-you're-talking-to?* She flashed an icy, ominous smirk that would've made Jayce shiver if it weren't so hot under the blazing sun. "Have you taken a look at my client list lately?"

"It's very impressive."

"And what about my contract? The contract *you* signed," she added pointedly. "Have you had a gander at that recently?"

"I'm familiar with the terms."

"Then you know there is no *we*. You've reached your level of fame because of *my* guidance. I make stars. It's what I do. And I'm pretty darn good at it. It's why you pay me the big bucks. And it's why you're going to trust me this time, just like all the times before. Right?" She'd sweetened her tone, but her smile still gave off supervillain vibes. She could be ruthless when she didn't get her way. He might be able to handle being on Gretchen's bad side, but what about Stacey?

He shot his co-star another glance. She'd gone from pale to putrid green. A dead ringer for how she'd looked on yesterday's sailing excursion right before she'd spewed her lunch all over the side of the yacht.

To make matters worse, Gretchen pinned her with her most persuasive smile. "Stacey, darling. You see the wisdom in my proposal, don't you? Please convince your shortsighted co-star that this is what's best for your career. For *both* of your careers."

Stacey's mouth fell open. She mirrored a limp fish gasping for air. "I—I—I—"

Great. She was stuck in a single syllable panic loop. He

needed to do something, but what? Gretchen wouldn't back down easily.

"I can't fake an engagement with Stacey," he announced before he'd formulated a coherent plan.

"And why not?" Gretchen crossed her arms with a *this-better-be-good* glare.

"Well, because, I—" *Come on, man. Come up with something. There's got to be a reasonable explanation in your brain somewhere.* "Because I'm already engaged," he blurted, then instantly winced. So much for reasonable—more like irrational. Idiotic. Irredeemably asinine. *What were you thinking?*

"You're engaged?" Gretchen's tone dripped with skepticism.

"Yep. Have been for a while now. To a girl back home." *Great. Just keep digging the hole deeper, dummy. Oh, the foolish things we do for friends.*

Stacey gaped at him, looking both shocked and grateful.

Gretchen scowled. "And why am I just now hearing about this?"

"She's a small-town girl. Not one for the limelight. She asked me to keep it on the down-low." Okay, so he'd stolen Stacey and Rob's story, but this way, they wouldn't have to go through with the fake engagement fiasco and Gretchen wouldn't find out the truth until after his friends tied the knot.

"And does your blushing bride-to-be have a name?"

"A name?"

"Yes, a name is the form of identification written on a birth certificate." Gretchen may not know how to conjure a sincere smile to save her life, but she could teach a master class in snark.

"Yes, she has a name. It's—" *Shoot.* He should've anticipated this question. *Pick a name. Any name. Don't overthink it.* "CeCe. CeCe Dupree."

Drat. Okay, so he should've thought about it a *little.* For more than five seconds, at least. Instead, he'd said the first name that came to mind—the one name *always* on his mind.

Jayce bit back a groan. *CeCe's going to kill me.*

Although, they'd had a fake wedding once already. In kindergarten. She'd worn a dandelion crown, and he'd borrowed his dad's tie, which he'd tucked into the collar of his T-shirt because he had no clue how to tie one. They'd invited all their favorite stuffed animals to the ceremony and celebrated with Oreos and juice boxes afterward. They'd had a blast.

Maybe he could appeal to her sense of nostalgia? Or her inner romantic? After all, didn't all women love weddings?

Chapter Three

ABBY

ABBY NEVER UNDERSTOOD the wedding hype until her entire world changed the day Logan proposed. Her first wedding had been all about her late husband, Donnie. He'd wanted the big shindig to show off to all his air force buddies, but without many loved ones to invite, Abby had hoped for a more intimate ceremony. Instead, she'd spent their reception smiling in snapshots with a bunch of pseudo friends and strangers. This time would be different, though. The people of Blessings Bay had become her family, and she couldn't wait to celebrate with them.

Buoyed by her blissful thoughts, Abby exited Sweet Blessings and paused on the sidewalk to soak up the summer ambiance. Across from Main Street, a grassy promenade underscored the vibrant blue hue of the Pacific Ocean.

She tilted her chin toward the sky and briefly closed her eyes, inhaling deeply. With only two weeks until the wedding, the sun felt warmer, the briny breeze smelled sweeter, and her heart swelled with joy. She couldn't wait to become Mrs. Logan Mathews.

Her steps light, she strolled down Main Street, headed toward home. On her right, the Victorian-style storefronts painted in soft shades of lilac, lemon drop, and periwinkle beckoned to her with their whimsical window displays, but she didn't stop to browse. Nor did she join the festive farmers market filling the promenade with music, laughter, and the mouthwatering aroma wafting from the various artisan vendors offering their wares.

In a few hours, Max's social worker, Carla Delgado, would stop by the inn to discuss the possibility of adoption. From the moment Abby welcomed Max into her home last December, Carla had approved of the placement, doing everything in her power to make sure Max could stay in Abby's care. Abby didn't doubt Carla would move mountains to ensure a smooth adoption process. Which meant, soon Abby would have the family of her dreams. After so much heartache, hope for a better future burned bright.

As had become a habit lately, a spontaneous grin spread across her face. She wanted to skip or sing or hug the next person who walked past. Before she could do either, the bell above a shop door jangled. Abby moved out of the way, making room for a tourist exiting the art gallery. As she sidestepped, she caught sight of a reflection in the gallery window—a tall, waifish figure that looked vaguely familiar. Was it the man from CeCe's café?

Abby turned around to wave, but Mystery Man halted midstep, quickly fixing his attention on a pretty watercolor painting in the window. He stared intently at the seascape, as if he'd never seen the ocean before. *Oh, well.* She'd say hi another time.

Resuming her stroll, Abby spotted Mystery Man's reflection again. He'd abandoned his perusing and followed a few feet behind. *Glad to see him out and about, enjoying the town for a change*, Abby mused with a smile.

After checking the time on her phone, she quickened her pace, anxious to get home to prepare a few snacks for Carla's visit. Was it her imagination or was Mystery Man also walking at a brisker clip?

She shrugged off the suspicion and turned right at the single stoplight in town onto State Street. The charming tree-lined lane bordered by beautiful historic homes sat high on a regal bluff. Where the houses ended, a nature trail began, traversing the rugged cliff side, providing miles of pristine coastline views. How did she get so lucky to live here?

Glancing over her shoulder to check for cars before she crossed the road, she noticed Mystery Man had also turned onto State Street. He froze when she spotted him, suddenly keenly interested in a hedge of roses. *Odd. Why does he stop whenever I turn around?* She tried to shake the eerie feeling he'd been following her. *He must be heading for the nature trail*, she surmised.

But as she continued her trek, she hastened her step.

Footsteps echoed on the pavement behind her.

Strange. He'd resumed his walk, too. Was the timing a coincidence?

She resisted the irrational urge to run the last few feet home. *This is ridiculous. Just stop and say hi.* Gathering a breath, she spun around, summoning her friendliest smile.

Mystery Man immediately dropped to one knee, pretending to tie shoelaces that appeared perfectly intact.

Abby's pulse pounded an uneasy rhythm. *Okay, something is definitely off with this guy.* She didn't care how silly or paranoid she appeared. Tucking the cake box tightly under one arm, she scurried down the street, just shy of breaking into a jog.

The elegant two-story Victorian with pale blue paneling

and a wide, welcoming porch greeted her like a safe haven from a storm. Her adrenaline surging, she scrambled up the steps and burst through the front door, plowing straight into a solid wall of muscle.

"*Oof*," Logan grunted as she collided with his chest. "Easy, Turbo. Are you trying to break the sound barrier?"

"Sorry," she panted, red-faced and flustered. "I—" She hesitated. *I—what? I thought I was being stalked by a strange man who likes to tie his shoes for no reason?* Suddenly, her fears sounded a little far-fetched.

She cast a surreptitious glance over her shoulder at the peaceful, empty street. Where did he go?

"Are you okay?" Logan asked, his teasing tone giving way to concern.

She peered one last time at the vacant stretch of road before closing the door on her vanishing Mystery Man. "I'm fine. I just — I was eager to get home."

Logan's strong features softened into an understanding smile that illuminated his brilliant blue eyes and sent the butterflies in her stomach into a frenzy. Somehow, the man managed to put her at ease *and* send her heart racing. "I get it. I'm eager to hear Carla's news, too." He dropped his gaze to the crumpled cardboard in her hand. "What's in the box?"

"Wedding cake samples." She pried back the lid, grateful they weren't smushed from the collision.

"Did you decide on a flavor?"

"I did. And wait until you taste it." Her grin returned, all tension from the unofficial footrace forgotten.

"Why wait?" Logan reached for the box, but Abby dodged his attempt.

"In the kitchen. With a fork like a civilized human," she teased, leading the way.

She watched with satisfaction as Logan devoured the rest of

the Toto cake, repeatedly praising her choice between bites. While he dug into the other flavor—with no regard for calories, Abby noted with bemusement—she prepared a tray of treats and appetizers along with a pot of Carla's favorite raspberry tea.

With each passing second, her apprehension mounted. What if Carla didn't have good news? What if the court denied their adoption request? Or deemed the timing too soon?

Her chest squeezed. She loved being Max's foster mom, and in her eyes—and heart—the foster status didn't make him any less her son. And yet, she couldn't deny the benefits of adoption. Most notably, the permanency. She'd almost lost Max before, and it had nearly broken her. She couldn't risk losing him again. Not when he claimed such a critical place in her heart.

Abby placed the steaming teapot on the sterling silver tray, her fingers trembling. She knew she shouldn't place all her hopes on an ideal scenario. Max had a tricky case. Even if Carla tried her best, there were extenuating circumstances outside their control. *Hurdles*, Carla had called them. She'd been careful not to make any promises.

The doorbell chimed.

Abby jumped, spilling some of the cream on the counter. Jittery, she quickly mopped up the mess.

Logan removed the damp dish towel from her hand and pulled her into his arms.

She melted against his chest, basking in the comfort of his embrace.

"No matter what Carla tells us today, it'll be okay," he murmured, planting a reassuring kiss on top of her head. "We're a family. And that will never change."

She buried her face in his soft T-shirt, inhaling his distinct scent of warm earth from tending the garden and the tangy peppermint of his pain relief balm.

Of course, he was right. So why wouldn't her hands stop shaking?

"I'll bring the snacks to the sitting room, if you can get the door," she said with the steadiest voice she could muster.

She gripped the cool silver handles with clammy palms, repeating a silent prayer. *Dear God, please let her have good news.*

Chapter Four

LOGAN

LOGAN MATHEWS CLASPED Abby's hand on the couch cushion between them, holding his breath as Carla rooted through her beat-up briefcase.

"As you know," Carla said, retrieving an overstuffed file, "Max's case is unusual."

"That's an understatement." Logan tried to sound light-hearted, while internally his pulse thundered as fiercely as the engine of an F-16.

Abby must have sensed his nervous energy through her fingertips because she tightened her grip.

"True," Carla conceded with a kind smile. "Between his mother's death as an infant, his father's disappearance last year, and the absence of extended family, his situation is one of my most challenging."

"Not to mention all the other garbage the poor kid's been through." The muscles in Logan's jaw still tensed whenever Max's traumatic past sprang to mind. The foster family who used him as manual labor and pocketed all the money from the state without spending a single dime on Max's well-being, all while they ran an illicit operation selling pilfered Social Security and credit card numbers. Then, more recently, the woman who posed as Max's long-lost relative and nearly abducted him, all because Max had unwittingly taken a notebook filled with stolen credit card numbers. The kid had been through the ringer, and Logan would do whatever it took to give him a better life.

"Exactly," Carla agreed, flipping open the file on her lap. "Max has experienced enough trauma, which is why we need to proceed carefully."

Uh-oh. Logan stiffened. *Proceed carefully* didn't sound good. Was Carla going to turn down their adoption request? At the possibility, a heavy weight pressed against his chest, matching the suffocating force of pulling high Gs. He needed to get off the couch, to walk around and shake it off, but he couldn't move.

Abby laced her fingers through his, pressing their palms together as if she could transfer her superhuman strength via physical touch.

He met her gaze, amazed by the hopeful resiliency reflected in her hazel eyes, tempering his own fear and uncertainty. Not for the first time, he marveled at the unfathomable blessing that a woman like Abby would choose him.

Whatever bad news Carla brought to the table, they would get through it together. Logan squeezed Abby's hand in solidarity.

"I've been researching your request, and here's where we hit a few snags." Carla glanced between them, her countenance soft and sympathetic. "If we were dealing with a general paternal abandonment case, Max would likely be eligible for adoption after six months, as long as his father didn't provide any financial support or communication during that time. However, Max's situation isn't that simple. Technically, his father is considered a missing person, and in most missing person cases, you need to wait five years before they can be declared deceased, per California law."

"Five years?" Abby whispered, the disappointment in her voice mirroring his own.

"But everyone knows Sam Bailey's fishing boat went down in a storm," Logan pointed out, battling his mounting desperation. He'd wait five years to adopt Max if he had no other choice, but he wasn't ready to give up on a quicker solution just yet.

"That may be true. But since neither a boat nor a body has been recovered, it's still a missing person case." Carla's round, pleasant features strained with regret. Logan knew the compassionate social worker didn't like the situation any more than they did. "However," she added with the slow, cautious inflection of someone choosing their words carefully. "I could pressure the court to evaluate the extenuating circumstances. There is precedence for what's called an expedited presumption of death based on the nature of the person's disappearance and their likelihood of survival. If the outcome is in our favor, it's possible adoption proceedings could begin much sooner. Would you like me to pursue this course of action?"

"Yes, of course," Abby blurted, breathless with even the slightest chance of moving things along. She fixed Logan with her eager gaze, waiting for him to voice his agreement.

But the words wouldn't come. Time seemed to slow, then spiral in reverse. Suddenly, he was seven years old again, listening to his grandparents recount the fatal car accident that took his parents away. He'd refused to believe they were really gone. For weeks, his naive hope and optimism had comforted him like a warm embrace, making the world bearable. When he'd finally confronted their deaths, the overwhelming sense of loss and emptiness had terrified him. It was the biggest, scariest emotion he'd ever felt, and more than anything, he'd wanted his parents to help him through it. And the fact that they couldn't only made it worse.

Max still clung to the belief that his father would come back for him. If they asked the court to declare Sam Bailey deceased, they would take that hope away. Logan's heart ached at the prospect of putting Max through that kind of pain—the kind of pain that had left a lasting wound on his own heart.

Yes, he and Abby would be there for him, to help him heal in any and every way they could. And yes, in the long run, the stability of adoption seemed like the healthiest route for Max. But what if they got it wrong?

What if, in trying to do right by Max, they only made things worse?

"Can I think about it?" he asked at last.

"Of course. This is a big decision. Take your time." Carla closed the file.

Logan felt Abby's gaze boring into him, but he couldn't look at her. Not when he could already picture the gut-piercing glint of betrayal in her eyes.

All Abby had ever wanted was to be a mother. Would she forgive him for getting in the way of her heart's greatest desire?

Chapter Five

CECE

I'M JUST CLOSING up shop. I'll run upstairs to change and feed Spock, then I'll head over.

CeCe sent the text to her mother, then flipped the sign in the window to Closed and locked the door. She rarely closed the café early, but tonight she'd make an exception. Her wayfaring father was finally coming home after spending several months at a dig site in— Where were they excavating this time? Argentina? Peru? He hopped so many continents searching for ancient artifacts she struggled to keep track.

As she climbed the back stairs leading to her cozy apartment above the café, her mother's familiar words swam inside her head. *Don't be so hard on your father. He loves us very much.*

Just not as much as he loves being Indiana Jones, she wanted to retort. But she never did. Why hurt her mother more? As hard as she tried, Durene Dupree wasn't the eternally happy housewife she presented to the world, content with her garden, volunteer work, and part-time job at the art gallery.

Growing up, CeCe had heard her mother's quiet sobs through the paper-thin walls of their tiny beachfront bungalow more nights than not. And when they said grace at dinnertime, when her mother prayed for the Lord to keep her husband safe in faraway lands, CeCe knew she'd really asked God to bring him home.

Tonight, they'd be celebrating the answer to her mother's prayer over her famous curry goat—a labor-intensive family recipe and her father's favorite meal. Not that he deserved it.

"Spock, I'm home!" CeCe kicked off her shoes in the small foyer. Early evening sunlight streamed through the balcony windows facing Main Street, illuminating the open floor plan.

Her feline roommate barely lifted his head from his perch on the wide windowsill, but what did she expect? She'd named him after her favorite *Star Trek* character, Spock, a half human, half Vulcan being with pointy ears and an aversion to displaying emotion. While the cantankerous cream-and-ginger kitten had grown into the personality of his fictional counterpart, his ears had not. As a Scottish Fold mix, Spock's ears pointed down, not up, an ironic trait CeCe found adorably endearing.

"Sorry, I can't stay long." She headed straight for the kitchen pantry. "Tonight's the big night, when the prodigal father returns. Mama's making curry goat."

Spock lifted his head, suddenly interested.

"I'll try to save you some. But until then, how does salmon and shrimp sound?" She withdrew a can of cat food and showed him the label.

Spock hopped off the window ledge, seemingly pleased with her selection.

"I feel guilty I'm not more excited to see him," she admitted, peeling back the tin lid. "But how excited can I be about a man I barely know? I mean, he's traveled so much of my life, I relate more to kids raised by single parents."

Spock settled on the ground by his water dish and listlessly licked his paw. He'd heard her melancholy monologue before.

"You're right. Who needs complicated human emotions?

Indifference is the way to go." She scratched his head before setting his dinner in front of him. "I'm happy for Mama, but I won't get my hopes up for some Hallmark-worthy family reunion. I doubt Dad'll be in town for more than a few days before he takes off again anyway. By the way," she said, straightening. "Mystery Man came back today."

Spock briefly glanced up from his food dish as though mildly curious.

"It was the strangest thing." CeCe poured herself a glass of chilled coconut water from the fridge. "I wanted to give him one of Abby's leftover sample cakes—she chose the Toto, by the way; no surprise there—but he bolted out of the café before I had a chance. He looked like he'd seen a ghost and left without finishing his latte."

Spock cocked his head, appearing contemplative, then went back to his dinner as if the mental effort to conjure an explanation wasn't worth his time.

"I know we get all kinds of customers in the café, especially during tourist season, but there's something off about this guy. I wish I could put my finger on it." She drained her glass and set it on the counter. "But that's a mystery for another day. Tonight's mission: pretend to be a loving, happy family with a man who'd rather spend time digging through dirt than getting to know his only daughter." She paused, frowning. "I sound bitter, don't I?"

Spock chirped in agreement.

CeCe sighed. "I'll work on it."

Her phone buzzed, and she pulled it from her back pocket.

Hi, sweetie. Dad called. He won't be home tonight after all. The expedition has been extended by a few more weeks, maybe months.

CeCe stared at the screen, her fingers clenched tightly

around her phone. He'd canceled. Last minute. *Again*. Did he even care what he put them through?

"Well," she said, her throat hoarse. At the crack in her voice, she swallowed her emotions. "I may have to work a little harder on not being bitter. Dad isn't coming home."

Spock sat back on his haunches, his amber eyes soft, almost sympathetic.

She blinked hard, fighting the urge to cry. *Indifference, CeCe. Don't let him get to you.* "It's fine. It's not like it's a big shock."

Spock hopped onto the counter and nudged her hand.

She smiled weakly, sliding her fingers through his silky fur. "You're more of a softy than you let on. You know that, right?"

Spock purred.

CeCe sniffled, already feeling bolstered by his uncharacteristic bout of affection. "On the bright side, if Dad isn't coming, that means more curry goat for me."

Spock mewed.

"And you," she added with a laugh. She quickly composed a response to her mother and hit Send.

Sorry to hear that, Mama. I'll be over soon, and I'm bringing dessert.

She'd made an extra four-inch Toto cake with lime glaze, knowing her parents would love it.

It's Friday night. I'm sure young people have better things to do than have dinner alone with their mother. I'm fine. I'll pack up the leftovers for you. Go out and have a good time. Maybe call that boy who asked you to dinner after church last Sunday.

Her mother added a winking emoji to her text, but CeCe knew an attempt at deflection when she saw one. She also knew her mother didn't want her to come over because she planned to spend the entire evening crying into her curry—the curry she'd slaved over for hours in loving preparation for her

31

husband who, once again, didn't have the decency to fulfill a promise.

The familiar flame of protective indignation burned hot inside her stomach. When would her mother realize he wasn't worth her tears?

I'm coming over. We can watch a movie or work on that puzzle you got last week.

She hated to think of her mother alone, wallowing over a man who probably wouldn't give her a second thought.

Really, sweetheart. I'm fine. I got a new historical fiction novel from the Unbound Bookshop that I've been dying to read.

But you won't actually read it tonight, will you? CeCe thought but decided not to press further.

Okay. Love you, Mama.

Love you, too, ma chouquette.

CeCe's chest squeezed at the sight of the familiar nickname —the nickname given to her at birth by her father, who'd been born in France. The endearment translated to *my little one*, and more literally referred to a small choux pastry. A pastry her father had taught her how to make, along with several other delicious French desserts. In truth, her love of baking began with those lessons, rare fond memories of her father from her childhood. But now, CeCe attributed her culinary passions to her mother and her mother alone.

After fixing herself a simple meal, she drew a hot bubble bath infused with coconut milk and lavender essential oils. While the tub filled, she threw her hair into a messy topknot and slathered a mixture of oatmeal and honey on her face— another one of her mother's DIY beauty treatments.

As she looked in the mirror, she tried not to notice the features she'd inherited from her father—her slightly lighter skin tone courtesy of her biracial heritage, the smattering of freckles across her nose, and the dimple in her left cheek. She was her mother's daughter, through and through, and that's all she wanted to be.

She slid her toes into the steaming suds, then paused when her phone buzzed on the bathroom counter. Balancing on one foot, she checked the message.

Just left some curry goat on your doorstep. Love you.

CeCe gazed longingly at the mound of fragrant foam calling her name. The curry would be fine outside for a few hours, wouldn't it? With a sigh, she slipped on her well-worn bathrobe, deciding it wasn't worth the risk.

She shot a warning glance at Spock, who sat poised on the edge of the toilet seat, ready to pounce. While he loathed water, he loved popping bubbles. "I'll be right back. Don't even think about going near the tub while I'm gone."

Spock leaned back on his haunches with a huff, but his coy expression said he couldn't be trusted.

Swiftly, CeCe skipped down the steps to the side entrance. A large plastic Tupperware sat on the welcome mat. Even though she'd already had dinner, her mouth watered at the sight, and she couldn't resist peeling back the lid for a quick whiff of the aromatic sauce. The savory scents of cumin, coriander, and turmeric wafted from the opening, bringing a smile to her lips.

A bright, startling flash of light caught her off guard.

The Tupperware slipped in her grasp, sloshing soupy sauce onto her robe.

Great. What a waste.

Another flash blinded her, followed by several more.

Then came the shouting.

"CeCe! CeCe Dupree! Over here!"

"How long have you been engaged?"

"When is the wedding?"

"Can we see the ring?"

CeCe squinted, shielding her eyes with one hand, struggling to reorient herself. Engaged? Wedding? Ring? What were they talking about? And who were all these people?

"CeCe, tell us. How did Jayce propose?"

CeCe's heartbeat stuttered. Jayce? *Her* Jayce? Wasn't he in Paris or somewhere filming a movie? They hadn't spoken in a few weeks, but she'd certainly remember a proposal.

Where on earth had they heard such a ridiculous rumor?

Chapter Six

JAYCE

JAYCE DEPLANED the private jet and scanned the tarmac for his usual driver, Carl. Instead, he spotted his lifelong friend, Mia Larsen, sporting a chauffeur hat and wielding a sign that read Dead Man Walking.

Rolling his carry-on behind him, he strode toward her. "Where's Carl?"

"I told him to take the day off."

"And he took orders from you?"

"You know he can't resist my homemade kettle corn." She flashed an impish grin.

While Mia had grown up in her mother's candy store, Sweet Blessings, and knew her way around confections, Jayce had a feeling Carl had been more persuaded by Mia's mile-long legs and million-dollar smile. If it weren't for her oddball style choices—today's ensemble consisted of a pink sequined shirt under scruffy overalls she'd sheared into cutoff shorts—she could be mistaken for a *Vogue* cover model.

"Why does the sign say Dead Man Walking?" He tossed his suitcase into the back seat of Mia's 1967 VW Beetle convertible. In the warm Los Angeles weather, she religiously rode with the top down. Although the butter-yellow exterior with hand-painted daisies on both sides drew more unwanted attention than his auspicious black Jeep, he couldn't deny the fun factor.

"Because by the time we get to Blessings Bay, CeCe's going to murder you. Or maim you, at the very least." She hopped into the driver's seat, ditched the hat, and secured her shoulder-length blond hair with a tie-dyed scarf. "You were planning to drive straight home to clean up your mess, right?"

"What mess?" He climbed into the passenger seat beside her. No way Mia knew about the fake fiancée fiasco. He'd explicitly asked Gretchen to keep quiet until he could tell CeCe he'd "spilled the beans" in person. In reality, he'd planned to beg for her cooperation—and forgiveness—while hoping she'd agree to ride out the bogus engagement for a few days, maybe a week, then they'd publicly announce they'd amicably parted ways. Of course, they'd have to figure out how to explain the situation to their friends and family, but first things first.

Mia tossed a celebrity gossip magazine on his lap. The cover photo showed CeCe in a stained bathrobe, her hair in a tangled topknot, and some kind of sticky goop on her face. Above the photo, the headline read, "Hollywood Heartthrob Jayce Hunt to Wed Homeless Woman." *Oof. That's rough.*

He cringed. "Maybe we should stop at a store for some body armor?"

"Unless they sell Kevlar at Dummies-R-Us, you're out of luck," she teased, heading off the tarmac. "How did this happen?"

Raising his voice to be heard over the wind, Jayce gave Mia the rundown.

Mia shook her head as she listened, but he struggled to read her expression behind her oversize sunglasses. "Why didn't I know Stacey was seeing someone? I thought we told each other everything."

Not everything, Jayce thought, with more than one secret in mind.

Ever since they were kids, Mia had followed Jayce around, along with their close friend, Evan Blake. They treated her like their kid sister, and when Jayce moved to LA to pursue his life-long dream of becoming Hollywood's next critically acclaimed screenwriter, Evan and Mia followed. Of course, life didn't go exactly according to plan, with Jayce stumbling upon a successful acting career and Evan eventually moving back to Blessings Bay to open his own business.

Mia, on the other hand, had accomplished her goal and had made quite a name for herself as a highly coveted foley artist. She re-created ambient sounds for multimillion-dollar block-busters, including all his own films, and was known for her creative, outside-the-box techniques that produced impressively realistic results. His most recent favorite: when she squished mashed potatoes and strawberry Jell-O between her fingers for one of his faux kissing scenes—grossly effective.

"Only a handful of people know about it," he assured her.

"So, you decided to avoid a fake engagement by faking another engagement?" she asked ruefully. "Please tell me you see the irony."

"Okay, so it wasn't my best idea. But in the moment, I couldn't think of a better one."

"Why didn't you ask me to play along? I'd be a fantastic fake fiancée." She pushed her sunglasses on top of her head, batting her eyelashes. "Why, Jayce, sugar pie, love of my life, of course I'll marry you! I thought you'd never ask."

"Is there a reason your impersonation calls for an exagger-ated Southern accent?" he asked with a laugh.

"It felt right for the character. Don't question my methods."

"Fair enough."

She shot him a sideways glance. "In all seriousness, not that I mind being passed over as your partner in crime, but is there any particular reason you chose CeCe as your wifey-to-be?"

"*Pretend* wife-to-be," he corrected. His neck suddenly burned hot. He tugged on his collar, avoiding her question.

"It wouldn't have anything to do with the fact that you've been madly in love with her since kindergarten?"

"Good grief," he groaned, "not again. How many times have we been over this?"

"Clearly not enough for you to finally admit the truth," she countered wryly. "Just confess already. Why fight it?"

Because I'd never do anything to hurt her. Rather than go down that road, he said, "You have a screw loose. CeCe and I are friends. *Best* friends. I'd do anything for her, and—"

"She'd do anything for you?" Mia finished for him.

Jayce sat in silence, staring straight ahead as cars zipped past them at breakneck speeds. A particularly reckless red Corvette wove in and out of traffic, putting everyone around him at risk.

Was he doing the same thing? Would his attempt to help Stacey ultimately do more harm than good? Or would the whole thing blow over in a few days, affording Stacey and Rob their chance to ride off into the sunset unscathed?

He instinctively tightened his seat belt. *Guess there's only one way to find out.*

Chapter Seven

ABBY

THERE'S ONLY one way to find out what he wants. Abby peered through her kitchen window, partially hidden by the damask curtain.

The mystery man from CeCe's café stood on the curb staring at the inn with an unreadable expression. First, he'd followed her home yesterday, and now *this*. What did he want? Was he stalking her? At the possibility, anxiety pooled in the pit of her stomach.

Whatever his intentions, she had an uneasy feeling despite her best attempts to explain away his odd behavior.

Heart racing, she reached for her phone in the back pocket of her jeans, ready to call Logan. Her hand stilled. Their interactions had been a little tense since their meeting with Carla. Admittedly, the tension was her fault. He'd wanted to talk after Carla left, but she'd been too emotionally bruised to trust her reaction. Deep down, she knew he'd made the right decision to wait and give their options more consideration. But closer to the surface, where every fiber of her being ached to be a mom, she hadn't wanted to listen to reason.

After a few more seconds of internal debate, Abby straightened, leaving her phone untouched. She didn't need to bother Logan; she could handle herself. Between growing up in a rough part of Boston and being a military wife, she'd learned a self-defense technique or two. She'd march right out the front door and demand answers.

Sucking in a breath, she stretched to her full five feet, five inches. Okay, so her petite frame wasn't exactly formidable, but she knew the power of a swift jab to the jugular. Or an eye socket. She'd be fine.

She continued her mental pep talk all the way to the front door. With one hand on the doorknob, she rehearsed her line of interrogation. "Who are you and why have you been following me?"

Shoulders back, she threw open the door, poised and ready to confront her potential stalker.

Turns out, someone had beat her to the task.

Her eighty-nine-year-old neighbor, Verna Hoffstetter, who lived in the lavender Queen Anne Victorian across the street, chatted amicably with the stranger. Or rather, chatted *at* him.

Mystery Man was too preoccupied by the pudgy snout plastered to the toe of his work boot to make casual conversation.

"Oh, don't mind him." Verna gestured to the chubby English bulldog leaving a trail of slobber along the worn leather. "Mr. Bingley is harmless. Sniffing is how he gets to know you. Remarkably, someone's shoes can reveal a lot about them."

If only Bing could pass along his intel, Abby mused, observing the exchange from the front porch, so far undetected behind the large pot of begonias.

"Are you new in town?" Verna asked while Bing moved on to chewing the man's laces. "I don't think I've seen you around before."

"Just visiting."

"Where are you staying?"

"Um, nowhere." He shook his foot, but the movement didn't deter the portly pooch. Bing clamped down even harder and shot the man a disgruntled glance. "I've been driving into town every day from Redton."

"Goodness! That's a three-hour drive, at least. More if you hit traffic on the highway." Verna shook her head, tousling her short tangerine-colored curls. "That's quite a slog."

"I don't mind." He shrugged his slim shoulders, and Abby noted how frail he looked, as if he hadn't eaten a decent meal in weeks. One of her hearty breakfasts would work wonders. At the thought, a new possibility occurred to her. What if he wasn't interested in her at all, but simply needed a place to stay? Maybe he'd heard she ran an inn and wanted to check things out before booking a room. The possibility helped calm her wariness.

"What brings you to Blessings Bay?" Verna asked as if she'd read Abby's mind.

"I don't know, exactly. There's just something about this place that calls to me, odd as that sounds."

"Not odd at all! Blessings Bay has that effect on people. If you hang around long enough, you may find you never want to leave. Isn't that right, Abby?"

Abby jumped at the sound of her name, stubbing her toe on the ceramic flowerpot. Her cheeks flaming, she stifled a whimper of pain. *Who looks like a stalker now?*

Verna's pale blue eyes shimmered with bemusement, as if she'd been aware of Abby's presence all along.

Mystery Man, however, didn't look amused in the slightest. In fact, he looked as startled as Abby felt.

With a sheepish smile, Abby hobbled down the steps to join them. "Verna's right. When I first arrived in Blessings Bay last December, I'd only intended to stay until the new year. Now, they couldn't run me out of town, even if they tried," she said lightheartedly.

The remainder of her apprehension vanished in Verna's calming presence. Plus, in light of the man's timidity around the squishiest and cuddliest dog in the world, it was almost comical she'd found him intimidating.

He cautiously offered his hand to Bing, who sniffed his fingers before giving them a lick. Abby made note of the pup's approval.

"Abby also runs the best bed-and-breakfast in the area," Verna added. "Possibly the country."

"Verna's my unofficial publicist." Abby beamed at the woman who'd become her surrogate mother over the last several months. "I don't know what I'd do without her."

"Your place does look nice." Mystery Man squatted to pet Bing. "Much too nice for a guy like me." He met her gaze with a playful smile of self-deprecation, but something about his eyes struck her—something she couldn't explain—and she couldn't look away.

Somewhere in the depths of warm, chocolatey brown, she glimpsed a humble vulnerability, perhaps even embarrassment, as if he didn't believe he deserved the finer things in life. What had he endured that made him feel unworthy of something as simple as boutique accommodations?

Compassion swelled in her chest. Maybe his eyes looked familiar because she recognized herself in them? A lost soul who'd experienced a string of unfortunate events outside his control who needed help finding a new path. She'd once been the wanderer who came to Blessings Bay in search of respite. And she'd found so much more than that—she'd found a home, a family, and a fresh start. Isn't that why she'd opened the inn? To share the same blessing with others who may need a new beginning?

"Don't be silly," she blurted before she could think better of her impulsive idea. "Everyone can use a little luxury every now and then. Besides, we have a special summer rate—first night free." Okay, so it wasn't an official promotion, but Logan would understand once she explained the situation, wouldn't he?

"Really?" His gaze traveled beyond her to the inn, taking in its elegant features, from the gingerbread trim to the pristine white shutters. "That's awfully generous, but even with a free night, I still don't think I could afford to stay here."

"Then stay the first night, at least," Abby insisted. "If you'd like to stay longer, we can work something out."

Mystery Man glanced at Verna, as if to gauge whether or not she'd heard the same offer.

Verna smiled. "I'd take her up on that, if I were you."

"Okay, I guess I will, then." Turning to Abby, he added, "That is, if you're sure it won't be too much trouble."

"I'm sure." She smiled, ignoring her simmering doubts.

What had compelled her to dismiss a very wise decision not to book any guests until after the wedding?

And how on earth would she explain her rash decision to Logan when she barely understood it herself?

Chapter Eight

CECE

"WE HAVE A PROBLEM," CeCe hissed into her cell, leaving Jayce a third voicemail that morning. "Have you seen the gossip websites? Do you know what they're saying about us? Also, the paparazzi have been camped out in the café since we opened this morning. I feel like I'm living the *Star Trek* episode 'Hide and Q' and can't leave the kitchen. Call me back." She hung up the phone, not thinking twice about her obscure television reference.

As kids, while Jayce had shared his love for Hollywood's legendary filmmakers, introducing her to classics like *Casablanca* and *Citizen Kane*, she'd made him watch every *Star Trek* episode—some of them more than once.

CeCe stared at the screen, hoping for a call back, even though she knew it might be a while before she heard from Jayce, especially if he was in the middle of filming.

"Yeesh! It's a madhouse out there." CeCe's assistant manager, Piper Sloane, slipped through the swinging door separating the kitchen from the main café, an empty pastry tray snug against her hip. "The pain au chocolat are completely sold out. And the kouign-amann aren't far behind."

"I made more." CeCe shoved her cell phone into the back pocket of her jeans and strode to the tall twenty-tier cooling rack. Sheet pans packed with fresh-from-the-oven pastries filled the kitchen with the delicious aroma of buttery dough and caramelized sugar.

Piper stole a moment to tuck a few strands of wayward blond hair back into her loose braid. "We haven't been this busy all summer. I don't think I've been off my feet once this morning."

"Sit. Eat something." CeCe set the tray of pain au chocolat on the large center island and slid out a stool, feeling terrible she'd had to sequester herself. But after last night's ambush, she hadn't wanted to risk another embarrassing Kodak moment and decided to sneak straight into the kitchen from her apartment upstairs. "Tammy can handle the floor for a few minutes."

"Thanks." Piper perched on the stool and grabbed a pastry. "Silver lining, I guess."

"What is?" CeCe dumped a ball of sticky dough onto the floured countertop.

"All the paparazzi. They consume three times the caffeine of our average customer. We're making a killing today." Piper cast her a sideways glance as she bit into the flaky crust, slowly making her way to the gooey chocolate center.

To her credit, Piper hadn't pestered her about the paparazzi, but CeCe knew she'd seen the tabloids and had to be dying of curiosity. "It isn't true, by the way. The rumors about me and Jayce." She concentrated on rolling the dough with smooth, steady strokes, even though she could feel both cheeks heating beneath the fluorescent lights. "We're just friends."

"Too bad. He's hot. And you two would make a cute couple."

CeCe glanced up in surprise. "We would?"

"Of course. He's all handsome and smoldering and you're

the epitome of the adorable girl next door. I would ship you two in a heartbeat."

CeCe's blush deepened. She enjoyed "shipping" fictional characters in books and TV, relishing the will-they-won't-they chemistry and the sizzling sexual tension. But she never imagined anyone would pair her and Jayce romantically. He was a big Hollywood movie star, and she was— She glanced at the flour covering her arms and the front of her faded *Galaxy Quest* T-shirt. Let's face it, she was a stone-cold nerd—right down to the cliché wire-rimmed glasses. Jayce could have any woman he wanted, probably one for each day of the week. He'd never view her as anything more than a friend. A fact he'd made abundantly clear the day he left town, leaving her alone at Lighthouse Cove.

"Well, thanks. But like I said, we're just friends. I have no clue where the media got the ridiculous idea we're engaged."

"I may have a hunch." The familiar voice sent a warm ripple down her spine. Jayce Hunt stood in her kitchen, filling the space with his larger-than-life persona. Even in jeans and a plain black T-shirt, the man oozed superstar sex appeal. Her stomach spun at the sight of him.

Starstruck, Piper froze, the last bite of pain au chocolat stuffed partway in her mouth. As she gawked, a glob of chocolate filling splattered on her apron.

CeCe felt for the poor woman, who'd obviously never seen a celebrity up close before. At least, not one this good-looking.

"Hi, Toto." Jayce met her gaze, his expression equally affectionate and sheepish.

His use of her special for-his-lips-only nickname would make her secretly swoon under normal circumstances, but this time, her Spidey sense tingled. "Jayce Harrison Hunt, what did you do?"

He winced. "*Oof.* Full name. I'm really in trouble, aren't I?"

"That depends. Is the rumor your fault?" Determined to appear stern, CeCe folded her arms in front of her chest, even though they ached to hug him. How long had it been since they'd seen each other? Eight—no, nine months? He didn't visit often.

"Don't I get a hello hug first?" Jayce asked, always able to read her thoughts.

Piper coughed, choking on her pastry as she suddenly regained control of her faculties. "I'm going to, uh, give you two a minute." She slid off the stool and awkwardly made her exit.

"New employee?" Jayce asked, watching her go.

"Yes. Her name's Piper. I'll introduce you later. Don't change the subject."

"Okay. Back to that hug we were discussing." He flashed his most endearing smile. The one he never showed the cameras. The one he seemed to reserve only for her. "I've missed you, Toto."

His sincerity weakened her defenses. "I've missed you, too." She sighed, relenting to his charm. "Welcome home."

He scooped her into a bear hug, and she melted against him, inhaling his scent. No matter how much money he made, he still wore the same inexpensive cologne—the brand she'd bought him as a graduation present. Starlight Storm. The fragrance resembled hints of the ocean after a midnight rain, deep and musky. She'd hoped to remind him of what he'd left behind.

He held her a little longer than usual before returning her to the ground.

She stepped back, smiling at the flour smudges smeared across his black cotton T-shirt that probably cost more than her car.

"What?" he asked, catching her bemused expression.

"Nothing. Except that your shirt looks like a Rorschach inkblot test in reverse."

He studied the splotches with mock seriousness, stroking his strong jawline with his thumb and forefinger, pretending to read the random shapes for hidden meaning. "Hmm... I see the outline of my best friend in the whole world forgiving me for something foolish I did." He glanced up, meeting her gaze with a chagrined smile.

"So, it *is* your fault." She slugged him in the arm. "Do you know they're calling me 'the Hollywood Hypnotist'? They're saying I hypnotized you into proposing." Well, one online blogger had made the claim. And she'd had to dive pretty deep into the blogosphere to find the article. But still. She wasn't thrilled with the accusation.

"That's crazy. If you were going to hypnotize anyone into proposing, it would be Chris Pine, not me. You've been in love with him ever since his role as Captain Kirk."

Oh, if only he knew how wrong he was.

"Besides," he added, "they're idiots if they think you'd have to hypnotize a man into marrying you. All you'd have to do is bat those beautiful dark eyes at him. And if that didn't work, you could bake him one of these." He reached for a pain au chocolat, but CeCe slapped his hand away, ignoring the way her skin flushed at his flattery.

"That's not the point. This whole situation is embarrassing. The photo—"

"Is not your best," he interjected. "But it's one unflattering photo. It happens to everybody. Any bozo can see how gorgeous you are."

Gorgeous? CeCe stared, caught off guard by the compliment. She involuntarily pressed a hand to her chest, hoping to slow her racing heartbeat. Did he really think she was gorgeous? No. That's absurd. Cute, maybe. But not *gorgeous*. Especially not compared to the models and movie stars he mingled with every day. "Stop trying to butter me up. I'm still mad at you. How did the rumor get started anyway?"

As she listened to Jayce's confession, and his impulse to help out a friend, her irritation softened slightly. That was so like him—always thinking of other people.

"I messed up," he admitted, throwing up his hands in a show of surrender. "I shouldn't have lied or dragged you into this, and I'm sorry. I have no right to ask you for a favor, but I'm desperate, so I'm going to throw myself at your mercy. Feel free to turn me down."

"What's the favor?" CeCe asked cautiously, a nervous suspicion brewing in the back of her mind.

"Would you go along with the ruse? Pretty please? For a few days. Maybe a week or two, tops. Just long enough for Stacey and Rob to get married and have their honeymoon in peace. Then we can come clean or stage an amicable breakup."

He gazed at her earnestly, looking so disarming and vulnerable, her better judgment wavered. *This is a horrible idea and will end in disaster.* But rather than share her concerns aloud, she said, "I won't lie to our parents. Or our friends."

"That's fair. And I wouldn't ask you to. We can tell them the truth and beg them to play along. The only people we have to convince are Gretchen and the paparazzi."

At the mention of the vultures circling her café all morning, CeCe realized it was unusually quiet. "Wait a minute. Where *are* the paparazzi?"

"I asked them to leave."

"And they listened? Just like that?"

"I may have promised each of them an exclusive interview and a press pass to our wedding."

"Jayce!"

"Our *fake* wedding. You know, the one that isn't really

happening. I figured it was a fair trade for some peace and quiet."

CeCe rolled her eyes. He always was too smooth for his own good. "You realize this scheme will most likely blow up in your face."

"Maybe. But think about how fun our last wedding was." His midnight-blue eyes twinkled, tempering whatever reservations she had left.

"It *was* pretty nice. At least that time you gave me a ring. Even if it was the twist tie off a bag of cotton candy."

"Oh! Thanks for reminding me." He reached into his front pocket and withdrew a tiny leather pouch. "Picked this up in Bali before my flight."

"Bali? I thought you were in Paris."

"That was last month."

"Right." She nodded along, trying not to draw the comparison between her father's globe-trotting tendencies and Jayce's. What was it about the men in her life and their inability to stay put?

She quieted the thought as he dropped to one knee. "Cecelia Desirée Dupree, will you do me the incredible honor of being my fake fiancée?"

Although she knew the proposal wasn't real, her heart beat a little bit faster as he revealed a stunning crescent-shaped diamond ring that looked like the moon surrounded by a dozen glittering stars. "I—" The words caught in her throat. What was wrong with her?

"Shoot. You don't like it." His face fell. "Obviously, this isn't the ring I'd give you if we really got engaged, but I tried to find one I thought you'd like."

Wait. What did he say? What did he mean by "if we really got engaged"?

"If you wear this one for now, I'll get you any one you want as a thank—"

"Jayce." She extended her hand, willing her fingers to stop jittering. *Get it together, CeCe. It's pretend.* "It's perfect. Thank you."

"You sure?"

"I'm positive."

"Great." With a look of relief, he took her hand in his.

The moment their fingers touched, her heartbeat faltered at a sudden and unexpected electrical charge.

An unreadable expression flickered across his face, as if he'd felt the same scintillating sensation that had skittered up her arm.

He cleared his throat then slid the ring onto her finger. A perfect fit.

Job done.

Why hadn't he let go?

And why hadn't she pulled away?

Their eyes met.

A strange current passed between them that confused and thrilled her.

In a matter of seconds, her simple, straightforward existence had become a lot more complicated.

And CeCe Dupree didn't *do* complicated.

Chapter Nine

JAYCE

JAYCE SWALLOWED against the dryness in his throat. How many times had he envisioned this exact moment? Down on one knee, offering CeCe his grandmother's ring—the art deco moonstone ring hidden in the bottom drawer of his nightstand. A secret reminder of his unspoken desire for something that didn't exist—a loving marriage that outlasted the twists, turns, and tragedies of life.

His gaze fell to her fingertips, still grasped in his hand. *Time to let go, before you make things weird.* On impulse, he gently grazed his thumb over her knuckle, brushing aside a smudge of flour. The intimate gesture made the hair on the back of his neck stand up.

Okay, now you've definitely made things weird. He cleared his throat, yanking his hand away before she could sense his rise in temperature. He jumped to his feet. "Now what?"

"You tell me," she said, studying the way the diamond sparkled in the overhead light. "This was your brilliant idea, remember?"

"Right." And if the last five minutes had taught him

anything, he'd need to be careful or risk getting lost in the con. "I guess we should get our story straight."

"Good idea. How long have we been engaged?"

"Let's say six months."

"And how long did we date before you proposed?"

"We didn't."

"We didn't?" CeCe balked.

"Nope. We've been friends our whole lives, and I've been in love with you for almost as long. When I finally gathered the courage to tell you how I felt, I skipped straight to the proposal." His neck burned hot, but he kept his voice steady and expression relaxed, recalling the advice from his acting coach. *To sell a scene, you need to draw from your deepest truth.* Well, he'd drawn from the truth all right. Hopefully, she couldn't tell.

A flicker of uncertainty flashed in her dark eyes, but it vanished as quickly as it appeared. "Seems far-fetched, but if you think the paparazzi will buy the story, it works for me. The fewer dates and details I have to remember, the better. Speaking of dates, when's the wedding?"

Tomorrow, he wanted to blurt, suppressing the familiar fantasy of CeCe's perfect curves conformed to the smooth sand, her dark curls tossed by the wind as they enjoyed their honeymoon on a private Caribbean island without another soul in sight. "How about October 15?" he said casually.

Was it his imagination or did her eyes spark with recognition? Jayce immediately dismissed the thought. No way she'd remember a random date that only held significance for him.

"What day of the week is it?"

"A Saturday. I *think*," he added hastily, not wanting to reveal how much mental energy he'd already put into this fake wedding.

"Okay. That works. What about nicknames?"

"Nicknames?"

"Yeah, what do we call each other? Babe? Bae? Sweetie?"

"Oh, right. I hadn't thought about that." He'd always called her Toto, after her favorite cake flavor, since her personality exuded the perfect blend of sweet and spicy. Not the cute little dog from *The Wizard of Oz*, like most people assumed. "What do you want me to call you?"

"Honestly, I love the one you already gave me. But do you think Toto works as a romantic term of endearment?"

He suppressed a smile. "I think it could."

"Okay, then we'll use it. What about you?"

"I've always been partial to Your Royal Highness or my lord," he teased.

"Keep dreaming. How about honey pie? Sweet cakes? Sugar dumpling?"

"You're making me hungry."

"I've got it!" She snapped her fingers. "How about *mi dawlin?*" she drawled in a sultry Jamaican accent.

Her eyes twinkled playfully. *She's just kidding around.* Obviously. He knew that. So why had he suddenly become the physical embodiment of the expression *weak-kneed*? He pressed his palm against the countertop for support, hoping she didn't notice.

This isn't real, he reminded himself. But he sure wouldn't mind hearing her whisper the moniker in his ear every morning. At the realization, guilt crept over him. *You shouldn't be having these thoughts about your best friend. It isn't right. Get it together, man. You're better than this.*

"Relax," she said with a laugh, misreading his look of discomfort. "I'm joking. We can go with something simple like babe."

He cleared his throat. "No, I like the last one."

"Mi dawlin?" she asked in surprise.

"Yep. Let's go with that."

"Okay." She shrugged. "Dealer's choice. Now, for the big question. How are we going to tell our parents?"

"I was thinking I'd mail mine a letter."

"Very funny. I'm serious, Jayce. You're asking everyone for a pretty big favor. You need to do it in person."

"You're right," he admitted, wishing she wasn't.

He raked his fingers through his hair, his muscles instantly tense. He loved his parents, but he loathed visiting them, a big reason why he rarely came home. No matter which parent he went to see first, the other one got offended. And no matter how hard he tried to keep the conversations neutral, his parents constantly complained about each other, pitting Jayce in the middle of their feud. It had been that way since sixth grade and only got worse when his dad bought the house next door after their divorce. He claimed he wanted to be close to his son, while Jayce's mother swore he'd done it to spite her. To this day, for reasons that could only be attributed to full-blown insanity, they remained neighbors—bitter, bickering, backbiting neighbors who fought over where to place their trash bins.

"What if you tell your parents at the same time? Two birds, one stone."

"I'd rather chew off my own hand than put them in the same room together."

"I realize it's like asking the Romulans and Klingons to get along," she conceded with another one of her adorable *Star Trek* references. "But what if I go with you and hold your hand so you aren't tempted to chew it off?"

"And ask you to fall on a grenade for me?"

"What are fiancées for?"

"Are you sure?"

"For better or worse, mi dawlin," she said with a playful grin, making his stomach spin.

Shake it off, man. "Where should we hold this doomed

rendezvous? The emergency room? You know things are going to get ugly."

"I was thinking somewhere a little cozier."

"How about here at the café?" he suggested.

"Ha! Definitely not. My staff has already endured a paparazzi infiltration. I don't need them to clean up a blood-bath, too." She crinkled her nose in concentration, just like she did when studying for a test in school. The endearing quirk still drove him crazy. "I know!" she cried in delight at her epiphany. "Sage and Flynn recently opened a bookstore on a vintage sail-boat. We could schedule one of their bookish sailing tours around the bay. It's a neutral location. And a novelty, so good for conversation. Plus, they can't escape unless they jump overboard."

"And what if *I* jump overboard?"

"A hollow threat considering you're deathly afraid of sharks."

"I'm afraid of being *eaten* by sharks. There's a difference."

"If you say so." She smirked.

"That's the last time I spill my secrets during a game of Truth or Dare with you," he grumbled.

"It's cute you think you have any secrets left."

Oh, if only you knew, he thought with another pang of guilt. Suppressing the swell of complicated emotions, he jokingly asked, "How about we book the tour a year from next Tuesday?"

"How about tomorrow morning?" she countered. "I'll call Sage and make sure she has an opening. In case the paparazzi come poking around again, you need to get this over with quickly."

"You have a point." Plus, knowing Gretchen, she'd conjure some weak excuse to show up unannounced and uninvited. He wouldn't put anything past her, especially after she leaked the engagement bombshell earlier than she'd promised.

"Where are you staying while you're in town?"

"I'm crashing at Evan's place. Mia's back, too, so we're having a Tinseltown Trio reunion tonight. You should come."

"Mia's home?" CeCe brightened at the mention of their mutual childhood friend.

"Yeah, she kidnapped me from the airport. If I hadn't already been planning to come see you the second I stepped off the plane, she would've dragged me back, by force, if necessary."

"And that's why I love her," CeCe laughed. "But I'm glad drastic measures weren't needed."

"I meant it when I said I'm sorry for putting you in this position. I realize it's asking a lot. So, thanks. Sincerely. I appreciate you helping me out."

"Anything for a friend." She smiled the kind of smile that made her warm, velvety eyes sparkle behind her glasses and her seductive dimple deepen. The smile that made his chest squeeze around his lungs, stealing his breath every time.

A friend...

That's all he was. And it had to be enough.

Because anything more would eventually ruin the best, most fulfilling and soul-quenching relationship in his life—a treasure too great to risk.

Chapter Ten

LOGAN

LOGAN RAKED a few fallen leaves from the flower bed with his blackened fingers. He didn't bother wearing gloves, preferring to feel the warm, gritty soil against his calloused skin. The grooves he'd created in the dirt released a deep, earthy scent that mingled with the salty ocean spray.

He'd lived at 1109 West State Street for several years, care-taking the property for Abby's late husband—and his old air force buddy—Donnie. He'd groomed the same acre of land overlooking the ocean, with its lush gardens and breathtaking view, but never quite appreciated its beauty until Abby opened his eyes, inspiring him to enjoy life again. He owed everything to Abby. And he'd do anything to make her happy. So why couldn't he make a decision about Max and his dad?

As he reached farther into the sweet-smelling gardenia shrub, his fingertips hit something hard and smooth. Several things, actually.

Logan gently bent back the branches, revealing a small stockpile of Max's treasures. Bits of sea glass, shells, interestingly colored rocks and artfully twisted sticks of driftwood. At the sight of each twig and stone, memories flooded Logan's mind of countless trips to the beach over the last few months. Beach-combing, building sandcastles, tossing a football in the frothy surf. The sound of Max's laughter, the brilliance of his smile, the way he enhanced the joy of every moment—Logan could never quite find the words to capture what Max meant to him.

He never imagined he'd become a father, not after his injury in the air force or all the emotional shrapnel he'd endured as a result. But now, he couldn't fathom an existence without Max. Raising a child had reframed everything in his life. He saw the world through a new lens—a new and improved lens. And it made him strive to be a better man, both physically—which had led him to pursue a nontraditional therapy treatment for his muscle spasms that seemed to be working—and emotionally. Was it so wrong to want Max to be a permanent part of their lives, of their family?

Even as the question crossed his mind, he knew it wasn't that simple. Declaring Sam Bailey deceased would change every-thing for Max. Perhaps forcing him to face a reality he wasn't ready to accept. Maybe they needed to be more patient, to give Max more time. Or maybe Max would never be fully ready to grieve his father's death. What if now was the right timing after all?

The soft padding of footsteps on the grass grabbed his attention. From his kneeling position, he turned to find Abby standing behind him.

"Can we talk?" she asked softly, tiptoeing across the invis-ible line of tension lingering between them.

In response, Logan stood and, with one long stride, closed the gap and took her in his arms. Bending down, he buried his face in her hair, inhaling the familiar scent of lilac. "I'm sorry," he murmured, relishing the feel of her body against his, of her intoxicating nearness. Feeling disconnected from Abby—even for less than twenty-four hours—had felt like cutting off a limb.

"Me, too." She slid her arms around his waist, clinging to him as if they'd been apart for years. "I hated not talking, but I didn't know what to say." She pulled back, tilting her head to meet his gaze. "I think it's because I knew you were right. Having Sam Bailey declared deceased isn't a decision we should rush. If I'm honest, I was being selfish." Her cheeks flushed, and she glanced at the ground. "I told myself it was best for Max, but I don't know that for sure. I only know it's what I want."

At her confession, Logan's chest swelled with heightened love and admiration for his future wife—for her honesty, humility, and sincere heart. He'd never met someone who loved so fiercely or who fought so hard for others.

He tenderly tucked his fingers beneath her chin and raised her gaze to meet his again. "It's what I want, too. And I may not have the right answer yet, but I know we'll find it together." Still cupping her chin, he brought her lips to his. They tasted sweet yet salty with the sharp tang of tears.

He kissed her harder, pressing his fingertips against her jaw and cheekbone, a willing conduit for her pain. If he could, he'd channel her sadness away and take on her agony, feeling it more deeply on his own.

Logan wasn't sure how long they'd stood there, finding comfort in each other's embrace, when the squeaking of hinges broke through the stillness, drawing their focus toward the sound.

French doors—slightly warped from decades of damp sea air—creaked open, and their new guest stepped onto the balcony overhead.

"Sorry about that," Abby said quietly, although Logan doubted the man could hear them.

"For what?" He matched her soft tone. "The interruption? Or breaking our no-guests-until-after-the-wedding rule?" He grinned, intending his questions to be playful, not accusatory.

"Both. I shouldn't have invited him to stay without asking you first."

"I know you had your reasons. What's his story, anyway?"

"To be honest, I'm not sure. He's shown up at CeCe's every morning for several days. From what I've seen, and what CeCe's shared, he rarely speaks to anyone. It's like he's waiting for someone—or some*thing*—but I don't know what."

"Mysterious." Logan studied the man with a critical eye. The raised, tense shoulders and clenched hands made him look wary, constantly on edge—a similar posture to airmen he'd known who'd returned home with PTSD, whether they'd admitted the diagnosis or not.

"Exactly. CeCe and I call him Mystery Man. His conversation with Verna this morning was the most I've ever heard him talk to anyone."

"Sometimes I think Verna missed her calling as an interrogator for counterintelligence," he teased, keeping an eye on their guest.

Mystery Man stood near the railing, staring blankly at the sea. Two cushioned bistro chairs offered comfortable seating, but the guy didn't seem to notice or care, completely transfixed by the vanishing horizon line.

"She is quite adept at subtly gathering information," Abby agreed with a lighthearted laugh. "I may see if she'll come over again and have another chat with him. Out of curiosity, I tried to look him up on the internet but couldn't find anything on Thomas Maineland."

"Not anything?"

"Nope. Not a single search result."

"That's weird." He made a mental note to have his own chat with the guy.

"Right? It's like he doesn't exist."

Or, Logan thought with an uneasy churn in the pit of his stomach, *he's hiding something*.

Chapter Eleven

CECE

"WHAT?!" Sage Harper cried into the phone, her dismayed squeal barely audible above the whoosh of wind.

CeCe pictured her friend aboard the Unbound Bookshop, her honey-blond curls whipping around her shoulders as her boyfriend, Flynn, expertly steered the svelte sailboat across the sparkling blue waters.

"It's a *fake* engagement to help a friend," CeCe shouted into her single earbud, gingerly navigating her fragile Fiat Jolly down her mother's pitted gravel drive. The wicker driver's seat creaked beneath her weight as the wheels rattled over yet another pothole. Her father had promised to refill the divots during his next visit—a visit that felt more improbable every day.

"It sounds like a terrible idea," Sage shouted back. "Your feelings for Jayce are complicated enough as it is. I don't want you to get hurt."

"I'll be fine," CeCe assured her, although she had yet to convince herself. For good measure she added, "I don't think about him in that way anymore," despite the claim not being entirely true. More like wishful thinking.

"Why don't I believe you?" Sage was the only living soul she'd told about her silly unrequited crush, and she'd been sworn to secrecy. But that still didn't stop her friend from having an opinion on the subject. An opinion that often involved encouraging CeCe to tell Jayce the truth. Advice she'd tried to take once, although it thankfully hadn't panned out.

"Because you're madly in love, which makes it hard for you to think straight," CeCe teased, tearing her thoughts from her unpleasant past.

Sage laughed. "Guilty. But I still can't say I'm on board with a fake engagement. Lies tend to cause more problems than they solve."

Sage had a point. And from the moment she'd agreed to Jayce's proposition that morning, she'd second-guessed her decision more than once. Deep down, her heart knew it wasn't wise. But something had compelled her to say yes. And she didn't want to admit—even to herself—that the impulse probably stemmed from those pesky feelings she purported to no longer possess.

"You're probably right," she admitted. "But I can't go back on my word now. I just need to know if you have an opening for a sailing tour tomorrow morning for me, Jayce, and his parents."

"For you, yes. Anytime. But, CeCe—" Another gust of wind barreled into the cell phone speakers, drowning out her words.

CeCe felt a pang of guilt at her relief. She couldn't stomach another word of warning to echo her own misgivings. "Sorry, Sage. I can't hear you. Too much wind. Plus, I'm almost at my mother's for dinner. Text me what time we should meet at the marina tomorrow. Thanks!" She hung up her phone the same moment she pulled up to her mother's tiny beachfront cottage.

In actuality, a beach shanty was a better description of the scant two-bedroom dwelling sitting on stilts. The peeling papaya-colored paint had seen better days, and some of the double-hung windows were warped shut, but the home still held a special place in her heart.

With the carefully boxed Toto cake in hand, CeCe rounded the side of the house, following the scent of grilled plantains to the backyard oasis. Caribbean music blended with the hum of the ocean, which could be reached by a narrow footpath down to the beach. Vibrant hammocks swayed in the gentle breeze beneath the trees, and flaming tiki torches glowed in the soft light of the setting sun, bringing an island feel to the rugged coastline of California.

Despite being a second-generation American, her mother held on to her roots in a way CeCe admired, and she'd loved visiting the Caribbean on multiple occasions as a child. But her mother's heritage wasn't the only influence in their home. Unusual artifacts from her father's travels taunted her from all corners of the house. *Treasures*, her father called them. But the souvenirs merely served as reminders of his true love in life, the career that kept him from her.

"You're here!" Her mother's beautiful face brightened when she spotted her. She stood barefoot at the grill in a blue cotton sundress, her black curls tied haphazardly with a silk scarf. Ageless in both appearance and spirit. "Just in time. Hand me the peppers, please." She gestured to the picnic table set with a colorful tablecloth and votive candles flickering in eclectic glassware, from assorted Mason jars to antique apothecary bottles.

After setting the pastry box on the table, CeCe grabbed the basket of Scotch bonnet peppers picked from her mother's garden and brought them to the barbecue. Brown stew salmon simmered in a cast-iron skillet on the side burner, sending the savory aroma of rich gravy and heady spices into the air.

Her mother set a whole pepper into the sauce to infuse its spicy flavor, then flipped the plantains.

CeCe cracked open a cold bottle of orange soda, watching her mother work. To a casual observer, Durene Dupree simply loved to cook. But CeCe knew cooking was a healing salve as much as a hobby. "How are you doing, Mama?"

"Fine, sweetheart. Why do you ask?"

Oh, I don't know, CeCe thought. *Maybe because your loving husband broke his promise, yet again.* Suppressing her urge for sarcasm, she asked, "Have you heard from Dad? Does he know when he's coming home?"

"Not yet. But I heard someone else is in town." Her mother tossed a smile over her shoulder. "Why didn't you invite Jayce to dinner? I haven't seen that boy in far too long."

"He had plans tonight. But he promises to come see you soon."

"Well, you should've joined him. I keep telling you a young woman should not be spending her weekends at home with her mother. Go out, have fun with your friends."

"And miss a delicious home-cooked meal? No thanks. Besides, there's something I need to tell you." Her mouth dry, she took another swig of soda. The creamy liquid did little to assuage her nerves.

"Help me get this food on the table first."

Grateful for the delay, CeCe obliged. Once seated, and after they'd said grace, CeCe waited for her mother to take her first bite of flaky salmon, hoping it would soften the blow.

Her mother chewed slowly, her expression unreadable as CeCe explained Jayce's predicament—emphasizing his altruism —and her agreement to help. When she'd finished, she sucked in a breath, her apprehension stealing her appetite.

Her mother set down her fork and dabbed her mouth with the cloth napkin.

Say something, CeCe silently pleaded, stewing in the agonizing silence.

Setting the napkin back in her lap, her mother met her gaze across the table. "Your salmon is getting cold."

CeCe's heart squeezed. "That's it? That's all you have to say?"

"And what should I say, *ma chouquette*?" She evoked the term of endearment with a heavy note of sadness. "Lying? Pretending to be something you're not? You're a twenty-seven-year-old woman, not a little girl anymore. You know better. This isn't how your father and I raised you."

"*He* didn't raise me," she mumbled under her breath, but not soft enough to go unheard.

"That isn't fair. He's your father and deserves your respect."

The shame of disappointing her mother mixed with lingering resentment creating a potent concoction that blazed hot across her skin. She could feel the fire of long-suppressed wounds—of a thousand unspoken thoughts—burning in her gut, threatening to erupt like emotional lava.

For too long she'd kept quiet, not making a fuss or expressing her feelings, simply accepting the status quo like a good daughter. "Then let's talk about pretending." Her voice quivered, hoarse with impending tears. "I learned from the best."

"And what is that supposed to mean?"

"*You*, Mama. You taught me how to bury the truth. Why won't you admit that Dad's actions—or lack thereof—hurt you? That every time he misses a phone call or postpones another trip home, it digs the wound a little deeper." CeCe's clenched fists trembled in her lap, but once she'd unleashed the words, she couldn't stop them. "I know his indifference, or lack of consideration, or whatever polite term you want to give it, kills you. But for some reason, you pretend like everything is fine and dandy all the time. At least *my* lie is to help someone. What does yours accomplish?"

Her eyes burned, but no tears fell, granting her an agonizingly unobstructed view of her mother's stricken expression. Why had she gone down this road? Hadn't she come to comfort her mother, not cause her more heartache? Or had she really come seeking her approval?

"I'm sorry," she whispered, struggling to stand as her legs weakened beneath her. She wanted to take back every word she'd said, to apologize and make things right between them, but the line between honor and honesty had irrevocably blurred.

Now that she'd spoken her mind, could she ever undo the damage? Where would she even begin? And for goodness' sake, why hadn't her mother said anything?

Strange shadows flickered across her mother's strained features in the candlelight, and her dark, glassy eyes glimmered like bottomless pools of black water. She'd retreated inside herself, so deep CeCe feared she couldn't reach her. At least, not in her current state of emotional emptiness.

By unburdening her own pain, she'd wounded the one person she most longed to protect. And after what she'd done, she wasn't sure how she'd ever live with herself.

Chapter Twelve

JAYCE

JAYCE LOUNGED in the Adirondack chair, sipping a tall glass of Mia's homemade lemonade that she'd spiked with a handful of sour gummy worms for some extra *oomph*, as she'd described it. The smiling faces of his friends—Mia, Evan, and his girl-friend, Nadia Chopra—glowed in the soft firelight, their silhouettes framed by the midnight-blue ocean behind them. A perfect evening.

Well, it *would* be perfect when CeCe arrived. She'd promised to join them after dinner with her mom. He expected her any second, to share in the bonfire-on-the-beach tradition they'd loved as teenagers.

While Mia and Nadia enjoyed a lively debate over who was the best leading man in the romantic comedy *The Holiday*, Jack Black or Jude Law, Jayce immersed himself in his surroundings, letting the sights and sounds transport him back to the past. The crackling logs and rumbling waves. The cool, silky granules beneath his bare feet. The earthy scent of sand, salty sea air, and smoldering embers.

His chest heaved at the memory of CeCe's moonlit figure, the way her dark eyes danced in the flickering flames. He often found himself transfixed by her, memorizing the way her windswept curls fluttered across her face. Even though he'd kept his emotions expertly hidden, he still sometimes wondered how she couldn't sense his feelings ran so much deeper than friendship. At times, they consumed him so wholly, he felt certain they'd bubble to the surface and give away his secret. But after all these years, CeCe still had no idea. It was almost as if she didn't realize how easy she was to love.

"Who doesn't adore Jack Black's character?" Mia cried so fervently, she yanked him away from his thoughts. "During that scene when they're in Blockbuster and he hums the scores from famous movies, I fell in love with him right alongside Kate Winslet."

"What about Jude Law's Mr. Napkin Head?" Nadia countered with equal enthusiasm. "Every woman in the world swooned when he put that napkin under his glasses and made his adorable daughters giggle." She cast a sheepish glance at Evan. "I mean, *almost* every woman."

"Hey, no jealousy here." Evan grinned an easy, slanted smile. With his blond hair still damp from a sunset surfing session and his tanned legs stretched lazily across the sand, he'd never looked more relaxed. Moving back home suited him. And so did the black-haired beauty sitting beside him.

Not for the first time, Jayce wondered if Evan had the right idea returning to Blessings Bay. Should he follow his lead? What had moving to Los Angeles accomplished other than providing the escape he'd so desperately needed? Sure, he'd distanced himself from the turmoil at home, but at what cost?

That wasn't your only reason for running away, a quiet voice reminded him. Silencing the intrusive thought, he tried to focus on his friends' conversation.

"The guy's a stone-cold stud," Evan freely admitted. "And

so is Jack Black. Although, I think the real superstar of the film was Eli Wallach, who played Arthur Abbott."

"True," Mia conceded. "He may have been ninety when they filmed the movie, but the man had charisma. And a sexy career as the Oscar-winning screenwriter who added the *kid*, to the famous *Casablanca* line, 'Here's looking at you, kid.' Pretty impressive. Right, Jayce?" Mia shot him a pointed look before taking a swig of lemonade.

Subtle, Mia. Really subtle. She didn't pester him about his sidelined dreams very often, but if a rare occasion presented itself, she wasn't beneath a carefully aimed jab or two. "It *would* be impressive if it wasn't completely fictional. That line was actually improvised by Humphrey Bogart during filming."

"Okay, but *someone* had to write the original line for Bogart to improvise," Mia retorted. "The script is the foundation of any good film. And with all the rubbish Hollywood is churning out lately, we need more good ones."

"No argument there." Jayce took another sip, ignoring the career-altering secret burning a hole in his chest. *It's too soon to tell.*

Noticing Nadia's confused expression, Evan explained, "Mia likes to remind Jayce that he originally moved to LA to pursue a career in screenwriting."

"Oh, that's right." Nadia's dark eyes glinted with recognition. "I remember you mentioning that." Turning to address Jayce, she added, "But then you took an acting class and discovered you had a knack for it, right?"

"Something like that." He'd taken the class to deepen his writing craft but had enjoyed the escapism of disappearing into new characters, especially as the feud between his parents fueled unhealthy stress levels in his personal life. At the prodding of his acting instructor, Gretchen came to a performance to observe him. With her killer powers of persuasion, she convinced him to pursue acting as a gateway into Hollywood, insisting he could return to his writing later. Then *later* turned into *someday* until it eventually became a distant memory. At least, until recently.

"Seems like you enjoy acting," Nadia offered kindly. "I love all your movies."

"Thanks. It's fun. The acting part, anyway. I could do without all the other junk that comes with the job."

"Such as?" Nadia asked in the genuine, caring tone of a newfound friend, not an intrusively curious fan, which Jayce appreciated.

"The three Ps," Mia interjected, ticking them off on her fingers. "Parties, publicity, and paparazzi."

"That about sums it up," Jayce agreed. Fame served as a curse more often than a blessing. And nights like this one—where he could count flickering stars instead of flashing bulbs—were few and far between. Thanks in part to the town's lack of lodging options, it mostly remained a safe haven from the prying media.

"All the posturing and pretense of Hollywood must make it difficult to find someone special." Nadia's gaze drifted to Evan, and they exchanged the kind of private, intimate smile shared between two people deeply in love.

Once again, Jayce marveled at how happy Evan looked. And not just happy, but *blissful*, with a depth of contentment that stemmed from being exactly where God wanted him to be—with exactly the right person.

Despite what he knew about the longevity of love, Jayce hoped beyond reason that their relationship would last. Or, at least, last for as long as possible. Nadia, with her well-intentioned knack for speaking her mind, had given Evan the nudge he needed to reassess his life choices. And perhaps even more crucially, she'd helped him summon the courage to make new ones. Everyone needed a voice like that, to prod and encourage them down the right path.

For him, that voice belonged to CeCe.

Missing her even more acutely than before, he said, "Excuse me a second," and pulled out his phone. They still needed to spill the fake engagement news to their friends. Why wasn't she here by now?

What's your ETA?

He hit Send on the text, then set the phone on the wide wooden armrest so he could easily keep an eye on the screen.

His phone buzzed a second later.

Sorry. Can't make it tonight.

What? It wasn't like CeCe to cancel plans at the last minute. Something must be wrong.

What happened? Are you okay?

He sent his response, then waited, his knee bouncing as the three text bubbles hovered on his screen.

Finally, after the longest pause known to mankind, a single word appeared.

No.

He instantly dialed her number.

The call went to voicemail.

Another text pinged.

Sorry. Can't talk. Eating my weight in Almond Joy ice cream.

Uh-oh. CeCe's comfort food.

Save me a scoop. I'm on my way.

Without a second thought, he stood, stuffing his phone in his pocket before she could text back telling him not to come. "Sorry, guys. Gotta bail."

"Really?" Evan asked in surprise. "Aren't you crashing here tonight?"

"Yeah, but something came up. Okay if I come in late?"

"Sure. Door's always unlocked. Everything okay?"

"Thanks. I'll catch up with you guys later." Ignoring Evan's question, he bid them all good night, avoiding direct eye contact with Mia. She knew him too well and would instantly guess where he was headed.

Breathing deeply to calm his racing pulse, he climbed into Evan's beat-up surfer van, grateful for the loaner vehicle even if it smelled like an odd mix of minty rash balm and musty wet suit.

The easy five-minute drive to Main Street felt like six hours as questions, concerns, and worst-case scenarios swirled in his head. His only consolation rested in the knowledge that if something truly catastrophic had happened, she would've asked him to come over. After all, despite the long distance between them, they were still best friends, right? He didn't want to exist in a world where he wasn't her go-to person. Although, deep down, in the dark corners of his subconscious he tried to avoid, he knew one day that role would belong to another man.

A man who would marry her for real.

Shoving the thought back into the filing cabinet of likelihoods he refused to acknowledge, he let himself into the café through the side door, using his spare key, then climbed the steps two at a time. He didn't bother knocking.

CeCe sat cross-legged on the couch, devouring ice cream straight from the carton, while Spock perched on the armrest as if impatiently waiting his turn. His feline friend mewed when he spotted him and leaped to the ground to greet him.

"Hey, buddy." Jayce scooped the cat into his arms, reciprocating the warm welcome with several scratches behind the ears.

"He never greets me like that," CeCe mumbled, her mouth full.

"We have a special manly bond." With a final rub under the chin, Jayce set Spock on the back of the couch, claiming the seat beside CeCe for himself. "Almond Joy, huh? Whatever's wrong, it must be a doozy."

She lifted her face, her cheeks puffy and tear-streaked. "Sorry, I just ate the last bite."

"Don't sweat it." He took the empty carton and spoon from her hands and set them on the coffee table before enveloping her in his arms. "What happened and how can I help?"

She leaned into him, melting into the crook of his arm. How did she fit so perfectly? "I'm the worst person in the world," she whimpered, resting her head on his shoulder as if she could no longer bear its weight.

His chest squeezed. He loathed seeing anyone in pain, especially someone he cared about. But with CeCe, the sight of her sadness wrecked him. "I doubt you're the worst," he joked, knowing she needed levity in moments like this one. "What about that guy who trolls *Star Trek* fan sites claiming Spock is the poor man's version of Grand Admiral Thrawn from *Star Wars*?"

"Okay, he's pretty bad." She sniffled, then laughed softly through her tears when Spock hissed, seeming to express his own disapproval of the troll. "But I'm a close second."

"Tell me what happened, and Spock and I can vote on where you rank in the Bad Guy Hall of Fame."

"I can't." She buried her face in her hands. "It's too awful. You'll wonder why you're even friends with me."

"It's clearly for the lifetime supply of coconut cake," he teased, lowering both of her hands. Cupping her chin, he tilted her face until she met his gaze. "Whatever happened, it's not going to change how I feel about you." He hadn't meant for his voice to sound so husky, but his emotions suddenly got the better of him.

Was it his imagination or did her pupils just dilate? Heat

radiated between them. He ached to kiss her, to draw her even closer into his arms and show her how deeply he cared. Instead, he cleared his throat and dropped his hand.

Be her friend, Jayce. That's what she needs right now.

"Tell me when you're ready. Or don't. Just know I'm here for you. Always."

A tear hovered near the corner of her eye, suspended in her thick lower lashes. Gently lifting her glasses, he gathered the tear on the tip of his finger, lingering against her soft skin a moment longer than necessary. What a cruel, exquisite kind of self-torment, to be so close to someone and yet still feel so far removed.

Someday, a man would come along to kiss her tears away. Then, one day, the same man would most likely become the reason for those tears. That was always the trade-off, wasn't it? Romantic Russian roulette, except every chamber was loaded with the barrel aimed right at the heart.

He couldn't protect her from every pain in life.

But he could strive to never be the cause.

Chapter Thirteen

CECE

CeCe's breath stalled in her throat, strangled by the scintillating sensation of Jayce's fingertips against her skin. His touch felt smooth yet strong, reassuring yet reckless. For the briefest moment, she allowed herself to imagine Jayce drawing her closer, angling his mouth to hers, kissing away every troubling thought. Heat surged through her, both from longing and mortification. *He's your best friend. You shouldn't want anything more than that.*

Dismissing the inappropriate fantasy, she swallowed hard. "Okay. I'll tell you."

He dropped his hand from her face. Even as he slid his arm around her shoulders, she could still feel the subtle pressure of his fingertips, lingering like an imprinted memory on her skin. His hand came to rest on her upper arm, a platonic gesture of comfort that unwittingly added fuel to her internal fire.

Focus, CeCe. She gazed into his striking blue eyes—the same deep hue as the sky after the sunset, before twilight gave way to the darkness. Part of her wanted him to see only the good in her, to appear flawless and above reproach. But at her core, where she yearned to be known and loved despite her imperfections, she valued the transparency of their friendship.

Over the years, they'd seen each other at their worst and bared the ugliest parts of themselves. Like in third grade, when she'd confessed to hiding her father's passport, which had resulted in a missed flight. Or when Jayce had admitted to cheating on a math test. In both cases—and many others involving similar poor choices—they'd encouraged each other to come clean and accept the consequences. CeCe didn't doubt that tonight would be the same.

Expelling a deep breath, she said, "I got in a fight with Mama."

"Really? You two never fight."

"I know. And I feel terrible about it. I think I really hurt her." She winced at the mental image of her mother's wounded expression—both shock and pain, like she'd been slapped without warning.

"What was the fight about?" He casually stroked her arm, as if the reflexive impulse to console her came to him as naturally as breathing.

"My dad." She scooted closer, resting her weight against him, gathering both solace and strength from his nearness. "He was supposed to come home the other night but didn't show. He told Mama the expedition had received additional funding at the last minute and had been extended. He didn't call me, though, which stings." Her last admission caught her by surprise. But the second the unconscious thought passed her lips, her heart ached. Why hadn't he called her? He'd simply expected her mother to pass along the message. Couldn't he spare five seconds to tell her himself? To apologize? To say he missed her?

But then, what else had she expected? Her father never called. Never texted. Never even emailed. A familiar feeling of unworthiness wormed its way into her heart, whispering long-held beliefs. *You aren't enough. You were never enough.*

Her eyes welled with unwelcome tears again.

Jayce squeezed her upper arm. "I'm so sorry, Toto. That's crummy. Your dad should've called."

Sniffling, she roughly rubbed the tears away. Why cry over someone who didn't deem her worth his time? "Yeah, well, instead of directing my frustration at my dad, where it belongs, I lashed out at Mama. I accused her of lying about her feelings."

"Is she?"

"Well, *lying* might be a harsh term, but she pretends like she doesn't care when Dad does stuff like this—when he's selfish and inconsiderate. But I know it breaks her heart every time. And I hate that she hides it." The words tumbled out of her now, unfiltered and unencumbered, rising from a wellspring of buried grief. "Whenever she gives him a free pass, when she makes excuses for him, I feel like I have to do the same. I've been doing it for as long as I can remember. And I don't want to pretend anymore. I'm hurt. And I'm angry. And—" She paused as a sudden realization crashed into her. "And I want Mama to finally confront him. I want her to tell him all the things I can't bring myself to say." Her fingers trembled with the release of repressed tension—tension she'd carried her entire life like a talisman of her inner turmoil. She curled her hands into fists in her lap to calm the shaking.

"And what do you want to tell him?" Jayce asked softly.

"I want to tell him—" She paused as a painful sob rose in her throat. *Don't cry. You've shed enough tears over him.* Swallowing past the uncomfortable tightness, she whispered, "I want my father back."

Despite her best efforts, tears fell as fragmented memories flooded her mind. Tiny, flour-covered hands kneading dough. A young girl, not yet tall enough to reach the counter without a stool. A father's smile—his laugh lines creased, his twinkling eyes fixed solely on her. Édith Piaf singing "La Vie en Rose" on an antique gramophone. The sweet, buttery scent of chouquettes browning in the oven. Happy, hazy snapshots her five-year-old brain had tried so desperately to preserve. The golden days before he left. Before he chose a career over his family.

"I want him to know it's not fair to say he loves us but not do anything to show it," she added, speaking for her childhood self—the little girl still longing for her father's affection.

Another less pleasant memory forced its way to the forefront of her thoughts. Her father on a phone call, wheeling a suitcase toward the front door. Not yet six, she'd run after him, tearfully pleading, tugging on his leg, begging him to stay. Distracted and agitated, his phone pressed to his ear, he hadn't said a word. He'd merely gestured to her mother, who'd knelt on the floor beside her, cooing in a consoling voice while she'd pried her fingers loose. That first expedition had lasted six months. And she'd cried herself to sleep for half of them, agonizing over a question she could barely understand at that age, let alone articulate.

Why wasn't I enough to make you stay?

Although she'd learned long ago how to put words to her wound, she couldn't bring herself to speak them now. How could she verbalize the question aloud when her father wasn't the only man she wanted to ask?

Jayce drew her closer, wrapping both arms around her, holding her tightly as she cried.

He'd never know half her tears belonged to her father.

And the other half belonged to him.

Chapter Fourteen

ABBY

ABBY STARED BLANKLY into her coffee cup, oblivious to the aromatic tendrils of steam wafting above the rim. Normally, she reveled in her morning routine, from sipping her favorite full-bodied Kenyan roast to preparing a gourmet breakfast for her guests. But today, not even assembling a lavish room service tray for Mystery Man—aka Thomas Maineland—could focus her fractured thoughts.

Max would come home from camp tomorrow. She couldn't wait to see him, but his homecoming also reminded her that she had no idea what to do about the future. Should they do whatever it took to pursue adoption, to give him a stable home and family? Or did she need to be more patient?

"Thinking about how to handle the situation with Max?" Logan entered the kitchen, fresh off a seven-mile run along the coastline. His skin glistened with sweat, and his blue eyes gleamed bright from the exertion.

"Is it that obvious?" She attempted a wry smile.

"It's all I can think about, too." He poured himself a tall glass of filtered water from the fridge, gulped half, then set the rest on the counter. Facing her with a steady gaze he said, "I think we should do it."

"Do what?" she asked hesitantly, too afraid to hope.

"I think we should pursue an expedited presumption of death for Sam Bailey."

"You do?" Her pulse quickened, and she suddenly felt lightheaded, her emotions swinging between joy and uncertainty.

"I was praying hard on my run, and I kept having the same thought: We've had so many close calls. Between a fake great-aunt and Carla having to pull strings with the foster care system so Max can stay with us, I don't want to risk losing our son to some phony relative, filing error, or flaw in the legal system. I want us all—me, you, and Max—to have security and assurance. And I think adoption is the best route to gain that certainty. What do you think?"

Her heart swelled. *Our son.* Had sweeter words ever been spoken? Too overcome with emotion to speak, she bobbed her head in a vigorous nod.

Logan beamed and swept her into his embrace.

She clung to him, arms wrapped around his neck, feet dangling above the floor, undeterred by his slick T-shirt or musky post-workout scent. Nothing could dampen this moment of joy and relief.

As he pulled back, Logan's smile vanished. "I know we're both excited by the possibility of moving forward, but we should try to regulate our expectations. The court might deny our request."

"I know."

"And there's still a chance the process will be really hard on Max."

The reality of his comment sobered her instantly.

He lowered her feet back to the floor, and her deflated

emotions followed. "But you still think we should go through with it?"

"I think if we don't, we're only postponing the inevitable. Sam's been missing for months. Even if he survived the storm, which would've required a miracle, he would've come back for Max by now."

"That's true." She'd come to the same conclusion many times. Although Max and his father hadn't lived in Blessings Bay for very long, and no one in town knew Sam Bailey well, he appeared to be a good father. At least, Max thought the world of him and often spoke about his dad as if he were some sort of superhero.

In fact, from the photo the authorities had circulated online in their attempt to locate Sam after his disappearance, he looked a lot like Jason Momoa in the Aquaman film—tall, muscular, and burly, with long dark hair and a bushy beard.

When Abby added Sam's skills as an avid sailor and swimmer, plus his affinity for the ocean and sea life—just like the aquatically inclined superhero—Max's father loomed larger than life in her imagination.

"So," Logan prompted, interrupting her wandering thoughts. "Should we call Carla and tell her we've made a decision?"

Abby swallowed one last lingering doubt. "Yes. Can you make the call? I need to take this breakfast tray up to Tom, and, now that we've decided, I don't want to postpone another second."

"Yes, ma'am." He flashed a teasing grin, perpetuating their playful inside joke where he called her ma'am in formal military fashion and she pretended to dislike it.

Rocking onto her tiptoes, she responded with a kiss. "I'll be back down in a second, so you can tell me what she had to say." Removing the Monte Cristo Casserole from the warmth of the oven, she served a heaping slice onto a fine china plate. She added the dish to the tray, placing it beside the seasonal fruit salad, lemon poppy seed scone, Greek yogurt topped with homemade maple pecan granola, and a glass of orange juice she'd hand-squeezed earlier that morning.

Anticipating her next move, Logan filled an antique teacup with piping hot Kenyan roast from the insulated French press and handed it to her.

She arranged the coffee on the tray next to a small sugar bowl and creamer, tweaked the tiny vase of tea roses, then gave a satisfied smile. *Perfect.* Hopefully, Tom would enjoy the selection. And maybe a big breakfast would help put some meat on his bones.

She carefully carried the tray upstairs and knocked on the door of their best suite.

The door swung open, and a freshly showered Tom stood on the other side. Water droplets beaded in his short-cropped hair, and he smelled like the fancy lavender soaps supplied in the en suite bathroom. Although squeaky clean, he wore the same oversize shirt and baggy jeans from the day before.

"Good morning," Abby said with a cheerful smile as she stepped into the room. *Wow.* He'd already made the bed with crisp hospital corners and arranged each throw pillow exactly in place. Apart from the open Blessings Bay travel brochure on the coffee table, the room appeared unused. "Would you like to eat in here or out on the balcony?" Most guests ate in the dining room, but a few, like Tom, opted to dine alone in their rooms.

"Outside would be nice, thanks." He followed her through the French doors to the balcony overlooking the garden and a breathtaking panoramic view of the Pacific Ocean.

"How did you sleep?" Abby set the tray on the cozy bistro table.

"Great. Something about the sound of the waves really knocked me out."

"I'm so happy to hear that." She hesitated, wanting to prolong their interaction to find out more about him, but blanking on casual yet meaningful topics of conversation. Especially since her thoughts lingered on Logan's call with Carla. "Well," she said, resolving to try again later. "Enjoy your breakfast. And let me know if I can suggest any outings or activities for the day."

"Thanks." He shifted his feet, still standing. "Thank you. For everything. You have a beautiful home. And I've enjoyed my stay."

Uh-oh. Sounds like a precursor to *goodbye*. She'd hoped to have more time to get to know Thomas Maineland, the mysterious man without a digital footprint. She couldn't shake the feeling he needed help of some sort. How could she find out for certain without scaring him off?

"I think I'll be on my way today, but I'm grateful for your hospitality."

As he confirmed her suspicions, her heart sank. He was leaving. Was he concerned about the price? Could she offer him another discount without offending his pride?

"I'd like to pay you for the room." He dug into his front pocket and withdrew a wad of cash along with a small, smooth stone. Aqua sea glass. He set it on the table to sort through the crumpled bills.

"That isn't necessary." She waved away his offer. "First night free, remember?"

"But this room. This breakfast. It's too nice. I can't accept—"

"You can," she interrupted with her warmest, most persuasive smile. "Just think of this as your lucky day." She nodded toward the pale blueish-green pebble. "My son, Max, collects sea glass. Aqua is his favorite color. He says it represents good luck."

"Your son, does he live here with you?"

"Yes, but he's away at summer camp. He comes home tomorrow." She couldn't stop her smile from spreading into a giddy grin of delight. "Sorry, I've really missed him. The thought of him coming home soon makes me so happy, it's hard to contain my excitement."

"You must love him a lot."

"More than I ever thought possible." Sensing an opening, she asked, "Do you have kids?"

He stared at her a moment without speaking, as if his mind had gone completely blank. After a long, awkward pause, he scooped the sea glass back into his pocket and said, "Actually, I'd like to stay one more night, if that's okay."

Taken aback by the abrupt change in topic, Abby took a moment to respond. "Um, yes, of course."

"Thank you." Without another word, Tom sat at the table and reached for his coffee, conversation over.

Flustered, Abby shuffled back through the French doors, trying to make sense of the strange shift in his demeanor. Had asking about his family been too intrusive? It felt like a natural segue. Why had such a simple question struck a nerve?

And even more perplexing, why had he suddenly decided to stay?

Chapter Fifteen

CECE

EARLY MORNING LIGHT fell across CeCe's eyelids, but she resisted the urge to open them. Her bed felt too snug and cozy, as if a soothing warmth radiated from the mattress itself. She couldn't remember the last time she'd slept so soundly.

Content in her cocoon of comfort, her thoughts drifted to the previous night. Jayce, holding her while she wept. He hadn't offered empty platitudes, only his presence. And, when the timing was right, the perfect amount of humor. Somehow, he'd taken her from tears to laughter, soothing the rough edges of her heart, giving her hope that eventually everything would be okay between her and her mom.

They'd ended the evening with popcorn—his trademark butter and Italian seasoning recipe—and a *Star Trek: The Next Generation* marathon. Then they'd fallen asleep and—

CeCe jolted from her half-awake haze, springing upright.

The figure beside her groaned softly but didn't stir.

Her cheeks flamed as reality swooped into focus. Her comfortable mattress looked more like Jayce's toned body stretched out on her couch.

Spock gazed down at them from his lofty position on the

back of the armchair, passing judgment on their compromising sleeping arrangement.

"It was an accident," she whispered, as if she needed to explain herself to a cat.

Frazzled, she searched for her glasses in the throw blanket and found them tangled in the fringe, luckily unharmed. Slipping them on, she glanced back at Jayce and swallowed, her mouth suddenly dry. His right arm arched above his head, bent in a way that accentuated his sculpted biceps. Just above his left temple, his thick, dark hair twisted in the most adorable cowlick. Her fingertips ached to untangle it. Truthfully, she longed to trace every inch of his beautiful face, from his full, perfect eyebrows to the chiseled contours of his jawline. Why did he have to be so sweet *and* so good-looking? At least the tiny dewdrop of drool in the corner of his mouth made him appear somewhat human. Should she wake him?

A knock at the door made the decision for her.

Her heart vaulted into her throat.

Jayce groaned again, but still didn't open his eyes. *Good grief.* The man could sleep through anything.

It must be Piper looking for her. She was usually down in the kitchen baking before sunrise, well before Piper started her shift.

"Wake up!" she hissed, shaking him by his exceptionally well-defined shoulders. *Yeesh.* How often did he work out?

"Five more minutes," he muttered, rolling onto his side.

Time for more drastic measures. She tugged off the throw blanket and tickled him in his weak spot, right below the ribs.

He instantly sprang to life, grabbed her hands, and pinned her backward on the couch.

She inhaled sharply, gazing up at him in surprise. Insanely fit *and* possessed catlike reflexes that could rival Spock's. *Impressive.*

He hovered above her, his body heat spanning the two inches between them. "What have I said about tickling me?"

"I forget," she lied, hiding a smile. His ticklishness had always been his Achilles' heel, and she'd unabashedly used it to her advantage more than once. Like the time he'd monopolized the Xbox when she'd wanted her turn. Or the one and only occasion he'd tried to read her diary when they were in second grade.

"I told you the punishment would fit the crime." He reached for her waist, but she blocked his attempt to tickle her in return, suppressing a laugh.

"Wait," she gasped, wriggling beneath his weight. "There's someone at the door."

With perfect timing, the knock sounded again, punctuating her point.

Jayce released her and sat back, his eyes wide as he appeared to piece together the events of last night. "Shouldn't we answer it?"

"And have someone think we spent the night together? I don't think so," she chastised under her breath. "Go hide in the bedroom until I can sneak you out."

"But we *did* spend the night together. And it was perfectly innocent. Can't we just explain that we accidentally fell asleep watching TV? Look." He pointed to her flat screen. The words *Are you still watching?* stared back at her. "See. There's proof."

"Great. Now you suddenly want a close relationship with the truth?" She rolled her eyes. "It still looks bad, and I'd rather not try to explain it." She jabbed her finger toward the bedroom. "Go."

He complied, albeit with some muttering, and Spock trotted after him. CeCe waited for her bedroom door to close before scrambling to greet Piper, her mind racing to form an excuse. *I fell asleep. Forgot to set an alarm. So sorry I—*

The words died on her lips the second she opened the door.

A bleach blonde in an expensive beige suit stood on the other side.

CeCe's heart stopped. She immediately recognized Jayce's shrewd and unsavory agent from photos on social media. Based on everything Jayce had told her, she'd never liked the woman at the best of times, let alone standing on her doorstep uninvited.

"You must be CeCe. I'm Gretchen Schroeder with SRT Talent Management. Jayce Hunt is one of my top clients." She peered over CeCe's shoulder as if she expected to see him. "Please tell him I'm here."

"It's nice to meet you, Miss Schroeder, but it's rather early in the morning, and I need to get to work."

"I'm sure your assistant manager, Piper, can handle things for a few more minutes. I really need to speak with Jayce, if you don't mind." She made a move to step inside, but CeCe didn't budge, blocking her from entering.

She *did* mind, thank you very much. And how did this woman know about Piper or that Jayce was in her apartment?

Eerily, as if she'd read her thoughts, Gretchen said, "I make it my business to know everything there is to know about my clients, including the people close to them. Which is why I'm still not sure how I didn't know about *you*." She swept an openly skeptical glance over CeCe from head to toe.

CeCe shivered beneath her brazen scrutiny.

"Frankly," Gretchen added coldly. "I find it hard to believe *you're* Jayce's fiancée."

Burning with embarrassment, CeCe tugged on the frayed hem of her oversize T-shirt as if the extra millimeter would cover the ice cream stain on her cotton shorts. The same shorts she'd owned since middle school. Why hadn't she updated her closet in the last decade? *Oh, right.* Because until this moment, she'd never cared about fashion trends. She loathed that this woman

—this *stranger*—had the power to make her second-guess her wardrobe.

"I think someone's ready for breakfast." Jayce strolled out of the bedroom, cradling Spock in his arms.

For a split second, CeCe enjoyed the flicker of shock on Gretchen's face. But her delight quickly faded, replaced by the mortification of the situation. She didn't want to give this woman the wrong impression of their relationship.

"Good morning, Gretchen. I see you've met my beautiful bride-to-be."

The way Jayce accentuated the word *beautiful*—with a casual confidence as if her beauty were the most obvious thing in the world—made CeCe stand a little straighter. Of course, she still felt compelled to set the record straight, and awkwardly blurted, "We fell asleep watching TV. He doesn't normally stay over."

Gretchen shot her a funny look that revealed her indifference to their lifestyle choices before glancing back at Jayce. "My sources said you'd be here, but I have to say, I'm surprised. You two must really be engaged."

"Happily." Jayce draped an arm around her shoulders, grinning like he'd won the matrimonial lottery.

From his perch in Jayce's other arm, Spock glared at Gretchen, his incisors bared.

CeCe's heart warmed. Between Jayce and Spock, she'd never felt more protected.

"What do you want, Gretch?" Jayce's tone had lost its cheerful edge.

"Now that the cat's out of the bag—"

Spock interrupted her analogy with an offended growl.

Startled, Gretchen paused and cast Spock a wary glance.

CeCe suppressed a giggle.

"Now that your engagement has been leaked to the press —" Gretchen amended.

"Earlier than we agreed upon." Now it was Jayce's turn to interrupt. He fixed Gretchen with a frown so stern, the Ice Queen actually squirmed.

CeCe had to admit, she didn't mind seeing the obnoxious woman thrown off her game.

Gretchen cleared her throat. "Based on some of the more, shall we say *unfortunate* headlines, I think we need to do some damage control."

To her credit, Gretchen refrained from detailing CeCe's disastrous debut in the spotlight. Was it possible the Ice Queen had a heart after all?

"I'd like to put our own spin on the press coverage," Gretchen continued. "Starting with some feel-good stories about how you two met, life in Blessings Bay, etcetera, etcetera. Let's really sell the sappy small-town fairy tale. But first," Gretchen added, turning to CeCe, "I'd like to meet the bride's parents. How soon can that be arranged?"

CeCe's stomach twisted. She met Jayce's eye. The shadows muddying his gaze mirrored her own fears.

If they didn't get Mama on board, their entire charade would fall apart.

Chapter Sixteen

JAYCE

JAYCE STRETCHED and curled his fingers, repeating the motion to help ease the tension creeping up his arms into his neck and shoulders. Midmorning sunlight sparkled across the water, bathing the marina in a golden glow, but he barely noticed, his mind stuck on earlier events.

His skin still singed hot whenever he recalled Gretchen's rudeness to CeCe that morning. He knew he'd been banished to the bedroom for good reason, but he couldn't hide while Gretchen insulted her. What planet did the woman live on? If someone was out of anyone's league, CeCe was out of his, by a long shot.

He'd said as much when he had a moment alone with Gretchen. He'd also made it clear he didn't appreciate her impromptu appearance. If she wanted to meet CeCe's parents —or anyone else in their lives—it needed to be on *their* terms, not hers. He wasn't sure how long he could keep her bulldog tendencies at bay, but he'd at least bought a couple more days to sort things out. Gretchen had headed back to LA in a semi-dignified huff, claiming she had a few other publicity angles to pursue. Hopefully, by the time she returned, his parents would be on board, and more importantly, CeCe and her mother would be back on good terms. CeCe needed her mom, and whether or not Mrs. Dupree participated in their plan, he wanted the two women to reconcile. But how could he help?

All ability to form a coherent thought, let alone brainstorm viable possibilities, vanished the second he caught sight of CeCe strolling down the pier toward him. Her legs looked incredible in cutoff jean shorts. And when he read the words on her graphic tee, he stifled a laugh. *I'm in My Nerd Era.* He loved the way she stayed true to herself despite the extra media scrutiny.

"Ready for this?" she asked, stopping beside him.

Clenching his fists again, he fixed his gaze on the end of the pier. The Unbound Bookshop gently bobbed in its slip, its polished wood and pristine white sails gleaming in the sunlight. He'd never seen a more beautiful boat. But the appeal of the vintage sailing schooner did little to ease his apprehension. It would be hard enough to sell his parents on his fake engagement scheme one-on-one, but contending with their constant bickering made the task feel impossible.

At least neither of them followed celebrity news and hadn't heard the gossip yet. Not that a blank slate to announce their sham engagement would make the morning any less unpleasant. "Is it too late to chew off my hands instead?" he asked wryly.

"I'm afraid so. But just in case..." She laced her fingers through his, giving his hand a firm squeeze.

Together, they trekked the remainder of the long pier. Jayce tried to steady his pulse, pacing each breath with the rhythmic lapping of waves against the wooden pilings. As they drew closer to their destination, agitated voices carried above the pleasant cadence of seagull cries, offering an ominous greeting.

"It's *The Curious Quest* of *Quinley Culpepper*," his mother insisted, putting extra emphasis on the word *of.*

"Actually, the title of the book is *The Curious Quest* for *Quinley Culpepper*," his father countered, his tone equally condescending as they debated the literary inspiration behind the day's themed brunch and sailing tour.

"Considering you've read five books in your entire life, please forgive me if I don't kowtow to your literary expertise."

"And forgive *me* if I'm not impressed by your pretentious vocabulary."

"Pretentious?" his mother snapped. "Is it my fault you don't know the meaning of *kowtow*? Or is it the words *forgive me* that you find so unfamiliar? Goodness knows you've never said them yourself."

Ouch. Jayce winced. Not even noon and they'd already dragged out the heavy artillery. "Ready to abandon ship?" he whispered to CeCe. "I think I'd rather be shark bait."

"Not yet," she whispered back. "But I'm willing to consider shoving you overboard as a last resort." Still holding his hand, she tugged him up the gangway.

His parents stood on deck, squared off like two buccaneers about to cleave each other to the brisket. However, if it weren't for their scowls and hostile posture, they could be mature cover models for Nautica or J. Crew. Both his parents still looked great, even in their unoriginal—and ironically well-coordinated —ensembles of linen pants and nautical striped shirts. Sure, they'd gained a few extra pounds over the last decade, but they carried them well. His father still had all his hair, even if it boasted a little more salt than pepper these days. And his mother had finally ditched her after-divorce dye job, trading the overly processed blond style for her natural chestnut waves. A good call, in his opinion.

Seeing them together conjured wistful memories—memories from a happier time, before all the anger and bitterness. Pre-split, his parents had the kind of gross, lovey-dovey, excessively affectionate relationship kids complained about but secretly appreciated because it made them feel safe. They'd been husband and wife, best friends, and equal partners. Until they weren't.

Now, they argued over prepositions in book titles. And chased people away with their toxic unpleasantness. He had a feeling Sage and Flynn had ducked below deck until the tension died down. He had half a mind to join them.

"Hey, Mom. Hey, Dad."

"Jayce!" His mother beamed, the literary feud momentarily forgotten.

"Welcome home, son." His father matched her shift in demeanor.

"Thanks for coming." Jayce tightened his grip on CeCe's hand, grappling for the right words. Despite rehearsing a hundred different variations of his speech, he had no idea what to say next.

"Of course! I wouldn't miss a rare opportunity to see my baby boy," his mother chirped, adding, "Although, I'm not sure why we had to meet *here*." Her tone and less-than-subtle glance at his father implied she also didn't understand why he'd been invited.

Jayce cleared his throat, glancing at CeCe for moral support.

She met his gaze with an encouraging smile.

Turning back to his parents, he squared his shoulders. *Best to rip off the Band-Aid.* "CeCe and I have something to tell you."

His mother's gaze shot to their entwined hands, settling on the large diamond glittering on CeCe's ring finger. Her dark-blue eyes doubled in size.

Shoot. He should've picked a different segue.

Covering her mouth with both hands, his mother squealed,

"You're engaged!" and rushed toward them. Yanking CeCe into a lung-crushing hug, she cried, "I've prayed for this moment for so long!"

Panic-stricken, CeCe tossed him a pleading glance that silently screamed, *Fix this.*

Heat scorched the back of his neck. *Peachy.* So far, they weren't off to a great start. "Hang on, Mom. It's not what you think. We're—" *We're what?* Why couldn't he get the words out?

"Don't tell me she's pregnant," his father said sternly.

"Dad!" Jayce cried, horrified by the suggestion. He seriously contemplated throwing himself and CeCe overboard to the mercy of the murky water below. Even becoming shark charcuterie had to be better than this.

CeCe made a wheezing sound, either from death by embarrassment or because his mother still hadn't relinquished her enthusiastic choke hold.

"We're not pregnant. Or engaged. Well, not technically. We're fake engaged." *Good grief.* He was floundering in his own work of fiction. The plan hadn't sounded so complicated in his head.

His mother finally released CeCe and took a step back. "Wait. What exactly are you saying?"

Jayce clumsily recounted the details of the situation, focusing on Stacey and her predicament and how he'd tried to shield her real engagement by fabricating a fake one so she and Rob had a fair shot at happiness. Somehow, the scenario sounded even more ludicrous the more times he explained it. When he finally reached the end of his monologue, he asked, "So, what do you think? Can you guys play along for a week or two?"

"Sure, why not!" his mother said so quickly and cheerfully, Jayce wondered if he'd hallucinated her response.

"Karen!" his father chastised, equally baffled by her gung-ho reaction.

"Oh, lighten up, Raymond." She gave a dismissive flick of her hand. "It could be fun." Sliding an arm around CeCe's waist, she added, "If the only way I get to claim this adorable girl as my daughter-in-law is by planning a fake wedding, then I'm going to plan the best fake wedding ever."

"That's sweet, Mom. But you won't really need to *do* anything. Just don't blow our cover if you're approached by Gretchen or the paparazzi. I'd actually prefer you say as little as possible."

"Nonsense. If you want me to play along, then I want to have some fun. That is, if your fuddy-duddy father doesn't insist on ruining it for everyone by being his usual stick-in-the-mud self." She flashed a smug smile, and Jayce suddenly realized, for better or worse, agreeing to the plan had become some sort of parental competition.

"Jayce didn't come by his acting abilities by accident, Karen. I did *Hamlet* in college, so I can certainly be a fake groom's father for a few weeks. More convincingly than you'll play your role, I'll wager."

"We'll see about that." Her eyes narrowed in a challenging glare.

Uh-oh. This didn't bode well. He'd wanted his parents to quietly cooperate, not perform a Shakespearean tragedy.

Around every corner, his well-intentioned plan only grew more complicated. Maybe he needed to call off the charade before things got out of hand. But whenever he looked at CeCe by his side, wearing his ring, he couldn't bring himself to take that step, as if their tangled illusion had become far more tantalizing than the truth.

Chapter Seventeen

LOGAN

SHIELDING his eyes from the sun, Logan scanned the marina for the *Jolly Regina*. Spotting the weather-beaten pocket trawler wedged between two svelte sailboats, he made his way down the pier, propelled by an intense urge he couldn't shake since his conversation with Carla earlier that morning.

A gruff-looking fisherman in grungy oilskins descended the gangway carrying two large coolers.

"Good haul today?" Logan asked, meeting him at the bottom of the gangway.

An indiscernible grunt served as a reply.

This wasn't going to be easy. "Garth, right? Garth Henderson?"

The man eyed him warily beneath his wide-brimmed boonie hat. Based on the behemoth's impressive girth and massive, scarred hands, Logan didn't want to get on his bad side. He had a feeling a tussle with Garth Henderson would rival wrestling a grizzly bear—a grizzly bear who smelled like diesel fuel and dead fish. *Tread carefully.* "I hear you knew Sam Bailey."

Without a word, Garth set the coolers down, then turned, prepared to head back up the gangway for another load.

Despite the man's surly, antisocial reputation, Logan couldn't let him walk away without answers. From the moment he'd told Carla to move forward with the expedited death certificate, an overpowering need consumed him—a need to learn more about the man he'd just propelled toward an official declaration of death. "I'm Logan Mathews, Max's foster dad."

Max's name stopped Garth's enormous rubber boots midstride. "You're taking care of Sam's kid?" He slowly swiveled back around.

"With my fiancée, Abby. We love Max like he's our own. I'm not trying to stir up trouble. I'm sure you were questioned during Sam's initial disappearance. I just want to—" Logan paused, struggling to verbalize his complicated string of emotions. Expelling a heavy breath, he confessed, "I just want to know more about Max's father. I want to know what kind of man he was. He'll always be a part of Max, and I want to honor that, to help keep his memory alive." His chest tightened as his jumbled thoughts gained some clarity.

He couldn't bring Max's father back from the grave, but he could do everything in his power to respect and preserve his role in Max's life.

Garth studied him a moment, his swarthy features softening beneath a bristly beard that covered most of his face. "Talk to Iris."

"Iris?"

"Iris Hodge." With a single name, Garth concluded their conversation and plodded back up the gangway.

"Wait. Was she a friend of Sam's? Girlfriend?" To his recollection, neither Max nor Carla had mentioned her before. At least, not by name.

Over his shoulder, Garth barked, "Landlady," and disappeared aboard his dilapidated boat.

Logan remained motionless, processing the information. Carla had mentioned they'd lived in a rental of some kind during their brief stay in Blessings Bay, but she hadn't been more specific than that. And he doubted she could legally pass along the woman's information anyway. But he needed to find her.

Pulling out his cell, he dialed the one person in town most likely to know Iris Hodge—his notoriously nosy neighbor, Verna.

His hunch paid off, and several minutes later, Logan found himself standing outside a quaint Cape Cod–style cottage on the outskirts of town. Four-feet-tall zinnias in vibrant pinks, purples, and reds lined a quintessential white picket fence. Impressed by the swath of colorful cosmos, salvia, and coneflowers, he made a mental note to ask Iris for gardening tips if he got the chance.

He knocked on the cheerful blue door.

A white-haired woman in her golden years—late eighties, maybe?—greeted him wearing a smudged gardening smock. "Hello?"

"Iris?"

"Yes, how can I help you?"

"I was hoping I could ask you a few questions about Sam Bailey."

"Sam?" Her voice softened, a note of warmth in her whisper.

"Sam and his son, Max, used to live here with you?"

"Yes. Briefly. In my guesthouse out back. Best tenants I ever had." Her pale silvery eyes clouded, as if the memories were bittersweet. "What is it you'd like to know?"

Logan sensed the woman cared for both Sam and Max.

And, unlike Garth, she seemed willing to talk. Impulsively, he asked, "May I trouble you for a glass of water?"

Iris countered his request with a pitcher of sweet tea and homemade shortbread cookies that she served in a back garden even more lush and vibrant than the one out front. While she freely shared stories about Max and Sam, Logan listened with interest, surveying his surroundings.

Max had played in this garden. He'd probably climbed that maple tree and fed the mottled koi fish lazily circling the small pond. The guesthouse, with its cutesy pink gingham curtains and overflowing window boxes, looked more like a granny's hobby shed than a home for a burly fisherman and his young son, but what it lacked in space and masculinity, it made up for in coziness. He could see Max being happy here.

"I miss Max's laughter and the sounds of his rowdy play," Iris admitted, her gaze sweeping the serene garden. "It's too quiet now."

"What about your new tenants?"

"I never had the heart to replace Max and Sam. Not after what happened." Her gaze fell to her iced tea. "Such a tragedy." She swiped a finger through the beads of condensation on the glass. "I suppose I'll have to find new tenants soon. I'm on a fixed income. But it's hard to imagine anyone else living there." A faint blush crept across her cheeks. "That must sound silly, since they were only here for a few months."

"Not really. Max makes an impression on your heart pretty quickly."

Meeting his gaze, she smiled as if they shared a special secret. "He does, doesn't he? You know," she said softly, glancing down at her iced tea again. "After what happened, I thought about taking Max in myself. But at my age, I didn't think I could offer what he needed." Her tone bore a note of shame. *Poor lady.* She'd carried that guilt a long time.

Logan reached across the table to pat her hand. "God worked it out."

She raised her chin and nodded tearfully. "I'm so glad Max found a happy home. You seem to love him very much."

"I do." A lump formed in his throat. *Yeesh.* When had he become such a softy?

He gulped the rest of his iced tea and set the glass on the table. "Thank you for taking the time to tell me about Sam." He now felt like he had a fuller picture.

From Max's point of view, Sam sounded larger than life, like some mythical figure from storybooks. Logan didn't mind. He wanted Max to admire his father. But now, in addition to Sam's supernatural skills at everything from fishing to soccer to belting popular sea shanties, he knew the man worked hard, long hours, but always made time for his son when he could. He'd even helped Iris with tasks around the house like heavy lifting, taking out the trash, and assembling a bookshelf, despite being spread thin. Although, he'd been banned from helping around the garden due to a deadly black thumb.

Logan also learned the man mostly kept to himself. He didn't do social media or dating apps or much of anything pertaining to technology. And in all the months they'd lived here, they'd never had a single guest over. Even though he'd supplied Iris with fresh fish without asking for anything in return, he'd never accepted her invitations to dinner.

"It was nice to talk about him," Iris said wistfully. "They had no one in their lives. And Max is so young. I worry that someday Sam will be forgotten."

"I'll make sure that doesn't happen," Logan promised. "By the way, what happened to their belongings?"

"Someone in law enforcement came to collect everything. I suppose it's evidence until..." She fell silent, but Logan could guess her unfinished thought.

Until Sam is declared dead.

"Iris," he said gently. "Based on what you knew of Sam and his skills as a sailor, do you think it's possible he survived that storm?"

Iris studied the cubes of ice melting in her glass. Finally, she met his gaze, her eyes filled with a profound sadness. "All I can say for sure is, based on how much Sam loved his son, *if* he survived, nothing in the world could keep him away."

Logan nodded in understanding. That's what he thought.

Sam Bailey sounded like a man he'd like to know. A man he respected.

How was it possible to mourn a man's death while also feeling gratitude for the unintended aftermath? Without Sam's tragic passing, life with Max wouldn't exist.

And what kind of life would that be?

Chapter Eighteen

CECE

AFTER A LONG CLOSING shift at the café, CeCe schlepped into her apartment and kicked off her shoes. "Today was the craziest day," she told Spock, who couldn't look less interested as he lazily opened his eyes then returned to his nap.

CeCe ignored his indifference. "You would not believe how well Jayce's parents reacted to the whole fake fiancée scenario." She flopped onto the couch beside Spock, disturbing his sleep again.

This time, he had the decency to at least *pretend* to listen while he slowly licked his paw.

"Mrs. Hunt even seemed excited by the idea." CeCe's cheeks flushed as she recalled the woman's reaction earlier that morning. *I've prayed for this moment for so long.* Did that mean what CeCe thought it meant? Did Karen Hunt want her and Jayce to be together? She'd always known his mother liked her. They got along well. But after all these years of being best friends with her son, did Karen Hunt hope for more?

CeCe couldn't help comparing Karen's instant support to her mother's stinging rebuke. Guilt immediately rose in her gut.

She should call. No, they should talk in person. But what should she say?

Suddenly achy, she heaved herself off the couch, exhausted from a morning of sailing in the hot sun followed by a busy workday—not to mention all the emotional stress—and made her way to the kitchen to fix Spock dinner.

She stopped short when she spotted a stunning floral arrangement adorning her small dinette set. The vibrant bouquet boasted tropical orchids and hibiscus, including her mother's favorite variety, the Blue Mahoe, which wasn't blue at all, but rather a deep crimson color.

Inhaling the delicate, fruity fragrance of the blooms, she plucked a tiny envelope propped against the crystal vase. The crisp white paper bore the logo from a fancy Los Angeles florist. Her pulse quickened as she slid out the note card.

I've heard flowers are the best way to mend fences.

CeCe smiled, pressing the card to her chest. Jayce wanted her to fix things with her mom. And he'd had an extravagant floral arrangement express delivered to aid her efforts. The sweet gesture must have cost him a fortune.

While he may have inadvertently caused all the chaos with his latest shenanigans, she appreciated his thoughtfulness. Even when his thoughtfulness sometimes led to terrible decisions, like faking an engagement to help out a friend.

After feeding Spock and grabbing a quick snack, she hoisted the massive vase into her arms and headed to her mother's house, hoping the right words would materialize on the way.

When she arrived—miraculously without tipping over the vase on the bumpy drive—she paused on the doorstep. Should she knock? Let herself inside? She and Mama never fought. What was the appropriate protocol for mother-daughter amends? *Don't overthink it.* She eased opened the door. "Mama?"

No answer.

Knowing Mama would usually be making dinner at this time of day, CeCe made her way into the kitchen.

Still no sign of her.

CeCe set the bouquet on the scuffed dining table surrounded by mismatched chairs.

That's when she noticed the album.

Her pulse fluttered. Hesitantly, she took a seat and flipped through the faded photos stuffed into shiny plastic sleeves.

Snapshots of happy memories.

Her parents, young and smiling against the backdrop of a pristine white sand beach. Mama wore a Blue Mahoe tucked behind her ear. Her father held her around the waist proudly, as if he knew he'd landed the most amazing woman in the world.

Mama, barefoot and beaming in front of their home, a brightly colored muumuu stretched across her round belly. She must've been eight or nine months pregnant.

CeCe, as an infant, her chubby hand curled around her father's finger.

CeCe's eyes stung as she studied the image. Her father's features radiated love and adoration, his gaze fixed intently on her pudgy little face, as if nothing else in the universe existed.

A tightness crept from her chest to her throat, making it hard to breathe.

More photos stared back at her.

Their first fishing trip. The time they'd baked beignets and he'd put her in charge of the powdered sugar—to disastrous yet comical results. Their pretend archeological dig in the garden, much to Mama's dismay.

These images, the hazy recollections, conflicted with others she'd held even more closely.

The countless Christmases he hadn't come home. All the birthdays he'd missed. Her high school graduation, when he'd watched her receive her diploma but caught a flight to Egypt before the celebratory dinner.

The photos in front of her depicted a loving, doting, *present* father. But her own memories told a different story. They revealed a man who had more pressing priorities than being present.

In her pain and resentment, she'd chosen that version of her father—the one who didn't spend enough time with his family —over the man in the photos. Perhaps because it hurt less than to try to understand how he could love them and still choose to leave.

CeCe jumped at the creaking of the screen door. She quickly dried her eyes as Mama came in from the back porch, a basket of fresh herbs slung over her arm.

Her mother's gaze fell to the photo album, then back to CeCe's tear-streaked face. She opened her mouth to speak, but CeCe beat her to it.

"I'm so sorry." She scrambled to her feet, her entire being exhausted from the weight of her bitter, long-buried burden. "I'm so sorry for what I said last night. There were a million better ways to handle that conversation. I let my feelings take control of my words. I wasn't kind. Or understanding. I lashed out at you, and that was wrong."

Her voice cracked, choked by emotion, by all the disjointed thoughts crashing together in her mind. "I've spent my whole life viewing my relationship with Dad in terms of black and white, right and wrong. I wanted the situation to be straightforward and uncomplicated, so I could hold on to my anger. Because anger was easier." Easier than what? Easier than talking to him, than facing a more complicated truth? She let the tears fall freely now, too off-balance and confused to bother wiping them away. "I don't know what I'm trying to say other than I'm sorry. I'm sorry I hurt you. You're the most important person in my—"

"*Ma chouquette.*" Her mother dropped the basket at her feet, rushing to embrace her. Holding her close, she cooed soft affirmations, stroking her hair as if she were five years old again while they cried together. "*I'm* sorry, my sweet girl. For not seeing how deeply this affected you. For not talking to you. For not *listening* to you. I thought I was being strong by—" Her voice broke with the strain of a rising sob, and CeCe couldn't bear it.

"It's all right, Mama. We can talk about it later. I just want to know that everything is okay between us."

"Always." Her mother pressed a kiss to the top of her head.

Sniffling, CeCe pulled back and attempted a smile. "I have something that might cheer you up." She stepped to the side, granting a full view of the flowers on the table. There would be time to dissect the deeper issues later. At least now, a dialogue had been opened. But for the moment, she simply wanted a chance to breathe and rest in their reconciliation.

Her mother's teary eyes brightened at the sight of the exotic blooms. "Blue Mahoe? How did you—?"

"I didn't. Jayce did. He knew I wanted to apologize, but didn't know how to take the first step. You know, since we so rarely fight." She grinned, offering some levity.

"That boy always did know the way to my heart." Smiling, Mama buried her face in the fragrant petals. When she'd finally had her fill of the sweet scent, she straightened, her features suddenly somber. "I still can't condone what you two are doing. And I won't lie for you. But I won't get in the way, either. If questioned, I'll stick with 'no comment.' Or answer in a way that's truthful, without revealing your secret."

"Wh-why?" As much as she'd hoped for the impossible,

CeCe hadn't expected her mother to change her mind so quickly.

Her mother caressed the crimson petals, answering her question with one of her own. "Did you know the Blue Mahoe is the national tree of Jamaica?"

"Of course." CeCe frowned, confused by her mother's change in topic. She'd made sure her daughter learned all about her heritage at a young age.

"It stands for strength and resilience," her mother continued, repeating a fact CeCe knew well. Mama stared intently into the heart of the flower, as if it held a hidden wisdom. "As a mother, you want to do everything in your power to protect your children, even from themselves. But sometimes, you have to let them learn from their mistakes, knowing God can use those moments to rebuild someone stronger than they were before." She let her fingers slip from the petal, meeting CeCe's gaze. "Hungry? I was about to start dinner."

CeCe blinked, startled by the abrupt shift in conversation. "Uh, sure."

Mama stooped to gather the herbs off the floor.

CeCe knelt to help, but couldn't shake her mother's words. Part of her wanted to be thankful Mama wouldn't blow their cover.

But another more cautious part couldn't help wondering if she should heed her mother's warning. How far was too far to go for a friend?

Chapter Nineteen

JAYCE

JAYCE STOOD ON THE CURB, staring at a tall lemon tree separating two distinct houses. The tree's trunk rooted firmly in the front yard of the home on the right, his mother's home, a pretty French provincial style with a flower-lined walkway. But the bulk of the branches arched into his father's yard on the left, a sturdy craftsman with a stone facade.

The lemon tree served as the focal point of their feud as well as their neighboring yards. His mom constantly accused his dad of covertly pruning the tree to his advantage, an absurd claim his father adamantly denied. More than once, Jayce offered to cut it down, curtailing the exhausting argument once and for all. But whenever he introduced the topic, his mother got all teary-eyed at the suggestion and changed the subject.

Ugh. Why had he agreed to come tonight? He usually avoided their petty conflicts at all costs. Regret mounted with each step he took up his mother's slate pathway, culminating in an intense urge to flee the moment his father leaned out his open window.

"Jayce!" His dad waved. "Stop by after dinner for some coffee and coconut cake I picked up from CeCe's place."

"Uh, sure, Dad." He gritted his teeth. And thus began the battle for his attention. Too bad CeCe couldn't join him as a buffer. He thought of the flowers he'd left for her, using his key, and hoped her night turned out better than his.

He reached for the doorknob, but his hand met dead air as the door swung open.

"Go back inside, Raymond," his mother barked. "Jayce is having dinner with me tonight."

"I know that, Karen. I invited him over for dessert."

"And what makes you think I didn't make a dessert to go with dinner? As a matter of fact, I made a lovely German chocolate cake."

Oof. Jayce winced. German chocolate cake. His father's favorite. Had she forgotten? Or was the dessert menu supposed to be another dig at his dad?

"Nothing wrong with having two desserts," his father countered. "He can come over afterward. Unless you plan on holding our son hostage."

"Don't be ridiculous." Rolling her eyes, she grabbed Jayce's arm. "Let's go, honey. Dinner is getting cold." Without another word, she yanked him inside and slammed the door.

Jayce spent the next ten minutes perched at the kitchen counter while she assembled a salad, shredding the lettuce with all the ferocity of a lion dismantling its prey. The roast, which wasn't in any danger of growing cold, crisped in the oven, filling the once-cheerful kitchen with the savory aroma of caramelized brown sugar, rosemary, and sage.

The ample space, with its tall cream cabinets, large maple island, and French cottage decor, used to be their happy place. Family dinners around the rustic farmhouse table. Enormous Saturday breakfasts when they'd all cook together, flipping flapjacks, baking homemade buttermilk biscuits, and slicing fresh fruit. They'd listen to classics from the sixties, and his parents would sing along or dance together, becoming especially mushy whenever "their song" came on. "Stand By Me" by Ben E. King. Talk about irony.

Now, the once bright and sunny room looked sad, somehow. Too large. Too empty. He couldn't wait to leave.

Seemingly oblivious to his somber mood, his mother slid the roast from the oven. "How's your grand plan working out?"

"So far so good." He stole a cherry tomato from the cutting board and popped it in his mouth. "I talked to Stacey this afternoon. She's attending the award ceremony on Friday, then she and Rob are eloping in Italy." Jayce smiled, recalling how excited she sounded. They wouldn't be able to avoid the paparazzi forever, but Stacey thought Rob would handle Hollywood life better once they were married. Jayce hoped she was right.

"No, not that. How's your *real* plan going?" His mother met his gaze, her eyes twinkling as she tugged off her oven mitts.

"What d'you mean?"

"Don't play coy with me, Jayce Harrison," she teased, evoking his middle name for emphasis. "I'm your mother. I know exactly what you're doing."

"And what am I doing?" he asked cautiously, stealing another tomato.

"You're hoping that by faking an engagement, CeCe will realize she's madly in love with you."

Jayce coughed as the cherry tomato caught in his throat. *What did she say?* He slammed a fist against his chest to dislodge the choking hazard, then reconsidered. Maybe losing his air supply would be preferable to wherever this conversation was headed.

His mother handed him a glass of water. "Don't be so dramatic. It'll be our little secret."

Jayce guzzled the cool liquid, then swallowed, finally able to breathe again. "Mom, I don't know what you're talking about."

She offered a patient smile. "Sweetheart, I've known how you feel about CeCe for years. I can see it in the way you look at her. It's the same way your—" She stopped short, her features strained as she glanced at the floor. Was she about to say *the same way your father used to look at me*?

Straightening, she wiped her hands on her apron, her calm countenance restored. "I think it's sweet you're going to such great lengths to woo her, but honey, real life isn't like one of your romantic comedies. Love doesn't require some elaborate ruse. You could've just asked her to dinner and told her how you feel."

"Mom, that's not— I don't—" He stumbled over his words, heat creeping up his neck. "That's not why I'm doing this." He noticed he hadn't denied being in love with CeCe, only that she hadn't been his motive for the fake engagement. "I'm just trying to help a friend." He tried to sound confident in his claim, but was it true? He'd thought so. But now, faced with his mother's wild theories, he wasn't so sure.

Thankfully, before she could press further, his phone rang.

He checked the caller ID, and his pulse quickened.

"Sorry, Mom. Gotta take this." He slipped off the stool and stepped into the next room.

"Mr. Delance, hi. Thanks for calling." Jayce wiped a sweaty palm on his jeans.

"Call me Victor." The man's rich, deep voice carried above the cacophony of a fancy dinner party in the background. "I gotta admit, kid. I almost didn't call. But Steve's a good friend of mine."

"I understand, sir. And I appreciate your time." Jayce's heart hammered in his throat.

"Steve's the best director in the biz," Victor Delance continued. "When he sends a project my way, I tend to trust his judgment."

Jayce nodded, even though the producer couldn't see him.

"He says you have a script I should take a look at. Why don't you—" Muffled voices cut off his sentence, momentarily drawing Victor away from their conversation.

With the phone pressed tightly to his ear like a permanent appendage, Jayce paced the carpet in the sitting room—a paisley wool pattern he didn't recognize. Another item his mother had replaced after the divorce. *Good grief. Focus, man.* Jayce forced himself to stand still, waiting in agonizing silence.

"Sorry about that," Victor said after the longest pause in human history. "Listen, kid. I won't make any promises, but bring the script and a synopsis to the award ceremony this Friday, buy me a drink at the after-party, and I'll take a look."

"Yes, sir. Thank you, sir. I appreciate it."

"By the way," Victor added. "What's it called?"

"What's it called?" Jayce asked dumbly.

"The script, son. I assume your movie has a title."

"Right. Yeah. Of course." *Smooth. You're a regular Aaron Sorkin.* After gathering a breath, he slowly released it. "*The Uncomplicated Café.*"

A weighty lull followed, during which Jayce reevaluated all his life choices. Why hadn't he titled his film something else? Something less obtuse. Less artsy. Who did he think he was? Woody Allen?

After a beat, Victor said, "Interesting. I like it. We'll see how it holds up."

And with that, the producer who cradled the fate of Jayce's fledgling screenwriting career in his hands ended the call.

Jayce didn't move.

This was the moment he'd fantasized about for most of his life.

The moment he'd been working toward ever since October 15 last year, when CeCe unknowingly pushed him to take the plunge—to finally face all the fears that had kept his dream on permanent pause.

Part of him couldn't wait to tell her the news. The other more vulnerable part didn't know how. Especially since she'd served as inspiration.

Plus, he needed to face one crucial but debilitating detail about his script: It didn't have an ending yet.

Chapter Twenty

ABBY

ABBY TAPPED her foot against the lawn in eager anticipation of Max's homecoming. Any minute now, Cynthia Richards would pull up to their curb with a van full of grungy eight-year-old boys, tired, unbathed, and overstimulated from two weeks at camp. Being the carpool mom wasn't for the faint of heart, and Abby couldn't be more grateful to Cynthia for her son's safe return.

She knew she'd miss him while he was gone, but she hadn't been prepared for how deeply. She'd waited her whole life to be a mother. And not just anyone's mother—*Max's*. The world seemed emptier without him, without his laugh, his silly antics, and his never-ending questions about random topics like the dietary preferences of pincher bugs.

Her foot tapped faster, as if her pent-up energy could hasten their arrival.

"Easy, Ginger Rogers," Logan teased, nudging her shoulder. "If you keep up with your tap-dancing routine, I'll have to patch a hole in the grass."

"Sorry. I can't help it. I can't wait to see him." She had the whole day planned down to the last detail in her mind. Most of the afternoon would be spent listening to Max recount his camp adventures, then they'd all attend the Bare Feet & Good Eats event at Blessings Beach that evening.

"Me, too," Logan admitted. "The past two weeks felt a whole lot longer."

Cynthia's silver van turned down State Street, and Abby bounced on her toes.

Logan laughed at her excitement.

The van parked along the curb.

Abby's breath hitched. *Only a few more seconds now.*

The side door slid open and a gangly boy with disheveled brown hair and rumpled clothes climbed out of the middle seat, lugging a sleeping bag, pillow, and duffel behind him. Was it her imagination or had Max grown six inches since he left?

Happy tears stung her eyes, and she bit her bottom lip. *Don't cry. You'll embarrass him in front of his friends.*

Max said goodbye to the other boys, and the door slid shut.

Abby waved her thanks to Cynthia before the woman drove away, then she turned her undivided attention back on Max.

His scruffy bangs stuck out on both sides, dirt covered his knees, and his T-shirt displayed more than one mystery stain. It probably smelled atrocious.

He's perfect.

With a gigantic grin, he scrambled up the lawn to greet them.

"Welcome home!" Abby beamed, flying her arms wide to embrace him.

"We missed you, buddy." Logan held out a hand to help with Max's bag.

But before he'd come within reach, Max froze midstride, his gaze laser focused on the house behind them. Uncertainty flickered in his light-brown eyes, followed by cautious confusion. He blinked slowly, squinting as if he didn't trust his own vision.

Then, in an instant, recognition flashed like a spark of blinding light.

"Dad!" Dumping his belongings in a heap, Max raced up the lawn, darting past Abby and her outstretched arms without a glance.

Bewildered, Abby spun around.

Thomas Maineland stood on the front porch, as still and expressionless as a statue.

"I knew you'd come back!" Max flung his arms around the man's thin waist, nearly knocking him backward with the force.

Tom stiffened, elbows elevated and bent at an awkward angle like a scarecrow on a stake.

Poor Tom looked beside himself with dismay and discomfort. Max had never looked happier.

Abby's heart ached, both baffled and broken by the worrisome scene.

Why had Max mistaken this man for his father? They looked nothing alike. Should she intervene?

Carefully weighing her words in her mind, she took a step forward then stopped cold.

In the span of a single second, Tom crumbled before her eyes. His features twisted as a flood of tears cascaded down his face, quickly escalating to an uncontrollable sob that shook his frail body. He fell to his knees and gathered Max to his chest, rocking back and forth as he wept.

Abby couldn't breathe.

The world turned upside down and inside out until all shapes and colors lost meaning.

"What just happened?" Logan echoed her tortured thoughts.

She swallowed against the tightness in her throat, her eyes burning. "I have no idea."

119

But one thing she *did* know: Nothing would ever be the same.

* * *

Abby sat pin straight on the sofa beside Logan, staring at the man across from her as if she'd never seen him before. Tom. Sam. Who was he?

He knelt on the floor beside Max, who cradled his lop-eared rabbit, Ron, in his lap. Max had been eager to introduce his new pet and hadn't stopped talking since he got home, enthusiastically regaling his dad with every detail he'd missed over the last several months. Tom, on the other hand, had barely spoken a word. He kept staring at Max as if he couldn't believe his eyes. More than once, Abby caught him wiping tears away. Tears that looked remarkably sincere.

If Max had mistaken the man's identity, Tom sure knew how to put on a good show. But they'd been down this road before, and all too recently. Everyone, including Carla, had been fooled into accepting a con artist as Max's distant great-aunt only a few months earlier. They'd almost lost Max for good. She couldn't let that happen again.

Abby jolted at a sudden knock on the door.

"Carla." Logan squeezed her hand and stood to answer the door. His features bore the same look of relief that she felt— Carla would put an end to this charade. She had access to DMV and medical records for Sam Bailey. She wouldn't be fooled by phony tears, no matter how convincing.

Her gaze flitted back to Max and Tom—aka Sam—on the floor. Her stomach knotted at the genuine glimmer of love in the man's eyes—warm brown eyes rimmed with amber. The same eyes staring up at him with unbridled delight. Max's eyes. How had she not made the connection before?

A wave of grief crashed into her as she instantly knew the truth, deep in her heart, in the dark corners of quiet intuition she'd tried to ignore. This wasn't a ruse or a misunderstanding Carla could fix.

Sam Bailey had returned.

"Sorry I took so long," Carla effused, although less than forty minutes had passed since they'd called with the news. "I had to run back to the office for some paperwork." She stopped short the second she caught sight of Sam and Max, visibly startled.

Abby knew how the woman felt. They'd all thought this moment would never come. And now that it faced them, it was difficult to process.

"Carla, look!" Max beamed up at her. "I told you my dad would come back."

"Yes, you did." Carla measured her response carefully. "Max, would you mind giving us adults a few minutes alone to chat?"

Max cast a worried glance at his dad. "But I want to stay with you."

Abby's chest tightened at the angst in his sweet voice. After all he'd been through, he didn't want to let his dad out of his sight again. She couldn't blame him. Max had suffered immensely in his father's absence, enduring more than any little boy should ever experience.

They all had the same question for Sam Bailey. A question to which Max, more so than anyone, deserved an answer.

"I don't mind if he stays," she said softly, trusting Carla to handle the delicate conversation with enormous care for Max's sake.

Logan nodded his agreement, reclaiming his seat on the couch beside her.

Carla looked at Sam. "And you?"

"I'd like Max to stay." Sam rose from his kneeling position on the floor and stood, offering his hand in introduction. "I'm Tom Main—I mean—" His sallow cheeks reddened slightly. He glanced at Max, then back to Carla, his flush deepening. "Sorry. I'm still a little, uh, disoriented." He cleared his throat. "I'm Sam."

"I'm Carla, Max's social worker." She shook his hand with a kind but reserved smile, then gestured toward one of the twin wingbacks. "Please, have a seat, Sam." She took the matching chair.

Sam tentatively eased himself onto the chair while Max sat on the floor by his feet, petting Ron.

His eyes wide and wary, Sam gripped the armrests, his body tense, like a trapped animal, unsure of its fate.

Abby's empathetic heart ached at his palpable discomfort. *Don't jump to compassion just yet*, she chided herself, trying to keep her expression unreadable. He'd better have a good excuse for his absence.

"Why don't we begin with you, Sam," Carla said gently.

"Okay." Sam's knee twitched with nerves. He cleared his throat again. "I, uh, don't really know where to start. I don't remember much of anything before I woke up in the hospital in Redton a few months ago."

"Were you sick?" Max asked in concern.

"Yeah, I guess you could say that." Sam leaned forward, resting his elbows on his thighs, looking more relaxed as he focused solely on his son. "You see, Max, my boat got caught in a storm."

Max nodded as if the information wasn't new to him.

"The storm sent my boat miles off course, and I don't remember exactly what happened, but I got lucky. A whale-watching tour found me, and I was taken to a hospital where I got the help I needed."

While Abby appreciated Sam's tactful explanation, she could read between the lines. Shipwreck victims often suffered from horrible ailments—dehydration, malnutrition, hypothermia, hypoxia, among many other possibilities. No wonder Sam looked so haggard. Her chest squeezed at the harrowing experience he'd endured.

"I know why you got lucky!" Max said proudly. "Abby and I prayed for you every night."

Sam's gaze flickered to Abby, then back to Max. He blinked rapidly as if to ward off tears. "Thank you," he said, his voice gruff with emotion.

"Plus," Max added. "You had the sea glass I gave you."

"The what?" Sam squinted as if he hadn't heard Max correctly.

"The sea glass," Max repeated. "The aqua piece I found. You always took it with you."

Sam shoved a hand into his pocket and withdrew a tiny bluish-green stone. "You mean this one?"

"Yeah. That's it."

"Y-you gave this to me?" Sam's voice cracked.

"Yeah. For good luck." Max cocked his head, perplexed by his dad's confusion. "You don't remember?"

"I—I remembered that it was important. That it meant something," Sam murmured, his glassy gaze fixed on the stone in his hand. Clenching his fingers around it, he closed his eyes, struggling to compose himself. When he finally opened his eyes again, they shimmered with tears. "They never found my wallet, or any form of identification. Only this." He uncurled his fingers, revealing the sliver of sea glass. "It was stitched into the watch pocket of my jeans. I had no idea—" His voice warbled, as if overcome by the revelation that he'd possessed a link to his son all this time. He swallowed, meeting Max's gaze. "When I woke up in the hospital, I'd lost my memory. I didn't remember who I was, where I lived, or anyone in my life."

"Oh." Max's face fell. "You didn't remember me?"

Sam shook his head, unable to speak, and Abby's heart broke for them both. She couldn't imagine what it would feel like to lose so much of yourself, to not even know what you'd lost. It had to be pure agony.

"I'm so sorry, Max," Sam croaked.

"But you remember me now?" Max asked hopefully.

"Yeah." Sam roughly rubbed the corner of his eye with his knuckle. "Yeah, buddy. I do."

"Good." Max nodded, satisfied with his answer. "Then you're all better now."

Sam smiled sadly. "Not quite. There's still a lot I don't remember. The doctors said my memories could come back all at once or in pieces, little by little. There's no way to know for sure. But there is one thing I know for certain." He held his son's gaze. "You're the most important person in the world to me. And as long as we're together, everything will be okay."

Max beamed up at his dad, and Abby's heart mended and broke all at once.

They'd finally witnessed the moment she and Max had prayed for—their miracle. And yet, while God had answered one prayer, He'd denied another. One family reunited meant the other one ripped apart.

How was it possible to be happy and heartbroken all in one breath?

"I don't understand." Logan's voice tore through her conflicted thoughts.

To anyone but her, his tone sounded calm and steady. But she caught the subtle undertone of tamped pain and felt the cold, clammy sweat on his palm pressed against her own.

They'd each lost something that day. Something they'd never get back.

"How did you know to come here, to Blessings Bay?" Logan asked.

"I can only describe it as an act of God," Sam confessed, addressing the adults for the first time. "After the coma, the hospital got me connected to a nonprofit that helps people in my situation. They set me up with a loaner vehicle, a place to stay, and a part-time job while I continued therapy and a legal aid worked on my case. They saved my life." His eyes glistened with gratitude. "One day on the job, someone mentioned this café he ran across on a day trip with his wife. While he raved about the coffee, I couldn't get the name of the place out of my head. It became an obsession. On my next day off, I drove out here, hoping to find out why I couldn't shake the feeling that it meant something. While that first visit didn't spark any memories, something told me to come back. So, I did. Day after day, praying for a miracle. Then Abby walked in." He met her gaze, communicating a world of appreciation in a single glance. "When you mentioned Max, something clicked inside here." He tapped his chest, over his heart. "I didn't know why or what it meant, but I had the same undeniable gut-level hunch when my co-worker mentioned the café. That's why I followed you, why I agreed to stay."

Abby reeled at his confession, unsure how to process the role she'd played in their reunion. What if she hadn't walked into CeCe's that day? What if she'd never mentioned Max? What would have happened?

"But it wasn't until you hugged me, Max," Sam continued, tousling his son's hair, "that some of my memories came back."

Max glowed with pride.

Straightening with an assertiveness Abby had never seen before, Sam told them, "God brought me back to my son. And words can't express how thankful I am to find him so healthy and happy." He glanced between Abby, Logan, and Carla. "I don't know how to repay you for taking care of Max when I couldn't."

Don't take him away, Abby's heart pleaded, but words wouldn't follow.

"We're happy to be here for Max," Carla said on behalf of them all. "And while I'm inclined to believe the events you described and can understand how such events would alter someone's appearance as drastically as they have yours, I hope you understand that there's a necessary protocol to follow. I'll need to contact the hospital and the nonprofit. And I'll need you to consent to a DNA test."

"Of course. I'll do whatever is necessary." Sam placed a hand on Max's shoulder. "I just want to be with my son."

My son...

Not hers. Not Logan's.

Their family no longer existed.

And she had no idea how to move forward from here.

Chapter Twenty-One

CECE

CECE SAVORED the last spoonful of her lemon bar ice cream, relishing the tart citrus burst blended with a sweet and buttery cookie crumble. The sun sank low in the sky, casting pinks and gold across the bay. A mirthful, raucous crowd mingled on Blessings Beach, dancing barefoot on the sand and broiling freshly caught fish in wire baskets over crackling bonfires.

She didn't usually enjoy such large gatherings, but tonight, with Jayce by her side, she'd never felt more at ease. They'd danced to classic cover songs by the local band, Blessings Beats, ate their fill of delicious food, and had even participated in the sandcastle competition. Sure, their attempt at re-creating the Starship *Enterprise* more closely resembled a pancake flanked by two deformed sausages, but they'd had fun. *Too* much fun. In fact, for the first time since Jayce left home, she'd wondered if he'd made the right decision. At least, the *safer* decision.

With half a state between them, she could more easily guard her heart. But being this close, spending so much time together, she found herself falling even deeper in love, despite her best intentions to keep an emotional distance.

Thank goodness for the paparazzi. Their presence—the

flash of bulbs and shouts to "hold hands" or "stand closer"—kept her grounded, reminding her that whatever currents of electricity she felt between them weren't real. The spine-tingling glances, the sultry smiles, even the intimate touches along her arm or gentle sweeping of hair away from her face, they were all part of the game. A game he played a little too well.

"Sorry about this," Jayce whispered, leaning in so close, she felt his warm breath graze the tip of her ear, making her shiver. "I promised them three hours of following us around, then they agreed to leave us alone for a while."

"It's okay." As they strolled the shoreline, watching the frothy tide tickle the sand, she tried not to focus on his heady scent—rich and musky with hints of sun and sea spray. "I'm actually amazed by the rapport you have with them. I've always viewed paparazzi as some feral species with no boundaries or common decency."

He laughed in his easy, infectious way. "We've come to an understanding over the years. They give me space and a little respect, and I make sure they get the photos they want. Occasionally, they'll go rogue, but I can usually rein them back in with a friendly conversation and a photo opp."

"Is there anyone you can't woo with your charm?" she teased.

"Just you." He cast her a sideways glance, but she couldn't read his expression. Was his tone purely playful? Or did she detect a hint of something more?

Best not to board that train of thought. "That's because I've seen you drink your weight in soda and burp the alphabet."

"Hey! I was fourteen. Give me a little credit. I'm a classy guy now."

She snorted in amusement, and they strolled a few more feet in companionable silence, enjoying the rumble of ocean waves as the celebratory cacophony dimmed in the distance.

"Look!" Jayce stopped abruptly and grabbed her hand, tugging her to stand beside him. Pointing toward the horizon line, he drew her attention to playful sea lions, ducking and diving in the water, silhouetted by the setting sun.

"Wow," she breathed. "They're beautiful." Her heart pounded in her chest. Jayce still hadn't let go of her hand.

"I had a good time tonight," he said softly, his tone low and rough.

"Me, too." Why did her throat feel so dry?

"Toto…" He turned toward her, meeting her gaze. Were his eyes always this blue? "There's something I need to ask you."

"You mean, besides if I'll marry you?" *Ugh*. Why did she have to joke at a time like this? He looked so sincere, so serious. And her heart couldn't handle it.

"Yeah, besides that." His lips scrunched to the side in a boyish smile. "It's another favor. The one I mentioned a while ago, when I called from Paris. You probably don't remember."

She did, although she'd pushed it from her thoughts. At the time, he'd made it sound like a big deal, claiming he'd be home in a few weeks to tell her about it. Then his filming schedule changed, and she hadn't heard from him again. She'd tried not to draw a parallel between Jayce and her father, despite the unsettling similarity, and had opted to give him the benefit of the doubt, deciding he'd simply changed his mind and no longer needed the favor.

He shifted his feet in the sand. Was he nervous? "There's this award ceremony at the end of the week, honoring achievements in the romantic comedy genre. I've been nominated in a couple of categories and—"

"Congrats, Jayce! That's amazing," she interrupted, unable to suppress her happiness and pride. Despite her own secret longing for an alternate reality where they could be together, she wanted nothing but the best for him. "Not that I'm surprised."

"Thanks. It's not a big deal, except that I have to attend or endure Gretchen's wrath. And she's unpleasant enough when she's in a good mood. I know you're not really into the showy Hollywood scene, but I was kinda hoping you'd go with me. As my date."

He held her gaze, his eyes soft and searching. The confident, cavalier, doors-always-open-for-me A-list celebrity wasn't standing before her. Just Jayce. The boy who'd climbed through her bedroom window the night his parents announced their divorce and slept on the floor by her bedside because he didn't want to go home. The boy who wasn't afraid to be vulnerable, to admit he needed someone.

He wanted her to attend the award ceremony. *As his date.* For moral support? Or something more?

"Toto?" He said her nickname again, as if she might have missed his question.

She briefly glanced away, collecting her thoughts, calming her racing pulse. She'd been down this road before, willing to bare her heart to him. And he'd made his feelings clear, with a single text, no less. But what if...? She looked into his eyes again. What if things had changed between them?

"Will you come with me?" he repeated.

"What kind of fiancée would I be if I didn't?" As soon as the teasing retort left her lips, she cringed inside. Once again, she'd used humor to hide the emotions simmering beneath the surface. Was it wisdom or weakness?

"I knew I proposed to the right woman." He grinned, matching her playful tone. But as quickly as the lighthearted sparkle in his eyes flickered to life, it dimmed. He turned solemn again. "There's something else I need to tell you."

He took a step toward her until they stood so close, she

could trace the faint outline of stubble along his jaw. She instinctively wet her lips. *Concentrate, CeCe.* "What is it?" Her own voice sounded foreign and far away, almost breathy, as if the ever-changing vibe between them—the emotional guessing game—had left her winded.

He raked his fingers through his hair. "I—"

"Kiss!" The shout preceded a flash of light.

CeCe jumped, her heart slamming into her chest.

"Kiss!" Another intrusive holler made the same demand.

CeCe flushed and stumbled a step backward.

Paparazzi clustered on the beach, cameras poised to capture their private moment.

Jayce waved them away, but they continued to chant in unison. "Kiss! Kiss! Kiss!"

"Come on, lovebirds. Give us a sunset smooch for the front page!" A man with a camera bag slung over one arm knelt in the sand, fixing them with his fancy lens.

Lovebirds... Is that what they resembled? That was the goal, wasn't it? The whole point of their ruse. Only, why, mere moments ago, had it suddenly felt real?

CeCe's cheeks burned hotter as the chant resumed. Conflicting emotions churned in her stomach, swelling and swirling with nowhere to go. Confused, flustered, and feeling exposed, she hissed, "It's fine. Let's just do it so they'll leave us alone."

Jayce tried to search her gaze, but she looked away. What if he could see the desire in her eyes? What if he could tell that, not so deep down, she actually *wanted* him to kiss her?

He took a step closer.

Her heart stopped beating.

The paparazzi cheered, expecting a show.

Cupping her chin gently with his fingertips, Jayce bent his head, his lips mere inches from hers.

Fire spread through her body, igniting every nerve ending like a torch touching a trail of kerosene.

This was it. He was actually going to kiss her.

Her eyelids fluttered, softly closing, then half opened, as if her brain couldn't discern between awake and dreaming.

"I can't," Jayce breathed, each syllable thick and labored. "Not like this."

Angling his face to hide their lips from view, he hovered his mouth over hers, lingering so close, she could almost taste him.

Her heart stung with the sharp prick of rejection, but a whisper of hope simmered beneath the surface.

Not like this...

Did a scenario exist where he *would* kiss her?

And if he did, what, if anything, would it mean?

Chapter Twenty-Two

JAYCE

JAYCE SQUEEZED HIS EYES SHUT, every muscle in his body straining, yearning to move one more millimeter.

How many times had he held this exact pose? So many, it had become rote, perfunctory, perfected to the point he could fake a kiss in his sleep.

So, why were his fingers shaking?

For the first time, he actually *wanted* to kiss the woman on the other side of the performance. So badly, the desire consumed him, almost pushing him to the point of no return.

But he couldn't kiss CeCe like this, tainted by paparazzi, under a guise.

It needed to be real. An undeniable, unyielding expression of his love for her. It needed to mean something. And if he crossed the line tonight, the opportunity for a perfect first kiss would be lost forever.

Satisfied with the photo opp, the paparazzi dispersed, leaving them alone on the beach once again.

Regretfully, Jayce dropped his hand, immediately missing the warmth of her skin. He took a step back in the sand, creating some much-needed distance between them. Maybe his heart would stop hammering if he could no longer feel the heat from her body.

Why did she have to look so beautiful in her casual cotton sundress with a plaid flannel button-up tied around her waist? She'd pinned back her curls with a clawlike clip, and he had a crazy urge to release them to the wind, to watch them dance around her face, to tangle them in his fingertips.

He cleared his throat, banishing the thought.

"Jayce?" CeCe murmured, her voice timid, tentative. She didn't quite meet his gaze. "What did you mean?"

His pulse throbbed as his own words rushed back to him.

I can't. Not like this.

Oh, no. Had he really said that aloud?

He'd been so focused on restraining his physical longing, he'd lost control of everything else. What explanation could he give her without revealing too much?

He decided to play dumb and rewind to an earlier part of their conversation, hoping she wouldn't press further. "You mean when I said I had something important to tell you?" He continued talking before she had a chance to respond. "I have a confession."

Her eyes widened, and for a split second, she looked wary, as if she wasn't sure she could handle whatever he had to say.

A pang of disappointment shot through him. Was she afraid he was about to confess his undying—and clearly unwelcome—love for her?

You're reading into things. Try to focus. He raked his fingers through his hair again, recentering. "Do you remember our conversation back in the fall? The one where you gave me some tough love?"

"The fifteenth of October," she said softly. "I marked it in my mind as potentially the last day you'd ever speak to me."

He smiled. If only she knew he'd fallen even more in love

with her that day. For her honesty. Her wisdom. And the way she pushed him to be better, even if it meant discussing the hard, uncomfortable truths most people tried to avoid.

In a world of shallow, selfish relationships that masqueraded as friendship, CeCe was the real deal. A rare treasure. Someone to be cherished and protected, no matter what.

"I'll admit, the convo was a gut punch. But one I needed."

They'd spent the evening on a video call streaming a documentary on George Lucas together. When it was over, CeCe recalled a quote in which Lucas said, "If you want to be successful in a particular field, perseverance is one of the key qualities." She'd looked him dead in the eye and said, "But perseverance is irrelevant if you're too afraid to take the first step."

"I'm not afraid," he'd countered, knowing exactly what she meant without her needing to elaborate.

"Yes, you are," she'd argued. "Acting is safe. You don't care if you succeed or fail at it. But writing is your passion. It matters. And that terrifies you. So you keep it locked in a box, untouched. Because you can't fail at something you've never tried. But that's where you're wrong. It *is* a failure. A failure to fight for the life you really want. Be a fighter, Jayce. Don't let your dream dwindle until your dying day, when all you'll have is *what if*."

He hadn't made any promises, but as soon as they'd ended the call that night, he'd dragged out his laptop.

"Does that mean what I think it means?" Her dark eyes glinted with hope, drawing him back to the present.

For a moment, all he could do was stare at her upturned face, noting the way the faint light of dusk illuminated her silky skin.

The tide had reached them now, bathing their bare feet, but he didn't even register the cold.

"I wrote a script. And I'd like you to read it and give me your honest opinion."

"As if I'd give you anything else," she said with a playful grin.

"That's why I love you." He tried to match her teasing tone, masking the deeper meaning of his words. "But it needs to be a quick turnaround. A director friend of mine talked to a producer he knows, and long story short, the producer wants to see a copy this Friday. I'm supposed to give it to him at the award show."

"Jayce! That's wonderful!" CeCe tossed her arms around his neck, hugging him tightly. "I'm so proud of you."

Jayce pulled her close, burying his face in her curls, inhaling the sweet, comforting scent of her coconut shampoo.

He'd missed this—missed *her*.

But in the same breath, he knew this feeling—the overwhelming desire to be near her, to be more than her best friend —was exactly why he'd left.

He'd once told her that he'd needed to move away to put space between him and his parents. But that had only been partially true.

The day he'd skipped town twenty-four hours earlier than he'd originally planned, he'd been running away from her.

Chapter Twenty-Three

ABBY

ABBY NESTLED DEEPER beneath Logan's arm, wanting to feel the full weight of it around her shoulders. She needed all the comfort possible after the emotionally exhausting day they'd had.

"Crazy night, huh?" Logan rested his cheek against the top of her head.

Both of their bodies sank into the soft sofa cushions, drained of energy. Faint moonlight filtered through the sitting room windows, signaling the day's end. If only she could wake up tomorrow and have life return to normal.

"Surreal," she agreed.

The Bare Feet & Good Eats event she'd looked forward to for weeks hadn't gone quite as she'd imagined. Between the presence of a big movie star, his gaggle of paparazzi, and the quickly spreading rumor of Sam's return, Abby struggled to relax and enjoy the food and festivities. Plus, it took all her willpower to be happy for Max instead of hurt that he'd wanted to spend the evening with his dad, not her.

She couldn't blame him, though. He'd lost so much time

with his dad. They were family. Of course they wanted to be together. But she couldn't help wondering what their father-son reunion would mean for their relationship. How did she factor into their world?

Their laughter spilled from the kitchen where they'd helped themselves to a late-night snack of apple slices and peanut butter, one of Max's favorites. At least Sam had agreed to stay at the inn until the DNA results came back. She wouldn't have to worry about saying goodbye to Max for a few more days at least. Well, she'd *worry*, but it wouldn't be a reality just yet.

She sat up straighter when Sam and Max strolled into the sitting room.

"When's your bedtime around here?" Sam asked Max. "And don't try to pull a fast one." He ruffled Max's hair in a surprisingly playful manner.

In such a short amount of time, Mystery Man had come alive, transforming into a completely different person—a happier, more vibrant one. He still didn't remember everything about his past, but he clung to his connection with Max like a lifeline, as if memories of his son were all he needed to feel whole again.

She couldn't imagine what he'd been through, how much he'd lost, how much he still needed to regain. She deeply regretted that she'd let her own sadness cloud her compassion for a man who deserved every ounce she had to give.

"It's already past our normal bedtime, but tonight seemed like a worthy exception," she told Sam with a smile. "Ready, Max?" She stood, eager to start their evening routine. While she and Logan usually took turns at bedtime, she'd asked for the honors tonight. She couldn't wait to pick up where they'd left off in *The Chronicles of Narnia*, tuck Max in, and savor her most coveted time together, nightly prayers.

Max looked up at Sam. "Can you read with me tonight?"

"Of course. What are we reading?"

"*The Voyage of the Dawn Treader*. You'll like it, Dad. Prince Caspian is a sailor, like you."

"Great. Lead the way."

Max gave his dad more backstory on the characters as he led him down the hallway toward his room.

Abby watched them go, fighting back tears, determined not to give in to her disappointment.

"Are you okay?" Logan asked gently.

"Yes," she lied, willing the words to be true. "It's important they have this time together." It *was* important. Sam was Max's father. Bedtime stories, nightly prayers, kissing Max's forehead before turning off the light—all parental privileges that belonged to Sam, not her. Why was it so hard for her to remember that?

"Want to watch a movie?" She tried to sound chipper as she collapsed back onto the couch beside Logan.

"Abs," Logan said softly, pulling her close again. "It's okay to not be okay. This is hard."

"So hard," she admitted in a hoarse whisper. "And I wish it weren't. I want to be happy. This is what's best for Max. It's a miracle. And I'm grateful for what God has done for both Sam and Max. But also—" Her voice cracked. She gathered a shallow breath, her lungs struggling to expand against the heavy pressure building in her chest. "I thought God brought Max to me —to *us*. I was so sure, Logan. All the signs. The way He orchestrated events, bringing us all together. I thought He wanted us to be a family." Tears pooled in her eyes, threatening to release. She blinked up at the ceiling.

"I believed that, too. I still do. Just maybe the family portrait is supposed to look a little different than we thought."

"What do you mean?" She shifted slightly so she could see his face in the glow of the floor lamp.

"Things are going to change. We can't deny that. But we're still Max's family. Maybe not in the way we'd planned, but we can still be a part of his life. What if—" He hesitated, his brow furrowing as he measured his words. "What if we asked them to stay here?"

"Here? At the inn?" They only had three rooms to rent to guests. The inn was their livelihood. She didn't see how they could make that work.

"In the bungalow. I assume I'll be moving into your room with you after the wedding," he teased.

She blushed, recalling the countless times she'd daydreamed about sharing her intimate space with him.

"I know the bungalow is small," he continued. "But it's not much smaller than where they lived before. We could help Sam find a job here, if he doesn't want to go back to fishing. And Max wouldn't have to move."

For the first time all day, the burden around her heart lifted. She beamed up at him. "You know, you can be quite brilliant sometimes."

"*Sometimes?*" he cried in mock offense.

"Well, you're a very intelligent man, in general. But in some cases, like this one, and when you picked me to be your wife, you're extra brilliant."

"I'm having another genius idea right now." His eyes twinkled as they fell to her lips.

"That's funny. Me, too." She tilted her chin. "Great minds think alike."

A throat cleared. "Sorry to interrupt." Sam hovered awkwardly in the hallway. "Abby, Max asked if you'd go in to pray with him."

"O-of course!" she stammered, simultaneously stunned and overjoyed. *Max wanted her to do bedtime prayers!*

Sharing in her joy, Logan smiled and squeezed her hand.

Floating down the hall, weightless with happiness, Abby freely allowed herself to hope.

Perhaps everything would turn out okay after all.

Chapter Twenty-Four

LOGAN

"Have a seat." Logan gestured to the armchair opposite the couch. "Can I get you anything?"

"I'm good, thanks." Sam settled in the vintage wingback, his posture stiff and uncomfortable.

"It's been a heck of a day for you." Logan tried to put himself in the man's shoes. Assuming everything he said was true, he'd been through the ringer. And despite his earlier resistance, Logan was inclined to believe him, if for no other reason than one—the raw and undeniable emotion he saw in Sam's eyes.

Sam loved his son.

"You could say that." Sam shifted in the seat, his hands gripping the armrests as if the chair might eject him into the stratosphere any second.

Why couldn't the guy relax around him? Sure, he'd been skeptical of his story in the beginning, but he'd come around.

"Abby and I were talking earlier, and we have an idea we'd like to run by you."

Sam repositioned again. *Jeez*. Did the guy have rocks in his pockets?

"I know you have a part-time job and a home in Redton, but we're hoping you might consider staying here, with us. I'll be moving into the house once Abby and I are married, which'll leave the bungalow vacant. It's not much, but I think you and Max could be happy there. Or he could keep his room here. You'd both be welcome to join us for meals, use whatever you need in the main house, and we'd help you find a new job in Blessings Bay." Logan leaned forward, his adrenaline pumping. The more he rattled off his idea, the more he wanted—no, *needed*—it to work. "Max loves his school, his friends at church. He's a star player on his soccer team. Plus, there's us. We're pretty great." He flashed a good-natured grin, hoping to cut the tension with some humor. "Max's also pretty fond of our neighbor, Verna, and her bulldog, Bing. What I'm trying to say is, Max has a full life here. And we'd like you to be a part of it."

Shoot. The moment the words left his mouth, Logan knew he'd said the wrong thing.

The muscles in Sam's forearms flexed as he clutched the chair tighter. "That's kind of you. And I appreciate all you and Abby have done for my son."

Uh-oh. Logan sensed a *but* coming. *Stay calm. Let the man say his piece. It won't be as bad as you think.*

"But," Sam continued with a forced confidence in his tone, "I believe the best thing for me and Max is to head back to Redton as soon as the test results are in. Then, when I've had some time to sort things out, we'll start over somewhere new."

Logan's pulse pounded in his ears like a warning blare. He needed to tread lightly. "May I ask why?" He refrained from adding, *Why would you want to take Max away from everything and everyone he's come to know and love over the last several months?*

Sam stared at the floor a few feet in front of him. "Max has been through a lot. So have I. We need time to reconnect and reestablish our relationship. As father and son. Away from"—his gaze briefly flitted to Logan's face then back to the floor before he added—"distractions."

Logan's jaw tensed. Distractions? Is that what Sam wanted to call the people who'd raised, loved, and cared for his son like their own? "And once you've sorted things out, where will you go?"

"I don't know yet."

"But you'll let us know when you decide?" When Sam didn't respond, Logan pressed, "We'd like to remain a part of Max's life in any way we can."

"I don't think that's a good idea."

Logan's stomach clenched, as if he'd been punched in the gut.

Sam awkwardly stood.

Logan sprang to his feet, unwilling to let this go. "You'd really cut us out of Max's life, just like that?" His heart screamed, *We're his family, too. He needs us as much as we need him.* Was this the loving man Iris Hodge had described—the man who put his son's best interest above his own? After the pain of losing his father for all those months, how could Sam rip two more people from Max's life? Logan couldn't believe what he was hearing.

"For a while, yes. I'm not saying it'll be permanent. But temporarily, at least, I think it's necessary. I hope you can understand." Sam turned toward the staircase.

Logan's chest heaved. *No. No, he didn't understand.* "Wait." His throat burned, and he swallowed against the sharp, acidic taste of pure panic in his mouth. "Our wedding is less than two weeks away. Max is my best man. Can you bring him back for the wedding? Please."

Logan had never begged a day in his life, but all pride evaporated in that moment, his thoughts fixed on Abby. He couldn't let her walk down the aisle without Max standing beside him at the end. He couldn't break her heart. Or Max's. Max wanted to be there. He *needed* to be there. The wedding wouldn't be the same without him. In truth, he couldn't imagine a single day without him, let alone the most important day of his life. What could he say to sway Sam's decision?

Sam glanced over his shoulder, his expression a mixture of pity and unwavering resolve. He shook his head. "I'm sorry." Conversation over, he strode toward the staircase without looking back.

Logan watched him ascend the steps into darkness, his insides ripping apart.

He'd felt powerless many times in his life. When his parents died, then his grandparents. After his accident, when he didn't know if he'd ever walk again.

But at that moment, his helplessness hit a new low.

This wasn't supposed to happen.

Their family portrait hadn't merely been altered.

It had been erased.

Chapter Twenty-Five

CECE

CeCe curled on the couch, reading beneath the light of the table lamp, Spock snuggled up beside her.

When Jayce handed her his script after the Bare Feet & Good Eats event that evening, she wasn't sure she'd be able to read it until tomorrow. How could she concentrate on anything after their disorientating almost-kiss? Her entire body still tingled at the memory of his lips mere inches from hers, from the warmth of his fingertips against her skin, his intoxicating nearness.

Then, those torturous and tantalizing words.

Not like this...

The implication behind the three short syllables had made her shiver, as if maybe he'd imagined a time and place for a kiss between them. But that didn't make any sense. They were friends. A fact he'd made all too clear over the years.

And friends didn't kiss.

She'd tormented herself with what-ifs for over an hour, then finally decided to shove the agonizing thoughts from her mind. After fixing a cup of tea, she'd settled on the couch with Jayce's screenplay. Her heartbeat had quickened as she'd folded back the title page.

For so long, she'd prayed for Jayce to take this step, to honor the longing placed on his heart. He'd been obsessed with telling stories since they were kids. He saw every plot twist ten steps ahead of the characters on screen and could determine the ending of the movie within the first twenty minutes. But beyond the bones of a story, he loved the relationships, the character growth, exploring the *why* behind the choices they made.

When she dove into the opening lines, she'd expected something deep, witty, and well-developed, but what she'd found inside the packet of crisp white paper contained so much more than she'd anticipated. An hour and a half later, as she neared the final pages, she reached for a tissue on the credenza behind the couch.

At her loud sniffling, Spock raised his head.

"I know, I know. I'm not usually a crier when I read," she admitted, dabbing her eyes. "But this script—*wow*. I knew Jayce would do incredible things with his creativity once he finally put pen to paper, but this is unlike anything I'd imagined." In a way, reading his words felt like glimpsing a piece of his soul—a raw, vulnerable, intimate piece; one she hadn't been privy to before now.

Spock cocked his head in curiosity.

"I don't even know how to explain it to you," she confessed. "It sort of defies genre. It's romance meets drama meets magical realism. Fun, quirky, and profoundly moving."

Spock gazed up at her, unblinking, as if he expected more.

CeCe sighed. "Okay, I'll try to summarize the plot as best as I can, but you really have to read it to fully grasp the emotional nuances."

Spock hissed, pointing out the obvious: He couldn't read.

"You're right. Sorry. That was insensitive." She scratched

behind his ears in apology. "So, the main character, Chloe, owns a café, where she lives and works."

Spock's floppy ears twitched at that little tidbit.

CeCe smiled. "I know what you're thinking. It sounds familiar. And I'm sure I inspired the character a little, but I see parts of Jayce in Chloe, too." And she suspected he'd infused even more of himself into the character than she even realized. At least, the depth of emotion poured onto the page felt too real and profound to be entirely make-believe.

"Chloe experienced some pretty serious trauma in her past," she explained, doing her best to recap the story succinctly. "And one day, she tells her quirky employee, Alvera, that she longs to live a simple, uncomplicated life, protected from everything—and every*one*—that could potentially lead to heartbreak. At the time, Chloe doesn't think anything of the conversation. But the next morning, strange things start happening around the café."

Spock sits up on his haunches, apparently intrigued.

"Overnight, Chloe's wish came true. Everything in her life falls into place like a flawless recipe. No complications. No messiness. No cause for heartache or angst. And she couldn't be happier. *At first*."

Spock mewed, as if he knew what came next.

"Exactly. Nothing perfect lasts forever, right?" CeCe crossed her legs beneath her and leaned forward with the script on her lap, relishing her role as storyteller to her enraptured audience. "One day, a hunky stranger comes into the café, and they immediately hit it off."

Spock mewed again, only this time in annoyance.

"I know you're not a fan of the mushy stuff, but this is where the story gets really interesting." She lowered her voice, laying on the theatrics. "As Chloe and Justin fall in love, the spell over the café starts glitching. Things go awry. Small things, at first. But the more time she spends with Justin, the more her life returns to normal, as it was before the protective spell. I just reached the part in the script where Chloe realizes she has a decision. She'll either choose love and break the spell forever, risking potential heartache again. Or she'll end things with Justin, thus restoring the spell and her haven of safety within the walls of her magical café."

Spock crawled closer and nudged the script in her lap.

CeCe laughed. "See, I knew you'd be interested in how things turn out." She flipped back to where she'd left off, then frowned. "Wait. This can't be right. Where's the rest?" She turned the page only to find a blank sheet of paper stapled to the back of the script.

She scanned the white space over and over as if she could summon the words onto the page by staring hard enough. That couldn't be the ending. There had to be more. Did Chloe choose love, with all its inherent risks, or self-preservation?

Her heart pounded, and suddenly anxious, she sprang from the couch. "It's just a story. A *fictional* story," she said aloud, pacing the carpet. "Maybe Jayce forgot the last page. Or maybe he wants it to be one of those movies where the viewer decides the ending for themselves?"

Ugh. She hoped not. How could she choose an ending for Chloe when she couldn't answer the thematic question of the film for her own life?

Was love worth the pain?

Did the good outweigh the bad?

Or was it better to remain alone?

Because, based on watching her mother all these years, love wasn't a cure for loneliness anyway.

Chapter Twenty-Six

JAYCE

JAYCE PLUMPED his pillow then flopped onto his back, staring up at the ceiling. He'd never had an issue sleeping on Evan's couch before, but tonight, he couldn't get his brain to switch off. He'd almost kissed his best friend, a move that would have been simultaneously glorious and disastrous.

Since the start of their fake engagement charade, he'd found himself riding a bullet train of bad ideas. On some level, he knew he needed to keep his feelings in check for CeCe's sake as well as his own. If he crossed the friendship line and things didn't work out, he'd never forgive himself. And yet, on a level becoming increasingly more difficult to ignore, he wanted to throw every caution to the wind and give a relationship with CeCe his best shot. What if they could succeed where others hadn't?

Restless, he flipped onto his side, gazing into the murky shadows of Evan's sitting room slash kitchenette. A dim glow from the porch light filtered through the bamboo shades covering the front window, illuminating faint outlines. The surfboard leaning against the wall. A stack of boxes containing jars of Evan's Epic Rash Balm that he sold online. Nadia's fancy copper pot with a built-in strainer sat on the stove. She'd used it to make him some masala chai when he first arrived.

There was something nice, almost comforting, about the way Evan's and Nadia's lives blended together, the way they easily shared so many parts of themselves. He wouldn't be surprised if his friend proposed soon. Did Evan ever have reservations about their future? Doubtful. What would it be like to experience that degree of blind assurance? Was it brave? Or foolish?

Jayce rolled onto his back, once again staring up at the ceiling. He'd better figure out the answer to that question before Friday, otherwise his script was doomed. No producer wanted to invest in a project without an ending.

A tiny stab of guilt pricked his heart for giving CeCe the script without a warning about the missing pages. But he needed her honest, gut-level reaction. He hoped that by the time she reached the blank page, she'd know exactly how she wanted the story to end. And maybe her thoughts would give him some guidance, pertaining to the script *and* real life.

He closed his eyes, allowing himself the pleasant memory of her perfect lips—their seductive bow shape, the tempting freckle that reminded him of a cake crumb. He imagined she tasted like coconut, cinnamon, and brown sugar.

She'd given him permission to kiss her, which had momentarily thrilled him. But she'd been under duress, panicked by the pressure from the paparazzi. Not exactly a recipe for romance. But what if he'd indulged anyway? What would it feel like to finally—

A soft tap at the door dragged him away from the tempting thought.

He squinted in the dim light. It had to be close to 2:00 a.m. Who would be knocking at this time of night? Maybe he'd hallucinated the sound.

Another gentle rap debunked that theory.

He kicked off the lightweight blanket and trudged to the door.

To his surprise, CeCe stood on the other side.

Her eyes widened, traveling from his bare chest to his baggy basketball shorts hanging low on his hips, then back to his chest.

He couldn't be certain in the amber-tinted glow of the porch light, but she almost looked flushed. "Toto, what are you doing here? Is everything okay?"

"No, it's not." She tore her attention from his naked torso to meet his gaze. "How could you do this to me?" she hissed, waving his script in his face. "There's no ending, Jayce. No ending!"

"You read it already?" He'd expected her to wait until tomorrow.

"Of course I did! I've been waiting my whole life to read your first screenplay. And it's brilliant, by the way." Her adorable, indignant whisper contrasted comically with her compliment. Plus, he found it endearing that even in her outrage, she didn't want to disturb Evan asleep in the other room. Could she be any cuter?

Jayce couldn't help a smile. "Thanks. What did you like about it?"

"Uh-uh. No way. You don't get any more praise until you give me the missing pages." She shoved the script against his chest, and the fleeting sensation of her fingertips against his bare skin sent a shock wave through his body.

The brief contact seemed to catch her off guard, too. She snapped her hands back and rubbed her palms down her thighs —shapely thighs clad in tiny cotton shorts. Jayce swallowed against a sudden tightness in his throat.

"Un-unless," she stammered, averting her gaze. "The lack of

ending was some artistic choice. And, in that case, may I implore you to rethink your decision? I—I mean, the *audience*," she corrected, "needs an ending."

"You're right. What do you think the ending should be?'

"Me?" She balked. "I—I don't know. You're the writer."

"And you're my best friend. I want your opinion. Do you think Chloe should choose love?" The second he asked her the question, an uncontrollable desperation clawed its way up his chest, like a caged animal unleashed. He wanted CeCe more than he'd wanted anything in his life. How could he continue to fight his feelings for her? It was too exhausting, too daunting. He silently begged her to say, *Choose love*, as if her words would somehow give him permission to risk a lifetime of friendship for a statistical shot in the dark. A shot in the dark he suddenly yearned to take.

He instinctively moved toward her, spanning the distance between them.

She inched backward, pinned against the doorjamb.

Compelled beyond rational thought, he bridged the gap until they stood toe to toe. "What should she choose?" he repeated in a raspy murmur, fighting for self-control.

She tilted her head to look up at him, light reflecting off her lenses.

He'd always loved her glasses, the alluring way they framed her beautiful eyes. But tonight, they felt like a barrier between them. His fingers itched to lift them from her face, but he didn't get the chance.

"I wish I knew," she whispered, dropping her gaze to the floor.

Her disheartened tone snapped reality back into focus. He'd let his emotions push him too far across the line. He needed distance. Two a.m. wasn't the time to make life-altering decisions.

"Me, too." He backed away. "I'll figure it out before Friday, though. Maybe I'll have her wake up and realize it was all a dream." He attempted a rueful grin.

"Keep workshopping that idea." She met his grin with a shaky smile. "Whatever you decide, I look forward to reading it." After an awkward pause, followed by a clumsily exchanged goodbye, she slipped outside, quietly shutting the door behind her.

Great. He'd made her uncomfortable. Or at the very least, confused by his odd behavior. He couldn't keep doing this, pushing the boundaries, cutting it too close.

After the award ceremony on Friday, when Stacey and Rob jet off to Italy to elope, he'd call it quits. They'd announce their breakup, and he'd take a vacation somewhere far, far away.

All he had to do was make it through the rest of the week without doing something rash, then things could return to normal. He'd lasted this long without kissing her. What were a few more days?

"You should've kissed her." The groggy voice broke through his resolved reverie.

He turned to find Evan in the doorway of his bedroom, rubbing his eyes.

"Sorry." His friend flashed a sleepy, sheepish grin. "I heard voices and caught the tail end of your conversation."

Fantastic. Just what he needed. "It's not what you think."

"I think you need to work on your acting skills. Even in the dark, I can see you're a lost cause." Evan sank onto a creaking rattan chair and kicked his feet onto the coffee table. "Why don't you man up and tell CeCe how you feel?"

"It's not that simple." Jayce collapsed onto the couch, too tired to maintain his denial.

"Who said anything about simple? Tell me, how many things in life that are actually worth doing are ever *simple*?"

Huh. Maybe Evan had a point. "Okay," he countered, verbally processing his muddled thoughts, "let's say I tell CeCe how I feel. And let's extend our imagination even further and pretend she reciprocates. Then what? We date, maybe get married, have a few kids. Then, one day, we wake up and realize we've drifted apart. We're different people, we want different things. If we're lucky, love fizzles to indifference. And if we're *un*lucky, it's worse. We wind up like—"

"Your parents?" Evan interjected gently.

Jayce winced. His friend could read him too well. "Sure. They're a prime example of friends-to-lovers-to-foes. And so is nearly every other couple I know."

"Okay," Evan conceded. "But nearly every couple you know is in Hollywood, which is its own microcosm of dysfunction. Their divorce rate is significantly higher than the general population."

"True, but the general divorce rate isn't exactly low, either." Jayce threw his head back against the couch cushions, the pressure between his temples building. He couldn't think straight.

"You're right," Evan admitted, "and that stinks. But you have to stop viewing yourself as one of the statistics, as if the outcome is inevitable."

"Isn't it, though?"

"Of course it isn't. You have a choice, Jayce. A choice to love CeCe with a fire that burns beyond the initial flame of infatuation. You can choose patience, forgiveness, grace, and perseverance. You can choose to see the good in her, day after day, long after the first rush of excitement fades. You can continue to be her best friend and her biggest supporter, to honor your commitment to stand by her, no matter what. That's on you, with God's help. And then you gotta trust Him for the rest."

Evan's words seeped into his bones, reshaping beliefs he'd long considered unshakable. As he stared up at the ceiling fan, watching it rotate round and round, his mind spun back to the past, transporting him to his childhood living room and the moment his family ripped apart.

"Your father and I are getting a divorce." His mother's voice still rang clear, cold, and unyielding.

"It's not anyone's fault," his father had chimed in, three feet away from his soon-to-be ex-wife on the couch while Jayce sat in the middle. "But sometimes, things change."

Jayce had noticed the change months before. They'd started snapping at each other more often, then the spats escalated into full-blown fights. They'd stopped laughing together, holding hands or even touching each other at all. The increased time apart and abandoned date nights soon devolved into separate bedrooms. He'd finally understood the expression *passing like two ships in the night*. Except, his parents were battleships that never passed each other without exploiting the opportunity to lob a missile.

When he'd asked them why, they'd exchanged a strained glance.

"Sometimes," his father had said with a pained expression, "love, no matter how strong it starts out, simply doesn't last."

It wasn't until that moment that his mother's stoic facade faltered. She'd blinked back tears, pretending they didn't exist while they insisted that their love for him would always remain the same.

But by then, their words carried little assurance.

In his young eyes, love had been reduced to a fleeting feeling with an unknown yet inevitable expiration date—a life lesson supported by countless other couples over the years.

But Evan's words that night chipped away at the scab around his heart, giving him hope.

And he finally knew exactly how he wanted his story to end.

Chapter Twenty-Seven

ABBY

Music and a myriad of voices swirled around Abby, but she barely registered a sound, aware only of the dense fog of emotion blanketing the backyard. The bittersweet blend of melancholy and merriment permeated Max's going-away party, and for a split second, Abby regretted hosting the event. What if they'd had a simple Friday afternoon together instead?

Her gaze swept the crowd of familiar faces. Verna and her eclectic book club, the Belles. Nadia and Evan. Sage and Flynn. Max's youth pastor, his teacher, soccer coach, friends and class-mates. Carla, Iris, and even grumpy Garth. So many people loved Max and deserved the opportunity to say goodbye.

Her throat tightened. *Goodbye.* How would she manage to say the word aloud, let alone to Max?

For the past few days, while they'd waited for the DNA test results, she'd tried to accept the inevitable, to come to terms with Sam's decision to take Max away, to sever their contact.

It's his call, she'd reminded herself. It's what Sam deemed best for Max. Even if she didn't agree with or understand his rationale, she needed to respect his decision. At the very least, for Max's sake.

And yet, nothing about the situation felt right. They could offer so much, both to Max and Sam. Their whole world had turned upside down. Sam would be starting over. And so would Max. Why didn't Sam want their help?

The stinging in her throat moved to her eyes. She blinked up at the crystal blue sky. *Strange*. Not a cloud in sight.

"Seems like a few gloomy rain clouds would be fitting, doesn't it?" Verna asked, handing her a glass of strawberry basil lemonade.

Abby managed a small smile. "It's like you read my mind. And thank you." She took a slow sip, letting the sweet, tangy liquid soothe her raw throat.

"How are you doing, dear?" Verna adjusted her wide-brimmed straw hat to shield her eyes from the sun. The long purple ribbon that matched her violet-hued pantsuit fluttered in the breeze.

"About as well as can be expected, I suppose. I just—" Her voice caught. She guzzled more lemonade, determined to get through the next few hours—and the rapidly approaching goodbye—without tears. "I just can't believe Sam's really taking him away after the party."

Her gaze instinctively found Max in the throng. He chatted animatedly with a few friends, Sam and Logan flanking him on either side. Logan stood so tall, so composed. Her rock. They'd get through this together, wouldn't they?

Her mind flew to their upcoming wedding. One more week until the happiest day of her life. At the thought, guilt crept into her heart, co-mingling with her grief. How could her wedding day joy be complete without Max's presence? A fresh wave of anguish crashed over her. Her throat cinched tighter. She gulped more lemonade, oblivious to the loud slurping sound of her straw sucking air.

Verna placed a gentle hand on her arm, wrenching her back to the present.

Abby jumped, jostling the ice in her glass.

Verna's gaze softened with empathy. "I know it feels like Sam is taking Max away. And I can't deny there's some truth to that. We're all going to miss him terribly. But the heart is a wondrous thing. It has the ability to hold someone close, to protect and preserve them. So no matter where they are, on this earth or in Heaven, they're never truly gone. And no one can take that away from you."

Undeterred by her cold palm, dampened by the beads of condensation coating her glass, Abby reached for Verna's hand. She gave it a squeeze. "Thank you. That's comforting. How do you always know the perfect thing to say?"

"Oh, probably due to several decades of saying the wrong thing," Verna teased, her eyes twinkling. "If you're lucky, you learn a thing or two."

Abby laughed, surprised by the surge of relief that followed. Her pain wasn't gone, but the edges dulled, making it easier to breathe. "Let's give Max the best going-away party possible."

Linking arms with Verna, she strode across the lawn toward Max, Logan, and Sam, repeating a silent prayer in her heart.

When the time finally comes to say goodbye, please don't let it be forever.

Chapter Twenty-Eight

LOGAN

LOGAN STOOD on the lawn beside Abby, watching their world detonate like a missile hitting its target. To think, not too long ago, they'd stood in that exact spot welcoming Max home. And now, he'd be leaving them again for who knew how long. Maybe forever.

Logan's jaw clamped tighter. *You can get through this.*

Max chatted cheerily as Sam loaded Ron's enclosure into the back seat of the run-down Camry. Strangely, Max had been in a chipper mood all day, completely unfazed by his impending departure. Not that Logan wanted the poor kid to be broken up about it, but he'd expected *some* show of emotion.

With all his belongings loaded in the car, Max skipped over to where Logan and Abby waited to say goodbye. "Thanks for the party! That was fun."

"Glad you enjoyed it." Abby smiled, but Logan knew she was dying inside. The woman deserved a medal.

Logan reached behind him for the *Top Gun* teddy bear he'd tucked into the waistband of his jeans. The scuffed leather jacket and aviator sunglasses had seen better days, but the gift from his grandmother had held up shockingly well over the years. "Here." He offered Max the stuffed animal. "Maverick wants to go with you."

"Really?" Max's eyes widened with delight. He'd slept with the bear every night since he'd arrived—when Logan lent it to him for comfort—despite needing the occasional reassurance that eight wasn't too old for stuffed animals.

Max had respectfully left the toy sitting on the bed when he'd packed up his belongings, and Logan had been surprised by how sharply the sight of the lone bear had affected him. "Yeah," he said, burying the mental image. "Mav told me he likes that you don't snore."

Max grinned and grabbed the doll, hugging it to his chest. "I'll take good care of him."

"I know you will." A lump formed in Logan's throat, but he choked it down. Dropping to one knee, he pulled Max into his arms, holding him close, committing every sensory detail to memory, from his distinct scent to the dimensions of his small hand splayed against his back.

He'd always heard having a child changed a person, whether they were prepared for the transformation or not. Over the last several months, he'd experienced that truth firsthand. Max's love—the pure, unconditional, unconstrained depths of it—had made him a better man in more ways than he could count. He'd do anything for Max, even give his own life—a sacrifice that, at that moment, seemed preferable to the piercing pain of goodbye tearing through him.

When Max started to squirm, he realized he'd reached the maximum time allotted for a reasonable hug. Closing his eyes, he whispered a barely audible "I love you, Max" before letting him go.

Max said goodbye to Abby next, fitting effortlessly in her arms.

She gently cupped the back of his head with her hand,

cradling him against her heart. "You will always, *always* have a place here," she murmured in a surprisingly steady voice. How had she managed to keep it together this long?

"I know," Max said brightly, as if he didn't quite understand their mushy display of emotion.

Sitting back on her heels, Abby reached for his hands, holding his gaze. For the first time that day—that Logan had noticed—she let the tears well in her eyes. "I love you, Max Bailey. Always and forever. I want you to know that."

Max cocked his head, his expression quizzical. "Why do you look so sad? I'll be back soon. Right after our trip. Right, Dad?"

Max glanced at his dad, who waited by the car.

Sam stared at the ground, his sunken cheeks flushed with guilt. *You've got to be kidding.* Logan's fists instinctively coiled. All this time, he'd kept Max in the dark?

Sam must have felt his glare boring into him, because he slowly lifted his gaze. The glint of contrition in his eyes confirmed his suspicion.

"You didn't tell him?" Logan growled.

"Tell me what?" Max asked, all innocence.

Logan fixed Sam with a look that said, *Either you tell him or I will*, despite a nagging feeling he'd be crossing a line. Even if Max deserved to know the truth before they took off, perhaps for the last time, it wasn't his place to interfere.

Wasn't his place...

No matter how hard he tried, Logan couldn't wrap his head around the new chain of command. His whole world had shifted around Max—around having a son. He'd finally settled into the role of fatherhood—relished it, even—only to have it snatched away in an instant. Only to be told to step aside, that he was no longer needed. Although Sam deserved to take his rightful position as Max's father, Logan couldn't suppress the internal war raging inside his heart.

"Max." Sam's voice shook. He cleared his throat. "Can you come here for a sec?"

Max shot a puzzled glance at Abby before shuffling over to the car. He stared up at his father with such open, unbridled trust, Logan found himself praying Sam had the right words to smooth all this over. The last thing he wanted was to see Max hurt.

"Max," Sam repeated, stealing more time to compose himself. "I don't know when—or *if*—we'll be back."

"What do you mean? We live here."

The confusion on Max's face clawed at Logan's heart. He wanted to step in, to intervene in some way, but knew he'd only make things worse.

A similar instinct must have gripped Abby because she slipped her hand into his and squeezed hard.

"I live in Redton now," Sam reminded him. "I have a job, a life there. I need some time to sort a few things out, then we'll start over somewhere new. Together."

"But—but I like it here," Max said in a soft, small voice.

"I know. And I can't tell you how glad I am that you've been happy here. But—" Sam hesitated, as if searching for words that eluded him. He gathered a breath, and his shoulders sagged with the weight of his exhale. "It's complicated, Max. I wish I could explain it all in a way that made sense to you. For now, I'm just asking you to trust me. As long as we're together, it'll all work out. Okay?"

The five-second pause that followed felt like forever. Abby's nails dug into the back of his hand, but Logan didn't flinch, too anxious to register the sensation. *Sam's a good dad. He loves Max. It'll be fine.* Although Logan knew the words to be true on a mental level, they did little to dull the ache in his rib cage.

Finally, Max nodded slowly.

"Great." Sam flashed a smile that didn't mask the uncertainty in his eyes. He opened the passenger door. "Ready to start our adventure?"

Max glanced over his shoulder to where they stood.

Logan clasped Abby's hand tighter, hoping to steady her trembling fingers. The vibration of her heartbreak traveled up his arm with the sharpness of a knife's edge.

"Come on, bud." Sam took the teddy bear from Max's hand and tossed it on the passenger seat, gesturing for Max to follow. The grooves on Sam's forehead deepened, as if he struggled against his own internal angst. Did he have doubts about his decision? Did he realize the damage he may inflict on his son if he went through with his half-cocked plan?

Logan's chest compressed as if he were back in the cockpit of an F-16, the pressure building rapidly with a sudden altitude change. *Take it easy, man. You're out of line. Max isn't your kid.* The mental reminder stung like a fresh wound. True or not, the facts didn't dampen the visceral reaction clawing at his stomach —the gut-level knowledge that Max claimed a permanent place in his heart, and he'd do anything to protect him.

Logan fought the urge to cry out, to say something to stop the wheels in motion. Nothing about the situation felt right. But what could he do? What recourse did he have?

Looking back one last time, Max hesitated. A flicker of indecision flashed in his eyes, then a spark of resolve. With all the speed his scrawny legs could manage, he sprinted back across the lawn, launching himself into Abby's arms.

He didn't speak or whimper or shed a tear; he simply clung to her with all his strength. The way Max's small fist fiercely gripped the back of Abby's shirt broke Logan in a way he didn't think could ever be fixed.

"Max," Sam said gently, tapping his son on the shoulder. "Time to go."

Max slowly slid his arms from around Abby's neck. His gaze

darted from Abby to Logan, then back to his dad, as if he didn't know what to do.

Sam took his hand, and together, they walked toward the car.

Max climbed inside.

The door shut with a resounding *slam*.

As the car pulled away from the curb, Logan's gaze followed Max's outline through the rear window, tracing his silhouette.

Abby leaned into him, and he drew her to his side.

Neither of them cried.

They merely stood in the silence of their shared suffering.

It was the silence that scared him the most.

Tears he could handle. Tears could heal.

But silent grief swept over a person like a noxious gas, promising to numb the pain while it quietly stole their life away.

Chapter Twenty-Nine

CECE

CeCe stepped in front of the full-length mirror in one of Jayce's several guest bathrooms, startled by the reflection staring back at her. The evening gown he'd bought her for the award ceremony fit beautifully. She twirled, swishing the silky fabric, mesmerized by the way light sparkled off the starry glass beads.

Between the ombre coloring that began with the palest blue at the fitted bodice and dripped downward into the deepest indigo, and the shimmering jewels, CeCe felt as if she'd been clothed in the Milky Way itself. To complement the striking gown, she'd twisted her hair into a simple updo with a few loose curls framing her face—a face she barely recognized after she'd carefully applied eyeliner, mascara, and a dramatic lipstick aptly labeled Red Carpet Ruby.

For the final touch, she'd replaced her basic wire-framed glasses with contact lenses. They irritated her eyes, but maybe, just maybe, she'd fit into Jayce's elegant A-list crowd after all.

At the thought, apprehension slithered up her spine. Tonight, she wouldn't simply brave a smattering of paparazzi, she'd be surrounded by Hollywood elite. A parade of perfect women. A conclave of stunning starlets whose collective bright-ness would illuminate all her flaws.

Would any of them really believe Jayce had chosen her?

The heat of anxiety radiated across her skin. Her flowy, lightweight gown suddenly felt ten pounds heavier, cinching around her rib cage like a corset. She clawed at the bodice, tempted to rip it off. Instead, she escaped onto the balcony for a rush of fresh coastal air.

The soothing hum of ocean waves and lilting seagull cries did little to assuage her misgivings. She should've stayed in Blessings Bay. She should've gone to Max's going away party. When she'd dropped off the desserts Abby had ordered earlier that morning and had spent a few hours with Max, saying her goodbye, she should've listened to the nagging voice telling her not to leave.

Going to Los Angeles with Jayce—leaving her cozy, uncom-plicated cocoon—would only muddy the emotional waters even more.

Turns out, Sage, her mother, and her own intuition warning her against agreeing to Jayce's charade had been right. She'd made a terrible mistake. She'd wandered too deep into the fantasy, foolishly reading into each glance, each word spoken and unspoken, fabricating a *happily ever after* that could never exist in the real world.

She'd even convinced herself that tonight meant something, that it wasn't simply another part of the ruse. That maybe his feelings for her had changed, had grown into something more. But who was she kidding?

Anxiety blended with embarrassment, burning through her body, making her stomach turn as she took in her surreal surroundings. Jayce's massive modern mansion claimed a prime stretch of sunny Southern California coastline, boasting a scenic beachfront backyard along with other opulent multimillion dollar homes—a slice of paradise few people could even fathom.

Jayce had built a life of dreams beyond the reach of most mortals. No wonder he'd left home and never looked back. No wonder he'd—

Her cheeks flamed as a sudden memory barged into her thoughts, dragging her backward in time almost a decade to the night of the big send-off for Jayce, Evan, and Mia.

They'd thrown a bonfire on the beach; a bittersweet farewell among friends. CeCe barely had a moment alone with Jayce all evening, but she'd consoled herself with their plans for the following day. A picnic, just the two of them, at their special secluded cove. She'd prepared all his favorite foods, baked his beloved Toto cake, and had rehearsed a speech finally declaring her feelings for him.

She'd waited at the cove—dressed in one of only three dresses she owned—a frazzled basket of nerves but also strangely excited, hopeful for a happy ending. A half hour later, with their toasted sandwiches soggy and cold, she'd received a text from Jayce.

CeCe closed her eyes, still mortified by the memory. As hard as she tried to block the mental image, it surfaced in her mind.

Hey. Decided to skip town early to beat the traffic. Sorry I can't make our picnic. Thanks for understanding. You're the best. I hope our friendship never changes.

I hope our friendship never changes. The words echoed loud and irrefutable all these years later.

To think, she'd planned to finally take Sage's advice—to tell Jayce she wanted more than friendship. To add to her embarrassment, she'd actually thought maybe—*just maybe*—he'd wanted more, too.

Then he hadn't even bothered to show up to say goodbye. *Traffic.* He'd been more worried about road congestion than spending time together. To top it off, he'd added the last line, solidifying his feelings for her loud and clear. His affection for her had a limit—a hard line he'd never cross.

A wave of sadness swallowed her whole as she surveyed the stunning panorama before her—the cobalt waters, pristine white sand, and swath of magenta blooms lining the meticulously groomed pathways. The kind of manicured perfection only absurd amounts of money could buy. If she couldn't compete with the possibility of avoiding a few extra hours stuck in traffic, how could she ever compete with all this?

"There you are." Jayce's rich baritone resonated behind her, startling her from her thoughts. "I was starting to think you'd gotten lost up—" His teasing tone died in his throat when she turned around. "Wow. You look—" He shook his head as if to dislodge words that wouldn't come. "Wow," he repeated, this time in a thick, raspy breath.

CeCe flushed beneath his admiring gaze, embarrassed by the urge to melt into a puddle at his feet. "You don't look so bad yourself."

He wore a sleek, impeccably tailored suit in a deep azure blue that enhanced the color of his eyes to mesmerizing effect. The supple, expensive-looking fabric formed to his muscular frame, accentuating his broad shoulders and toned arms as he moved closer, meeting her up against the balcony railing. "I knew the dress would look great on you, but *dang*. I think I missed my calling as a personal stylist."

Flustered, she tucked a wayward curl behind her ear, directing her gaze back to the ocean. The sun dipped low in the sky, dusting the waves with gold. "I didn't realize you'd picked it out yourself. I figured you had people who did that sort of thing for you."

"I do. I gave them specific parameters, then chose my favorite out of twenty or so options."

"What kind of parameters?" she asked, curious how they'd selected a gown so perfect.

"I told them I wanted something unique but classy, like the Academy Awards in the Golden Era of cinema. I believe my exact words were, 'Dress Hedy Lamarr as if she were attending the Oscars in outer space.'"

CeCe laughed. "You didn't actually say that."

"I did. And I think they knocked it out of the park. Except, you look even more beautiful than Hedy Lamarr."

Her skin sizzled despite the breeze and slight drop in temperature as the sun slowly set. Why did he have to say such lovely things? They were alone on the balcony. No paparazzi to placate. No Gretchen to fool.

She tried to think of a silly, sarcastic retort to hide the effects of his flattery, but as he inched closer, his nearness rendered her speechless.

"Thanks for coming with me tonight." He kept his gaze on her face, despite the gorgeous display of color cascading across the water. "I know you had to give up the going-away party. And this kind of event isn't really your thing. Not to mention all the pressure of pulling off a fake engagement." His voice softened, as though blanketed by a building intimacy between them. "It means a lot to me that you came."

"Of course." Why was her throat so dry? She gripped the railing tighter, intently studying the horizon line like a light-house keeper on the lookout for lost ships.

You're being ridiculous, she scolded herself. *This is Jayce. Relax.*

"Before we go," he said, suddenly sounding as nervous as she felt. "There's something I need to tell you."

An unexpected urgency in his tone made her turn around. His impassioned gaze pinned her in place. What was happening? He wasn't looking at her like a friend. He was looking at her like—

The wind picked up, flinging a speck of sand in her eye. She flinched. "Ow." Her eyes watered, trying to extricate the foreign object grating against the already irritating contact lens.

"Here. Hold still." Jayce cupped her chin, tilting her face toward him. She felt the firm pressure of his fingertips all the way to her toes.

As he gazed into her eyes, searching for the tiny grain of sand, she held her breath, the stinging sensation no longer her most pressing concern. She couldn't keep doing this, riding an emotional roller coaster with no end in sight. After tonight, they needed to stop playing pretend and return to a friendship sustained over sporadic phone calls and text messages. A status quo that kept her safe.

"Got it." With a quick sweep of his finger, Jayce removed the offending granule.

"Then why do my eyes still feel like they're on fire?" Blinking rapidly, she resisted the urge to rub her eyes and ruin her mascara.

"Probably the contacts. If they're bothering you, you should take them out. I've always liked your glasses, anyway."

Ugh. There he went again, saying all the right things. Did he have to be so sweet?

"In fact," he said hoarsely, stroking a loose curl away from her face. "I like everything about you, Toto. I always have."

The tenderness in his voice, in his touch, in the way he leaned in toward her, left little room for doubt or debate.

This wasn't pretend.

And it wasn't platonic.

The invisible line of friendship filled the shallow expanse between them, fragile and tenuous, and she silently begged him to cross it.

Chapter Thirty

JAYCE

JAYCE COULDN'T EXPLAIN the electrical current radiating through his body like a rogue signal from his brain, pushing him to the edge of reason. Before he could stop himself, he'd claimed CeCe's mouth with his own—no artful angling or skilled illusions. He could taste her sweetness, feel the soft pressure of her perfect lips. When they gently parted, welcoming him to deepen the kiss, he eagerly accepted the invitation, succumbing to every long-anticipated sensation.

He cradled her face with both hands, as if he risked losing her if he dared to let go for even a second.

Her arms slid around his shoulders, and her fingertips found the sensitive skin at the nape of his neck. His head swam and his muscles tensed with a mounting urgency that heightened at her touch.

After years of envisioning this exact moment, he never imagined it would feel like this—so feverish and all-consuming. A level of passion far beyond friendship, built over a lifetime of longing. A longing they'd evidently shared in silence. How had he never noticed before?

Squelching his regret over lost time, Jayce resolved to lay his heart bare, once and for all. He loved CeCe. With the kind of ardent, steadfast, unconditional love Evan described the night he'd called him out on his cowardice.

All this time, he'd been afraid to risk their friendship. But in reality, he'd jeopardized something even more valuable—the kind of connection that ran so deep, so transcendent, it not only transformed them from the inside out, forging the best versions of themselves, but radiated outward, beyond their relationship.

Being together didn't simply make *them* better—it made *everything* better.

And his fears needed to finally move out of the way.

With concerted effort, he broke off the kiss. Breathless, he pressed his forehead to hers, stealing one last second to bask in the glow of pure bliss.

They couldn't have shared a more earth-shattering first kiss. And he prayed it wouldn't be their last.

"Toto, I—" Before he could finish his thought, a cell phone trilled from the other room, trailing through the open balcony door.

"Hmm?" CeCe murmured, her voice hushed, almost reverent, as she ignored the call.

He lifted his head, meeting her gaze.

Her dark eyes glistened with a happy, dreamy glaze, as if she still couldn't believe what happened. As if she, too, had conjured the kiss from the depths of her own deep-seated desires.

His throat cinched with emotion, hindering his ability to breathe. Was it really possible this woman standing before him —the most remarkable, beautiful, incomparable woman he'd ever known—loved him in return?

RACHAEL BLOOME

He took her hands in his, prepared to find out, when CeCe's phone rang a second time.

"Whoever it is, I'll call them back," she said softly, squeezing his fingers, encouraging him to continue.

Jayce cleared his throat, an excited energy rippling through him. He felt a shift in the air. From this moment onward, everything would change. And now that he stood on the precipice of new possibilities, he couldn't wait to take the plunge. "I—"

Once again, an intrusive cell phone cut him short. Only this time, the custom Caribbean-themed ringtone emanated from his coat pocket. *Strange.* "That's your mom's ringtone."

"Mama?" CeCe's brow knit with confusion. "Why would she be calling you?"

"I don't know. Maybe when you didn't answer your phone, she tried mine?" He suppressed a groan of impatience as he reached into his pocket, reminding himself that he'd waited this long. He could survive two more minutes. *Maybe.* "Do you think you should answer in case she needs something?" *Hopefully, something quick,* he added silently, eager to get back to their life-altering conversation.

"That's probably a good idea."

Jayce noted a faint warble of worry in her voice when she said, "Mama, it's CeCe. Is everything okay?" As she listened, her eyes widened. She slumped against the railing. Terror splashed across her stricken features.

Panic revved through Jayce's body, triggering a surge of adrenaline. "What's wrong?" He instinctively gripped her free hand. It felt so small. So cold.

The phone still pressed to her ear, she whispered, "It—it's my dad. The dig site collapsed. He—he's still inside."

Their eyes met, and her look of helplessness tore through his chest like a chain saw.

Suddenly, nothing else mattered except solving the current crisis.

CeCe couldn't lose her dad. Not now, when the two had so much to say, so much to mend.

But what could he do from half a world away?

Chapter Thirty-One

CECE

Numb, CeCe leaned against the railing, the phone limp in her hand. Was Mama still talking? She wasn't sure. The world faded in and out of focus.

Your father and three others are trapped in the dig site. They were working late. Something went wrong. We don't know much else yet. They've promised to keep me posted.

Her mother's words still pounded in her ears, increasing the pressure between her temples. Her father would be okay. He had to be okay.

She scrunched her hot, tender eyes shut, hoping for relief.

Jayce took the phone from her hand. "Durene, we're on our way."

CeCe's eyes fluttered open. What did he say?

He anchored his arm around her waist, supporting her weight as he slid the phone back into his coat pocket. "Come on. I'm taking you home."

Dazed, she shook her head. "You—you can't. The ceremony. The screenplay." Her thoughts came in ragged fragments, her emotions torn between conflicting desires. She needed to be with her mother. But Jayce needed to be here.

"Neither of those things matter right now." He led her off the balcony, back inside.

Too stunned to resist, CeCe wordlessly relented as he helped her into the car—Mia's brightly colored VW Beetle he'd borrowed for the weekend. The cheerful daisies painted on the side seemed to mock the dire mood.

Instead of driving back to Blessings Bay, Jayce parked at the airport where a private jet waited for them. Normally, she would've asked about the logistics—How would they return Mia's car? How would they get from the small local airport near Blessings Bay to her mother's home?—but tonight, she didn't care. Jayce would figure out the details.

CeCe sat perfectly still, staring at her cell, barely registering the plush leather seat or her opulent surroundings. She didn't even remember Jayce getting her phone from the bathroom. He'd grabbed her glasses, too, and although her eyes enjoyed the reprieve from the scratchy contacts, she still hadn't shed a single tear. She existed in a state of emotional limbo, praying her mother would call with another update before takeoff.

Jayce sat beside her in supportive silence while her thoughts flooded with all the words she wished she'd said to her father. All the *I'm sorrys*. All the *I love yous*.

What if she never got another chance to tell him? What if she'd seen his strong, sun-worn features for the last time? Or never again inhaled his familiar earthy scent of sandalwood soap and dry clay and soil?

At that moment, the abundance of anger she'd carried for so long gave way to an intense ache in the center of her chest. All the milestones he'd missed, the countless times he hadn't called, the once-close relationship he'd allowed to slip away, suddenly paled in comparison to an entire future lost. She'd give anything for a do-over, a chance to begin again, to fix what they'd broken.

What *they'd* broken, she reminded herself. The distance between them wasn't all her father's fault, was it? Over the last few years, she hadn't made much of an effort to stay connected, either. She'd placed the burden of responsibility squarely on his shoulders, reasoning that he was the parent, after all. But did she really deserve a free pass?

The quiet self-reflection continued until they reached her mother's doorstep. One glance at Mama's swollen pink eyes released the floodgates holding CeCe's own tears at bay, and for a moment, they merely stood in the doorway and wept in each other's arms.

Pulling away, Mama wiped her eyes on the sleeve of her sundress. "Come in, come in. I'll make us some tea."

As Jayce stooped to kiss her mother's cheek, something stirred in CeCe's heart. For the first time that evening, her mind made room for thoughts beyond her father's safety, to what had transpired between her and Jayce on the balcony—what would've been the most glorious, pivotal moment of her life before her mother's call. She couldn't help reading into every glance, every display of love and support.

"Thank you for coming." Mama welcomed Jayce's embrace, seeming to gather strength and comfort from his presence.

"Of course." He squeezed her tightly, the way a son would hug his mother.

He'd always been a part of their family, but had things changed between them since their kiss? Was this the beginning of something more? He hadn't hesitated to come with her, putting her needs above his own. Was it possible he'd give up Hollywood? That he'd choose to stay—with *her*? Was it foolish to even hope?

The sharp ring of a cell phone interrupted her rumination.

Her mother rushed to the kitchen table to answer it. "Hello? Yes, this is she."

CeCe held her breath.

Jayce reached for her hand.

Together they stood side by side, studying Mama's face, searching for clues.

A strangled sob escaped Mama's lips, and she collapsed onto the chair. Tears cascaded down her cheeks. "Thank you, Jesus," she murmured, her strained features suddenly softening with relief. "Oh, sweetheart, thank God you're all right."

CeCe's heartbeat stuttered, barely daring to ask. "Dad?" she whispered.

Mama nodded, holding out her hand for her daughter.

CeCe hastened to her side, sinking onto the chair next to her, her heart racing, ready to burst. *He's okay! Hallelujah, he's okay!*

Gripping her mother's hand with all her might, she eagerly waited for her turn to talk to her dad, mulling over everything she wanted to say, anxious to hear his voice.

After a few short minutes, her mother said, "Of course, honey. I understand. She's here now. I'll tell her."

Tell me what? CeCe silently wondered. *Why can't he tell me himself?*

Before she could ask her question aloud, her mother hung up the phone.

CeCe's heart crumbled.

"Your father had to go, but he wanted us to know he's okay. They got everyone out safely. They're being evaluated by medical personnel as a matter of precaution, but he's fine."

"That's great." Her tone sounded tense to her own ears, and she forced a shaky smile, determined not to give in to her disappointment. *It's not personal. There's a lot going on. He'll call you when he can. Just be grateful he's alive and well.*

She took a moment to say a silent prayer of gratitude, allowing her racing pulse to settle. Resolved to focus on the positive, she turned toward Jayce. At least he was here. Maybe now, in the solace of her father's safety, they could explore whatever had happened between them.

The front door closed. The latch clicked.

CeCe sat in stunned silence. Had Jayce just left?

Her phone buzzed on the table where Jayce must have placed it before he snuck out.

Her stomach knotted with nerves as she warily glanced at the screen.

Glad your dad is okay. Sorry to slip out. There's somewhere I need to be, and I didn't want to interrupt. Talk soon.

The disappointment she'd suppressed suddenly rose to the surface again, like a geyser erupting. She struggled to tamp it back down.

Of course he had to leave. He probably still had time to catch the end of the award ceremony. Or, at the very least, give the producer his script during the after-party.

This was Jayce's big break at his lifelong dream. Could she really begrudge his desire to chase after his greatest passion? Even if it meant leaving her behind?

Chapter Thirty-Two

CECE

"Where's Jayce?" Mama set a pot of hibiscus tea on the table to finish steeping.

"He left." CeCe tapped twice on Jayce's text and selected the thumbs-up icon to indicate she'd read his message.

"Back to LA?"

"Probably. He's supposed to give his script to a producer tonight." She placed her phone face down, wondering when she'd get to read the end of Chloe's story. Jayce had said *soon* kind of mysteriously, as if he'd had a specific moment in mind. "I'm really proud of him," she added with an urge to defend his sudden absence. "Screenwriting has been a lifelong dream of his. I'm happy he's finally making it a priority."

Mama smiled softly as she set two mismatched mugs on the table.

"What?" CeCe prompted, trying to read her mother's cryptic expression.

"Nothing." Settled back in her seat, Mama added a drizzle of wildflower honey to their mugs.

"No, there's definitely something," CeCe prodded. "What is it?"

"It's nothing," Mama repeated, pouring the deep-red liquid over the thick swirl of honey. The aromatic steam filled the air with its fruity fragrance. "I just find it interesting, that's all."

"What's interesting?" CeCe frowned. Why wouldn't her mother come out and say whatever was on her mind?

Mama set the colorful ceramic teapot back on the trivet and met her gaze. Her dark eyes shimmered with a mother's love—gentle and understanding. "You've supported Jayce's passions since day one, even when it meant moving away. Why is that?"

"Because I care about him." CeCe shifted on the rickety chair. Where was this conversation headed? And why did she feel compelled to further explain herself? "I want to see him succeed, to be fulfilled in life. Screenwriting—*storytelling*—is what he loves. Whenever he talks about it, he lights up. And he's good at it, Mama. Really good. You should read his script. It's amazing." Her heart swelled with pride as she recalled the beautiful words he'd written. The humor and subtext. The meaningful message behind the entertaining story. "Yes, I miss him. And I wish he lived closer. I wish—" She paused, on the verge of saying too much.

A surge of heat flooded her body as the memory of Jayce's kiss interrupted her thoughts. What did it mean? After all these years, he clearly had feelings for her, too—feelings that far surpassed the safe simplicity of their friendship. But what kind of future could they possibly have together? She couldn't give up her café and life in Blessings Bay any more than he could abandon his successful career in Hollywood.

She took a sip of tea, and the sweet, tangy liquid stung the rawness in her swollen throat. Would pursuing a future with Jayce condemn her to a life like her mother's, constantly torn between love and loneliness? Or did she and Jayce have a shot at doing things differently?

Taking another sip, she willed the soothing herbal tea to

center her troubling thoughts. "I wish we could see each other more often," she continued, sticking to the abbreviated version of her complicated emotions. "But I would never want him to give up something that brings him so much joy."

Mama smiled again—a knowing smile bordering on amused.

CeCe squirmed, feeling exposed. "Why do you keep smiling like that? Is it so strange that I want him to be happy?"

"Of course not, sweetheart. It's perfectly natural. It's how I feel about your father." The subtle implication of her mother's words floated across the table like a feather-soft tendril of steam —a tendril that pierced CeCe's heart with an unexpected sharpness.

She inhaled a quick, cutting breath.

Mama pushed her mug to the side and sighed deeply. "We should've had this conversation a long time ago."

CeCe held the air in her lungs, too nervous to exhale. Was it finally happening? Was the heart-to-heart she'd had with her mother a million times inside her own mind about to become a reality? She'd both feared and desperately longed for this moment.

Mama met her gaze again. This time, her eyes were glassy with a potent mixture of guilt and sadness. "I told myself I was doing the right thing. That I was protecting you. When your father quit his job at the university and started traveling more as a contract archeologist, you were so young. I didn't know how to help you understand—" She hesitated, glancing at her clasped hands on the table. Twisting her wedding band, she admitted, "I couldn't help you understand what I wasn't willing to accept myself."

For a moment, the confession lingered in the silent space between them. When her mother finally spoke again, her voice strained with barely suppressed emotion. "Those first few years were so hard. I missed your father terribly. I wanted things to go back to the way they were, before he quit teaching. I wanted our family to be together again, but I didn't know how to tell him —didn't know if I *should* tell him." She wiped a tear from the corner of her eye before fidgeting with her ring again. "I knew the university job wasn't enough for him. I saw the fire in his eyes die a little more every day he spent behind a desk. He needed to be on the front lines of discovery. In the trenches." She flashed a sad, wistful smile. "He wanted us to go with him."

"He did?" CeCe sat up straighter. Why hadn't anyone ever told her?

Her mother nodded. "He begged me more than once. But what kind of life would that be for a little girl? Always traveling from one country to the next. No school. No friends. No stability." Her voice cracked, and she reached for her tea. After a long, bolstering sip, she set her mug back down. "I realize now, we might have been able to make it work. Other people have. But I was... scared. Terrified, actually. To give up our life here. Our friends. Our community. Everything we know and love for a world of uncertainty. So, I—I chose to stay."

CeCe sank into the chair, her mind reeling. Her father wanted them to join him? If she'd known earlier, would the realization have changed anything between them?

She tried to envision her life if her mother had agreed to her father's request—all the adventures, the excitement. But what about the potential isolation and loneliness? Not to mention the domino effect such a decision could elicit. Where would she be now? Would she still own her café? What about Spock? And her friends? And *Jayce*?

Her heart wrenched at the possibility of losing so much.

Without the ability to live out both scenarios and then decide, she suspected her mother had made the right decision. And yet, the mere knowledge that her father missed them—that he *wanted* them by his side—helped to soothe the fractured edges of her soul. If only she'd known sooner, maybe they wouldn't have drifted so far apart. "Why didn't you and Dad ever tell me?"

"I don't know. I suppose because it took so long to work through our own issues as a couple. You were right, sweetheart. For a long time, I *was* pretending. At least, partly." For the first time since the conversation began, her mother's hands stilled, resting calmly on the table. Her steady gaze sparked with conviction.

"I love your father. And I truly believe God designed him for the work he's doing. But I still struggled with hurt and resentment. Not resentment toward your father," she added hastily. "I resented the time we spent apart. And I didn't know how to both support him *and* be honest about my feelings. So, instead of asking him to call more often, to try harder to come home on time, and essentially, to be more present in our lives, I bottled all those desires inside. And I see now that you suffered from my silence. And I'm so sorry, honey."

CeCe nodded slowly as her mother's words seeped into her wounds like a welcome salve while also stirring her empathy. She, too, struggled to support the man she loved while yearning for more.

What would it look like to be a priority in Jayce's life without expecting too great a sacrifice? What did a healthy balance even look like? Was it possible?

She reached across the table for her mother's hand. "It's okay, Mama. I feel like tonight has been the wake-up call I've needed. Maybe one we've all needed. I don't know what the future holds. But I do know it's finally time to express all the things I've been too afraid to say."

Both to her father.

And Jayce.

Chapter Thirty-Three

ABBY

ABBY PUSHED a plump strawberry around her plate, regarding the merriment of her bridal shower with the detached eye of an outside observer. The other women seated at the table, sipping tea and nibbling tiny cakes and sandwiches, laughing and chatting together, faded into the background, despite her best intentions to focus on the festivities.

Guilt swirled in her stomach, mixing unpleasantly with the mango-peach tea she'd recently consumed. She *wanted* to be emotionally present. Her friends had gone to so much trouble to plan the perfect afternoon tea party to celebrate her upcoming nuptials. Even working within the truncated timeframe of their extremely short engagement, her friends had thought of every detail. But despite her immense gratitude, Abby's heart still lived in yesterday's grief, in the perpetual pain of Max's goodbye.

At the depressing memory, her sorrow sunk even deeper into her soul. If she couldn't summon an ounce of joy here, in the gorgeous garden of the Honeybee Retreat—an oceanside oasis specifically designed for wounded women to heal after heartache—how could she enjoy any of the festivities leading up to her wedding day?

Her mind flooded with images of Logan. The smile that crinkled the corners of his eyes. His calloused, capable hands, so quick to reach for hers. His broad shoulders, steady and strong, always willing to support the weight of her burdens.

Over the past several months, he'd become the single most important person in her life. And he deserved her heart *and* her unhindered happiness.

Determined to lift her spirits, she sat a little straighter, smoothing the folds of the fancy cotton sundress Nadia had convinced her to wear in lieu of her usual jeans and T-shirt. Across the garden, her stylish maid of honor stood out like a vibrant rose among the fragrant lavender and hollyhocks. With her dark hair and dusky complexion, no one could pull off a red cocktail dress quite like Nadia. Beside her, Sage and Mia—looking equally lovely in their elegant tea party ensembles—helped set up what appeared to be Bridal Shower Bingo.

A groan welled in her throat, but she quickly squelched it. A game would be fun. It would take her mind off Max. *Maybe*.

"Here. This might help." CeCe placed a pretty porcelain teacup in front of Abby before taking the seat beside her.

"What is it?" Abby sniffed the earthy aroma. She didn't really need any more tea.

"It's Bissy tea. Mama's relatives send bags of the stuff from Jamaica. It's a common remedy for countless issues, including boosting energy and elevating mood."

"Well, I could definitely use that." Abby lifted the teacup to her lips, willing to try anything to improve her melancholy mood.

"Me, too." CeCe joined her in taking a sip.

Abby softened with sympathy. Her friend had recently confided in her regarding her own troubles—her father's harrowing experience, Jayce heading back to Los Angeles so soon thereafter, and her inability to reach either of them by phone. "Still haven't heard from your father or Jayce?"

"No, but I'm sure everything's fine. They both have a lot on their minds. They'll call as soon as they can." CeCe smiled and sipped her tea, but Abby detected a glint of unease in her eyes—unease Abby felt in her own heart.

Even though she knew better than to expect a call from Sam so soon—if ever—she couldn't help checking her phone multiple times that day. What if he'd changed his mind? What if he wanted to return to Blessings Bay and accept their offer to live in the bungalow? More than anything, she wanted Max back in her life, in whatever capacity possible.

It took every ounce of self-control she possessed not to bombard Sam's cell phone with inquiries about Max—How was his first night in a new place? Did he like Redton? How was his rabbit, Ron, adjusting? Could she send them a boxed set of *The Chronicles of Narnia* so they could continue reading the series together? And the one question her heart longed to ask but she'd never dare to voice aloud: *Does he miss us?*

Reading her mind, CeCe interrupted her thoughts with her own lingering question. "Do you think Sam will bring Max back for the wedding?"

"I don't know." Abby's chest squeezed, and she tightened her grip on the teacup. "He said he'd think about it, but from his detached, noncommittal tone, I didn't get a hopeful impression."

"That's so strange." CeCe frowned, mirroring Abby's sober expression. "Why wouldn't he want Max to be a part of your wedding?"

"Logan and I have wondered the same thing many times. All I know is, Sam made a big deal about the importance of starting over. He seems to think the best thing for him and Max is a completely clean slate."

"And you and Logan, there's nothing you can do?"

Abby took a slow, deliberate sip of tea, focusing on the slightly bitter flavor as it slid down her throat. *This isn't the time or place for tears*, she told herself for the hundredth time. After swallowing the tea along with her emotions, she said evenly, "Unfortunately, no. We have zero influence in Max's life now."

As a foster parent, she knew the risks. Permanent placement was never guaranteed. In fact, parental reconciliation was usually the goal. A foster parent willingly opened their heart to a child with the full understanding that one day, they might have to say goodbye forever. So why did she feel so much resentment toward Sam for taking Max away? Why could her mind acknowledge, and even accept, his decision while her heart railed against it?

"I'm so sorry, Abs. I can't imagine what it must feel like to welcome a child into your life and family and then wake up one morning and have everything change." CeCe hesitated, her brow knitting before she asked quietly, "If you could go back and do it all over again, would you?"

Abby set the teacup back on its saucer and met her friend's gaze. Without a flicker of doubt, she answered honestly, from the depths of her heart. "Yes, I would. The time we had with Max was worth all the pain we're enduring now. I'd never give that up, even though it's hard." She paused thoughtfully before adding, "After losing Donnie, and everything we've gone through with Max, I think I'm finally starting to realize something about loss. Healing isn't always about erasing the sadness. It's about learning to let the joy back in."

Abby thought of the darkest moments in her life; how she thought she'd never see light again. And yet, the light always found a way, filtering through the cracks, at first, then beaming brightly, eradicating the shadows. "Loving someone isn't always easy, but it's a blessing unlike any other because it transforms us, from the inside out. It's worth cultivating, whatever the cost."

Abby clung to that truth throughout the day's festivities. It carried her through the games and the opening of gifts. She'd even managed to nudge Max from her thoughts long enough to actually enjoy herself for a few hours.

She perched on a white wicker chair while her friends sat in a semicircle around her, oohing and ahhing over embroidered linen napkins and monogrammed bath towels. When she finally finished opening the last present, Abby thanked them all profusely, touched by their love and generosity.

"Hold on," Nadia said, snatching a card off the table. "There's one more." She handed her a plain white envelope with the words *A Wedding Gift* scribbled across the front. "Logan found this inside your mailbox this morning. He thought if you opened it today, it would be one less gift to keep track of after the wedding."

Abby smiled. And one less thank-you note to write after the wedding, too. Her fiancé, ever the pragmatist. "Who's it from?" She couldn't think of anyone who would leave a card inside her mailbox instead of handing it to her in person.

"No clue," Nadia said. "But I know how you can find out." She tapped the corner of the envelope.

Her friends collectively leaned forward, their expressions openly curious as Abby tore the seal and slipped out the card. When she flipped it open, a small piece of sea glass fell into her lap.

Her heart froze at the sight of the familiar aqua stone. "It's from Sam," she whispered in a barely audible breath.

Swallowing the lump of emotion lodged in her throat, she read his note aloud. "'I don't really believe in good luck charms. But this sliver of sea glass is my most valuable earthly possession.

190

And the only thing I own that could possibly convey my gratitude for everything you've done for me and my son. I hope it brings you good fortune on your special day.'"

Tears welled in Abby's eyes, betraying her best efforts to keep them at bay. She curled her fingers around the smooth stone, allowing the man's kind gesture to soothe her wounded heart.

Sam Bailey was a good man. And that needed to be good enough for her.

"Are you okay?" Nadia asked softly, placing a gentle hand on her shoulder.

"I will be." She smiled up at her friend, wiping her damp cheek with the ruffle of her flutter sleeve.

For the first time since Max left, she actually believed she would be... eventually.

Chapter Thirty-Four

CECE

CeCe pulled into her private parking spot in the small courtyard behind the café, her thoughts lingering over Abby's words from earlier that day. What had she said about love? *It's worth cultivating, whatever the cost.*

Her friend had made the claim with such heartfelt conviction, CeCe couldn't help comparing Abby's outlook with her own reticence toward any emotional risk.

A romantic future with Jayce finally floated within her reach, solid and tangible and oh so tempting. She could still taste his lips on her own and feel his fingertips cupping her face, firm and intentional, driven by an all-consuming desire she'd only ever experienced in her dreams.

Did she dare take the next step despite all the uncertainty? The answer had seemed so clear last night, before the doubts of daylight had crept in, threatening her fragile confidence. Especially considering he'd left so abruptly and still hadn't called.

Mired deep in her thoughts, she trudged to the side entrance of the café, her heavy footsteps traversing the habitual path in the dusky haze of twilight. As she reached the dimly lit door, the streetlamps flickered to life, illuminating the shadowed alleyway.

That's when she noticed the shrouded figure leaning against the side of the building.

The man straightened when he spotted her, his angular, stubbled features silhouetted in the soft amber glow of lamplight.

Her chest swelled, strangling her breath. Struggling to process the strange apparition, she blinked several times, waiting for the vision to vanish.

"Hi, chouquette." The familiar yet foreign voice triggered a deluge of memories, like a beloved childhood melody unlocked from deep within her subconscious.

"Dad?" she asked warily, not trusting her own eyesight. How was it possible? She wanted to throw herself in his arms, to hug him tightly and never let go. But he couldn't be real. Her brain simply wouldn't accept such an outlandish scenario.

"You look nice." His warm, wistful gaze slowly took in her appearance, as if he could picture his little girl behind the grown woman wearing a simple blue sundress, her unruly curls twisted into a knot at the nape of her neck.

"Thank you. You look—" She faltered, still adjusting to the shock. The man standing before her looked exactly the same as she remembered, even though she hadn't seen him in several months. Somehow, her father never aged. Or was it simply because she still looked at him with the eyes of youth, trapped in the past?

"Like I was buried alive?" He finished her sentence with a wry grin, making light of his traumatic ordeal as he brushed dust from his wrinkled khaki pants.

"Don't remind me." Her throat tightened, the worry still fresh in her mind. "I thought—" Once again, words failed her.

She wanted to say, *I thought I'd lost you*. But, in so many ways, it felt as though she'd lost him long ago.

"I know." He grimaced, his features etched in empathetic apology. "I'm sorry I put you through that."

"Have you seen Mama?" She still couldn't wrap her head around how or why he'd materialized on her doorstep.

"She knows I'm here. But I came to see you first." He hesitated, shuffling his feet. "May I come inside so we can talk?"

For a moment, CeCe merely stared. He'd come to see her first? So they could talk? Surely, she had to be imagining the surreal exchange. "Sure," she said at last, unlocking the door in a daze. She stepped aside, so he could enter first.

As he slipped past her, she inhaled earthy notes of soil and sandalwood. The strong urge to hug him struck her a second time, but she didn't act on the impulse. They hadn't hugged since her childhood. She used to bury her face in the curve of his shoulder, her little hands wrapped around his neck. She'd felt so safe, so content. Now, all these years later—after decades of emotional distance— she had no idea how to initiate something as intimate as an embrace. And even if she did, how would he react? Would he hug her back?

She led her father into her apartment, trying to recall if he'd ever stepped foot inside her home before. Only once, that she remembered, shortly after she'd bought the café. The previous owner had offered her a generous arrangement that had allowed her to pay off the purchase price in installments over a ten-year period. Partly because she'd worked as a dedicated employee since high school, and partly because the owners were eager to retire near their grandchildren in Michigan.

As she'd given her parents a tour of the café and upstairs apartment, excitedly detailing all her hopes and dreams for revamping the run-down space, she'd been so proud to show her father what she'd accomplished at such a young age. Not many women ran their own business before the age of thirty. But rather than extoll his praise, he'd spent the afternoon glued to his phone, distracted by updates from the team at his latest dig site.

At the memory, a surge of disappointment threatened to resurface, but she stifled the unwanted sentiment. "Can I get you something to drink?"

"Water would be wonderful. Thank you." His gaze swept her apartment, surveying the cozy, mismatched furniture and eclectic decor, including her framed vintage *Star Trek* artwork. "Nice place."

"Thanks." She filled two water glasses in the kitchen, strangely nervous as her father settled on the couch. What did he want to talk about?

From his perch on the opposite armrest, Spock raised his hackles, eyeing the intruder with a skeptical scowl.

"Still as friendly as ever, eh, Spock?" Her dad tried to pet the frosty feline, but Spock hissed, and he withdrew his hand.

CeCe stifled a laugh at the cat's overprotective behavior. She may be willing to mend fences with her father, but Spock was slow to forgive.

She handed her dad a water glass then sat beside him on the couch, a cushion's distance between them.

Spock nudged her arm as if to ask if she was all right. She scratched his head in response. "Don't take this the wrong way," she told her dad tentatively, "but what are you doing here? *How* are you here?"

He sipped his water then smiled. "It's amazing how quickly you can get somewhere in a private jet."

"A private jet?" she repeated, still not understanding.

Her father's eyes twinkled. "That boyfriend of yours sure knows how to travel in style."

"Boyfriend?" Nothing her father said made any sense. "Wait. Are you talking about *Jayce*?"

"I sure hope so. Unless you have another boyfriend with a private jet I don't know about."

CeCe gulped her water, trying to wrap her head around the news. Jayce had flown to South America to see her father? Why hadn't he told her?

"I deduce from your expression that you weren't apprised of his plans?" her father asked.

CeCe shook her head, reeling as another realization struck her. With Jayce in South America, he'd missed the award ceremony in Los Angeles. And his meeting with the producer. Her heart squeezed at his selflessness, and she wasn't sure how she felt about such a generous gesture. Touched? Grateful? Guilty? Distressed by how much he'd sacrificed for her sake?

"What did Jayce tell you?" she asked, wondering what had possessed him to do something so drastic—and potentially detrimental to his career.

"Nothing."

"Nothing?" CeCe balked. "He traveled all that way and said *nothing*?"

"He asked me a question."

CeCe raised both eyebrows, silently indicating she expected further explanation.

Her father set his glass on the coffee table, his countenance solemn. Shifting on the cushion to face her, he met her gaze. "He asked me what went through my mind the moment the excavation site collapsed."

"I don't understand." CeCe frowned. "Why did he need to hop on a plane to ask you that?"

A knowing smile teased the corners of his mouth. "There may have been a bit more to our conversation, but I'll leave the rest for Jayce to tell you. For now, all you need to know is Jayce's question made me reassess my life in a profound way."

"How so?" she asked cautiously, not daring to hope.

"They say when a person faces their final moments on earth, their life flashes before their eyes. Most notably, their deepest regrets," he said. "I expected my greatest regret to be related to my work—that I have yet to make the one career-defining discovery. Instead—" His voice cracked, his formerly rich, smooth baritone now a rough, dry croak, as if he'd swallowed sand.

"Instead," he said again, with considerable effort to keep his words from warbling. "My one and only regret was that I hadn't spent more time with you and your mother. That I may never get another chance to see your face or hear your laugh."

A burning sensation tickled the back of her throat. She sipped her water, but it didn't help.

"I realize I haven't been much of a father to you over the last several years," he continued, his gaze glassy. "I've been absent. Distant. I told myself there would be time. That I could dedicate myself to my work now—that I could leave my legacy—then settle down with you and your mother. I convinced myself that you were happy. That your mother was right, and you were both better off here, where you belonged. That you didn't need me."

CeCe felt her own tears swell, and she blinked hard, determined to fight them off. Her father's words weren't a surprise—not after her recent conversation with her mother. And yet, hearing them aloud stung more than she expected.

"I'm sorry, chouquette. I should have fought harder to stay connected, to be in your life. I've missed so much. I've missed *you*." He attempted a small, sad smile. "I've always considered myself a wise man. But it took a young man half my age to reveal an obvious truth: I'd already found my two greatest treasures. And I'd foolishly left them behind."

At his words, a tear escaped the corner of her eye and slid beneath her glasses, tumbling slowly down her cheek.

"My work is a part of who I am," he continued softly. "And I believe it's a God-given passion. But I also believe He's called me to be a husband and father, first and foremost, and I'd lost sight of that calling. It's time I rectify that mistake." He placed his hand on the cushion between them, palm facing up like an olive branch. "I dig up the past so the things we learn from history can inform and shape the future—a better future. And if you'll let me, I'd like to build a better future with you."

For a moment, CeCe studied his open hand through her tears, tracing every callous and scar. Each one told a story. A story of a man she barely knew. A man she desperately wanted to know. Now, she'd have her chance. And she knew exactly who to thank.

She slid her hand into her father's.

His fingers folded around hers.

She wasn't sure who moved first, but she found herself in his arms, her cheek cradled in the same comforting curve of his shoulder she recalled from all those years ago as a child. How was it possible that even as an adult, she still fit as perfectly in his embrace as she did in her youth?

For the next two hours, they worked on mending their relationship, chatting about anything and everything. When she finally walked him to the door to say good night, her steps felt lighter. He said he'd be spending a few days in town before heading back to Peru, but he planned to return in two months for a longer visit. For the first time in years, she actually believed he'd honor his word.

After bidding him good-night—with plans to bake together

in the morning, just like old times—she turned to head back inside.

A stack of papers sitting on the welcome mat caught her eye.

Her breath hitched.

Jayce's screenplay! Had he finally finished it?

She scooped the script off the doormat and scurried inside. Plopping onto the couch, she quickly flipped to the final pages. Her heart racing with unfettered curiosity, she eagerly devoured each line, picturing the vivid setting of the café's kitchen in her mind as the character, Alvera, narrated the scene in voiceover.

INT. THE UNCOMPLICATED CAFÉ – KITCHEN – DAY

CHLOE and JUSTIN kiss, sealing their commitment to one another.

A POT BOILS OVER on the stove behind them.

Unnoticed, ALVERA steps in and switches off the burner, a gentle smile on her face.

ALVERA (V.O)

And so it was that the complicated became uncomplicated once more.

She lifts a tray perfectly plated with an **affogato** and slice of **coconut cake**, previously prepared by Chloe.

ALVERA (V.O.)

Not safe or simple. But straightforward.

She exits the kitchen and walks toward a CUSTOMER seated at a cozy corner table.

ALVERA (V.O.)

An understanding that love—*real* love—casts out fear.

GENTLE RAINDROPS dapple the windowpane as Alvera sets the tray before the customer.

ALVERA (V.O.)

And when the storms come, we can face them

with faith, fortitude, and, if we're lucky,
a creamy affogato and slice of coconut cake.
Alvera turns toward the camera.
She breaks the fourth wall and SMILES.
ALVERA (V.O.)
At least, that's how we do it here
at The Uncomplicated Café.
She WINKS.
FADE TO BLACK.

With the giddiest grin—the kind that made her cheeks hurt in the best possible way—CeCe reread the last page, savoring each soul-quenching sentence.

Chloe had chosen love over the safety of Alvera's spell. She'd weighed the risks and still offered her heart, without restraint.

CeCe couldn't help drawing a comparison to Abby's words from earlier, and the similarities made her laugh.

Spock mewed, nudging her hand, as if he wanted to be let in on the joke.

"God must think I have a pretty thick head," she said with a smile. "He's laying on the life lessons a little heavy today." She scratched Spock behind the ears. "To be fair, I have been a bit dense."

Spock mewed again in agreement.

CeCe chuckled. "Point taken. No more waffling. It's time to be brave and tell Jayce how I feel."

Spock purred his approval.

"How should I do it?" she asked, continuing to stroke his fur. "Have any bright ideas?"

To her surprise, he hopped off the couch.

"Some help you are," she huffed.

Ignoring her, he swatted at an index card lying on the ground.

Cece frowned. How did that get there?

As she plucked the card off the carpet, her heart skipped. She immediately recognized Jayce's handwriting. The card must've fallen out when she'd hastily rifled through the screenplay.

Meet me at Lighthouse Cove after your shift tomorrow. I'll bring lunch.

Her mouth went dry. Lighthouse Cove. Their special spot. The spot where she'd planned to confess her feelings all those years ago, but Jayce never showed.

"Okay, God," she murmured. "Message received."

She knew what she needed to do.

If only she could predict the outcome.

Chapter Thirty-Five

JAYCE

JAYCE STOOD on the edge of his mother's lawn, momentarily mesmerized by the serene setting. In the pleasant dim of twilight, his parents' homes appeared tranquil, as if the occupants weren't waging an eternal war. He'd never noticed how both of his parents' porch swings hung in opposite directions, facing each other. Did the decision reflect their inner desire to remain connected somehow? He certainly hoped so.

He tread quietly across the soft grass. The gentle hum of the ocean just beyond the sleepy street muffled his footsteps. As he moved in relative silence, his thoughts drifted to CeCe. Once again, he prayed over her conversation with her father, hoping for the best. *Let tonight be a night of reconciliation,* he internally pleaded, thinking of more than one relationship in desperate need of repair.

He stopped beside the lemon tree, his heart beating wildly, anxiously anticipating his next move. Was he doing the right thing? He wasn't sure. But he couldn't shake Mr. Dupree's words from earlier that morning—words that had reshaped a long-held perception of his parents' feud.

Jayce could still see the stark sadness in Mr. Dupree's eyes when he'd offered to fly him home in his private jet.

Mr. Dupree—or Paul, as he'd asked to be called—had dropped his gaze, staring blankly into his steaming mug of Peruvian coffee. "I don't think CeCe wants to see me."

"What?" Jayce had balked, asking, "What makes you say that? She may be angry with you, but—" Before he'd had a chance to finish his sentence, Paul's head jerked up in surprise.

"She's angry with me?" The man's voice had carried an unexpected twinge of hopefulness.

"A little, yeah," Jayce had confessed, confused by Paul's reaction but also guilt-ridden he'd accidentally betrayed CeCe's confidence. It was her place to tell her father how she felt, not his. "But forget I said anything. And don't let it discourage you." The last thing he wanted was his blunder to deter Paul from coming home.

"Discourage me?" Grinning, Paul had removed his thin wire-framed glasses and wiped the coffee steam from the lenses with his frayed bandana. "My boy, you've given me phenomenal news."

"I have?" Jayce had suddenly wondered if all those hours trapped underground had affected the man's mental faculties. "How is CeCe being angry with you a good thing?"

Paul had looked at him with borderline pity, as if he'd been the one missing brain cells. "Because, dear boy, indifference is the road to death. But anger—ah, anger!" His voice rose an octave with unusual gusto. "Anger is a strong emotion. It means something matters, that there's hope." His eyes had danced with the delight of an archeologist who'd just discovered the Holy Grail.

Jayce had dwelled on Paul's words for the duration of their travels home, mulling over the implications in his own life. Could the man's philosophy be true? Did his parents' perpetual hostility and inability to move on mean they still had feelings for each other?

There was one way to find out....

Jayce pulled the ripcord on the chain saw he'd borrowed from Evan. It revved to life, disturbing the evening's tranquility.

Widening his stance, he drew in a deep breath, braced for the impending showdown.

The loud rumble lured his intended targets.

"What's going on out here?" his father asked with gruff annoyance. Jayce suspected he'd roused him from the TV.

"Jayce?" His mother gawked, her bewildered gaze darting between the whirring chain saw and her beloved lemon tree. "What are you doing?"

For a split second, Jayce hesitated. His parents stood on their respective porches, staring at him as if he'd lost his mind. Had he? Was his experiment too wild to actually work? Or would the lemon tree—which he'd long suspected to hold deeper meaning—serve as the impetus to get them talking again?

Angling the saw's spinning chain toward the sturdy trunk, he decided to put his theory to the test.

"Stop!" his mother shrieked. Horrified, she covered her mouth with both hands.

"Son, what are you doing?" his father demanded sharply, striding across the porch, poised to intervene.

"I'm tired of you two bickering over who rightfully owns this blasted tree," Jayce told them. "Either you sort it out, once and for all, or I chop it down."

His parents shared a quick glance of concern before his father narrowed his gaze in Jayce's direction. "You wouldn't."

"I would. It's for your own good." He suppressed a rueful grin at the irony of the situation. How many times had his father used the same line on him during his childhood? *Jayce, this timeout is for your own good. Jayce, we're revoking your video game privileges for your own good.* Now, he finally understood.

His parents exchanged another glance, silently debating how to handle their renegade son.

Finally, his father turned to him. "Put the chain saw down."

"Can you two agree on the rightful owner? Or is it *arrivederci* lemon tree?"

"The tree belongs to your mother. I'll stop pruning it to favor my yard."

"I knew it!" His mother jabbed a finger at her underhanded ex-husband. "I knew the growth pattern had nothing to do with optimal sunlight on your side of the fence."

His father flashed a sheepish smile. "I had a feeling you wouldn't buy that excuse. You're too smart for that."

The compliment seemed to mollify her slightly. "Then why even attempt it? Why go through all the trouble of pruning the tree in the first place? You don't even like lemons that much."

His father hung his head.

Jayce cut the engine, and the chain saw rumbled to a stop. *Come on, Dad. Fess up. Tell her you still care.*

After a long pause, his father lifted his head, meeting his mother's gaze. "Do you remember when we got this tree?"

"Of course," she said with unexpected softness. "You bought me a sapling for our fourth anniversary, since the traditional fourth anniversary gift is fruit. You said, as our love grows and bears fruit, so will our tree."

His father nodded. "I really believed that. After four years of marriage, my love for you had only grown stronger. I thought it always would."

"But it didn't, did it?" The pain in her voice sounded as sharp and poignant as the day they'd announced their divorce.

Jayce wanted to look away, to give them privacy as they

hashed out their broken relationship from across their two porches. But he couldn't. He needed to know what happened.

His father released a deep, guttural sigh, his entire body sagging with the force of his exhale. "That's what I told myself. I didn't know how else to explain the disconnect, why our marriage fell apart. Except that you'd stopped loving me."

"Me?" His mother flinched in surprise. "You're the one who stopped loving me."

"What? No." His father shook his head, as if the motion might shift the fractured pieces of his memory back into place. "That's not what happened. You must have forgotten."

"Forgotten?" His mother's voice warbled with emotion. "How could I forget the worst moment in my life? When you said you wanted a divorce—"

"No," he interrupted. "I asked if you thought we *should* get a divorce."

"Because you wanted one," she fired back.

"Because I thought *you* wanted one."

His parents stared at each other in stunned silence as the walls of their misconceptions came crashing down around them.

Jayce's heart squeezed, compressed by the crushing weight of grief. So much misery. Decades of heartache. All because two people didn't know how to communicate. Or weren't willing to try.

He couldn't help wondering, if everyone in the world compiled a list of their regrets, would more people regret the things they said? Or the things they *didn't* say?

He knew which way he'd land.

Luckily, he'd get a second chance to say all the things he should've said long ago.

He just prayed it wasn't too late.

Chapter Thirty-Six

CECE

THROUGHOUT HER MORNING shift at the café, CeCe struggled to keep her mind on work. Why did Jayce want to meet at the cove? Was it simply to have a picnic lunch on the beach like old times? Or did he have something else in mind?

Only one thing served to calm her erratic thoughts: her father's help in the kitchen. He'd arrived early, wearing the white linen apron she recalled from her childhood—the one he claimed belonged to a distant relative who'd worked as a *maître pâtissier*, or master pastry chef, in France in the 1800s.

She'd smiled when she spotted the familiar stains on the bib. He had a colorful story explaining each one, and although she remembered them, she'd asked him to repeat the imaginative tales while they baked.

Together, they made chouquettes and pain au chocolat, and CeCe updated her father on major milestones he'd missed, including the recent situation with Jayce. While the kitchen flooded with sweet memories and the comforting scent of warm, sugary dough, her heart started to mend.

To her great surprise, her father offered to cover the last hour of her shift so she could leave early to change. She accepted gratefully, and spent a little extra time getting ready for her lunch date—was it a date?—with Jayce.

After she finally settled on a white jersey-knit dress, she ambled down the beach, her sandals in hand. Her bare feet sunk into the soft sand, and the sharp, briny breeze brushed against her skin. She couldn't have asked for a more beautiful afternoon, and her mind raced with possibilities for the day ahead. Would they finally discuss their earth-shattering kiss? Would he reveal what else he'd discussed with her father in Peru?

Nearly bursting with anticipation, she rounded a bend, slipping through a narrow crevice in a craggy rock formation, and emerged in a secluded cove beneath the Blessings Bay Lighthouse.

Her breath caught.

Jayce sat waiting on a quilted blanket, but he wasn't alone. A dozen of her childhood stuffed animals sat beside him, arranged in a semicircle around a buffet of Oreos and juice boxes.

"What's all this?" She flashed back to their pretend wedding in kindergarten, comparing the detailed memory to the display before her. Jayce had even remembered to stick a tiny bouquet of bougainvillea into the threadbare arms of Space Bear—the astronaut-themed teddy bear she'd dubbed her maid of honor. "And where on earth did you find all my stuffies? I thought I'd donated them years ago."

"Turns out, your sentimental mom couldn't part with them. She dug them out of storage for me." He sprang from the blanket, and CeCe noticed the silk tie tucked into the collar of his T-shirt.

She laughed. "Pretty sure you know how to tie one of those by now."

"True," he conceded with a boyish grin. "But I was going for authenticity." Proving his point, he held out a clumsily knotted dandelion crown. "It's been a while since I made one of these. And your head's a lot bigger than when we were five. I hope it fits."

"Hey! My head's not that big," she protested playfully.

Jayce settled the crown on top of her curls, then stepped back to admire his handiwork. "Perfect. I was worried I wouldn't have enough dandelions to make it all the way around."

"If this is your idea of whispering sweet nothings on our wedding day, you have some work to do," she teased, her whole body tingling in hopeful expectancy. Surely the nostalgic tableau meant something.

"You're right. Pointing out the increase in your cranial circumference isn't very romantic, is it? How's this?" He cleared his throat and met her gaze. His expression shifted from playful to purposeful, and the intensity gave her chills.

"Nearly a decade ago, I stepped through that slit in the rocks and saw you standing in this exact spot, waiting for me."

Her heart jolted. He was here? All those years ago, he hadn't left early to avoid traffic after all? But instead of joining her, as planned, he'd left her on the beach alone. Why?

"When I saw you standing there, staring at the ocean, so beautiful, so painfully perfect, I knew I couldn't do it: I couldn't say goodbye. Not in person. Not looking into the eyes of the woman I loved."

As he spoke, the world around her spun. Loved? He loved her? Did he still? Her head swam, struggling to process the revelation.

"I'd watched my parents' relationship devolve from steadfast devotion to disgust, and the thought of repeating the pattern with you—" He broke off, shaking his head as if he couldn't bear the thought. "Out of fear, I conflated their situation with ours, believing we'd face the same fate. And I couldn't lose you, Toto. So, I chose the coward's way out. For the next ten years, I gave the greatest performance of my life as a man who wasn't wholly, desperately, undeniably in love with his best friend."

At the sincerity in his eyes, her breathing slowed. Tears blurred her vision. All this time, she'd clung to her own misguided conclusion, convinced he hadn't met her on the beach that day due to disinterest—that she hadn't meant enough to him. She thought of the text he'd sent, claiming he didn't want anything to change between them. She'd been so quick to believe him, so willing to bottle her feelings back inside. And why? Because of insecurity? Because she couldn't fathom the possibility that someone like Jayce could actually care for her as much as she cared for him?

Her chest ached for what could have been, but she pushed the regret aside, not wanting a single what-if to mar this moment.

"Cecelia Desirée Dupree, I recently asked you to be my fake fiancée, but what I didn't tell you was that, more than anything, I wanted our engagement to be real."

Her eyes widened as he dropped to one knee in the sand.

"Thanks for holding on to this, Space Bear." He withdrew a small square box tucked behind the bouquet in the bear's arms.

CeCe wasn't sure if she was awake or dreaming as Jayce flipped open the box, revealing an antique moonstone ring—his grandmother's ring. A ring she'd admired—and even tried on—on more than one occasion.

"I've spent a lifetime fighting my feelings for the sake of our friendship," Jayce admitted, plucking the ring from its velvety resting place. "And in the words of the great Mr. Spock, to continue to do so would be highly illogical."

Caught off guard by his *Star Trek* reference, CeCe laughed, joy bubbling out of her as light and airy as the frothy surf lapping the shore. Was this really happening?

"Before you ask if it's too soon, or point out that we haven't even been on a date yet, let me make my case." He held her gaze, more earnest than she'd ever seen him before. "We know everything there is to know about each other. We've stood by each other at our worst and our best. There's nothing a first date will tell me about you that I haven't already known for years. Most importantly, I know that I love you. And I don't want to spend another second pretending I don't. Besides," he added with a mischievous grin. "I already have your father's blessing."

"You do? When did you…" Her voice curtailed as she answered her own question. Her father had alluded to there being more to his conversation with Jayce. Had Jayce really flown all the way to South America to ask for her hand in marriage?

It all felt too surreal, too close to a dream come true. She tried to anchor herself in the feel of the warm sand, the wind in her hair, anything to cement reality.

"So, what do you say, Toto?" He grounded her with his loving gaze. "Will you be my best friend *and* my wife?"

For several seconds, she merely stared, overwhelmed with emotion. How many times had she longed for this exact moment, believing it would never happen? How deeply had she loved this man without ever breathing a word?

And now, he'd reached across the invisible line of friendship, offering her his whole heart.

She extended her hand, beaming down at him. "Make it so."

He laughed at her *Star Trek* quote, looking equally relieved she'd finally answered and overjoyed by her response.

Switching the faux engagement ring to her right hand, he

replaced it with his grandmother's moonstone, then sprang to his feet.

Enveloping her in his arms, he drew her lips to meet his with a firm, unwavering hand—the hand of a man who knew exactly what he wanted.

And he wanted *her*.

She met his kiss with all the pent-up passion bottled inside for years, finally releasing her worries to the wind.

He responded, matching her need, and she fell even deeper into the dreamlike euphoria overtaking her.

Every surrounding sensation, from the gentle swish of the soothing tide to the salty scent of the sea, faded into the background as they lost themselves in the pure bliss of the moment.

A moment that would forever reshape their friendship.

And their future.

Chapter Thirty-Seven

JAYCE

JAYCE LACED his fingers through CeCe's, relishing the closeness of their entwined hands as they strode up from the beach onto Main Street. It took all his self-control not to announce the good news to the first person he saw.

He'd proposed to his dream girl, and she'd actually said yes! He still couldn't believe it. A luckier guy had never lived, and nothing could dampen his good mood.

Ugh. Spoke too soon. His cheerful optimism faltered the second he spotted Gretchen seated at a patio table in front of the café.

"Hey, Gretchen. To what do we owe the pleasure?" he asked dryly.

"You weren't at the award ceremony last night." Her sharp, accusatory tone popped his blissful bubble. This clearly wasn't a social call.

He sighed. "Yes, I'm aware."

"Are you also aware that your failure to attend puts you in breach of contract?" She stood, her unnaturally flawless features puckered in a disapproving scowl.

"I left a voicemail explaining the extenuating circumstances." He'd called Stacey and Victor, too. Stacey had been quick to support his decision, and Victor, to his surprise, had also been understanding. He'd even told him to email the script as soon as he had a chance.

Comparing their compassion to Gretchen's coldness, he added with thinly veiled irritation, "CeCe's dad is fine, by the way."

She dismissed his comment. "I don't care if *you* were the one trapped six feet under. I'd still expect you to attend one of the most crucial PR events of the year, even if you had to dig your way out with a plastic spoon."

He bristled. "Come on, Gretchen. That's a little callous considering what CeCe and her family have been through." He glanced down at CeCe, who'd stiffened by his side. Her strained expression said it all. If she gave in to her baser instincts, Gretchen would be the recipient of a hard jab to the nose. Lucky for his agent, CeCe had self-restraint.

"Well, Jayce. Since you mentioned your *fiancée*," Gretchen snarled, somehow managing to make the endearing title sound like a dirty word. "I think it's time we face facts. This little experiment has run its course, don't you think?"

"Experiment?" What was she talking about?

"Fling. Fetish. Whatever you want to call *this* anomaly." She gestured to CeCe as if drawing his attention to a wad of gum on the bottom of his shoe. "You're not seriously going to marry this PR nightmare, are you?"

At her nasty comment, the irritation simmering below the surface boiled into full blown outrage. His jaw clenched. "What did you say?" he growled, daring her to repeat herself.

She took an instinctive step backward, startled by the flash of anger in his eyes. *No more Mr. Congeniality.* "I—I just think everyone will be better off if we—"

"There is no *we*, Gretchen. My personal life has nothing to do with you. The woman I choose as *my wife* has nothing to do with you. And frankly"—he gathered a galvanizing breath—"I no longer want anything to do with you."

"Excuse me?" She blinked, her eyes wide and questioning, as if she'd misheard.

"Don't look so surprised. You've done nothing but insult CeCe since the day you met. Which not only reveals your lack of character, but your lack of judgment, too. CeCe is the kindest, most incredible woman I've ever met, and if you can't show her the respect she deserves, then I can't work with you."

There was no misunderstanding now. He'd made his stance abundantly clear. Gretchen glowered. "We have a contract."

"Yes, we do. With a fairly detailed morality clause that I'm sure a few talented lawyers could prove you've violated. More than once."

"Oh, please," Gretchen scoffed. "You're bluffing. You're not going to fire me. You wouldn't have an ounce of success without me."

"Maybe not. But I've been thinking about a career change anyway."

"To what? Don't tell me it's screenwriting." She actually laughed.

CeCe squeezed his hand as if to say, *Don't let her get to you.*

"It's none of your business. As of this moment, you're no longer my agent." The decision filled him with surprising relief. He should've cut her loose years ago.

"Fine." The single syllable slithered off her tongue. "But don't say I didn't warn you."

"What's that supposed to mean?" He immediately regretted taking the bait.

"Jayce, darling," she said with an ominous lilt. "You know I'm not afraid to get my hands dirty. In a town this small, it will take me two seconds to dig up dirt on you *and* your precious fiancée."

"Good luck," he grunted. But even as he said the words, a cold feeling of dread swept over him.

"Everyone has a secret." She slid her purse over one arm. "And I'm going to have fun finding yours." With a vicious smirk, she made her dramatic exit.

"That can't be good," CeCe whispered, putting words to his own apprehension.

He'd not only poked the bear, he'd served himself on a silver platter.

Chapter Thirty-Eight

CECE

A FEW DAYS LATER, CeCe exited the café and stepped onto Main Street. The setting sun splashed a gilded palette of pinks and yellows across the shimmering sea. She loved this time of day, when evening approached, promising cooler breezes and quieter streets.

She smiled, recalling her stolen moments with Jayce—her *fiancé*—in the still hours of nightfall. They'd watched movies, made dinner together or simply talked, late into the early morning when the sleepy sun slipped back into the sky.

On her urging, they'd decided to wait until after Abby and Logan's wedding to share the news of their no-longer-fake engagement—apart from with their parents, who'd been ecstatic—not wanting to pull focus from their friends. Plus, after years of secretly pining after one another, there was something sweet about savoring the newness of their relationship in the serene, protective sphere of their silence.

However, she realized she'd only been able to keep the secret by avoiding her friends, secluding herself with the excuse of prepping for Abby's wedding—she'd be supplying assorted desserts in addition to the cake.

Tonight, her powers of restraint would be put to the test during Abby's bachelorette party. Hopefully, her friends would be too preoccupied celebrating Abby's upcoming nuptials to be suspicious of her secret.

Resolved to give her full attention to the night's festivities, not dwell on her own relationship or Gretchen's ugly threats, which had thus far proved hollow, she stepped into the lobby of East Street Cinema. Now defunct, the historic movie theater sat vacant except for the occasional special event.

To the right of the lobby, a large room with arched windows faced East State Street. Formerly a small eatery frequented by moviegoers before and after films, it now sat empty. For tonight's celebration, Nadia had cleaned and polished the long mahogany bar top that once served concessions. Now, it offered gourmet charcuterie boards, spritzers, and colorful mocktails, all in keeping with the night's elegant Audrey Hepburn theme.

CeCe added her contribution to the smorgasbord—a pastry box filled with flaky croissants à la *Breakfast at Tiffany's*—before joining the rest of the party in the main auditorium.

Abby, Nadia, Sage, and Mia all congregated at the front of the room, each clad in their favorite pajamas. CeCe smiled at their eclectic ensembles, from Nadia's two-piece set in crimson silk to Mia's rainbow-colored onesie with a unicorn head for a hood. She'd opted for her usual cotton shorts and oversize T-shirt, which thankfully hadn't drawn too much attention on her brief walk from the café.

"Wow, Mia," she breathed, admiring the run-down yet, somehow, still regal space. "You've really worked your magic. It looks beautiful."

Since the theater equipment was no longer in operation, Mia had rigged a portable projector that connected to her cell phone to stream the night's movie selection onto the big screen. She'd also hung twinkle lights strategically along the stage and arranged plush pillows and cozy blankets across the worn stadium-style seats.

"Thanks." Mia flipped on the projector and the opening credits for *Roman Holiday* rolled across the screen. "I can't believe the owner shut this place down. It's criminal."

"To be fair," Sage interjected, "with everyone streaming movies at home, the business wasn't very sustainable."

"Maybe," Mia conceded, "but it's still a shame to have it just sit here, unused, unless someone wants to rent it out for a random event once in a blue moon."

"What do you suggest they do with it?" Abby asked.

"I don't know," Mia admitted. "Reopen it as a historic landmark?"

"Sounds expensive," Nadia pointed out.

"Maybe Jayce would have an idea," CeCe offered. "He loves this place." As kids, they'd spent multiple nights a week in the theater, feeding Jayce's insatiable fascination with the film industry. He'd be sad to see it close its doors for good.

"Hang on." Mia narrowed her blue eyes into a scrutinizing squint. "Did something happen between you two?"

"What do you mean?" CeCe flushed, grateful no one could tell in the dim lighting.

"The way you said Jayce's name just now sounded different," Mia asserted, studying her closely.

"Don't be silly," CeCe deflected. *Great.* She hadn't counted on Mia's superhuman sleuthing skills.

Mia swiped the flashlight feature on her phone and aimed the beam directly in CeCe's face like a police interrogator. "Spill."

"There's nothing to spill." CeCe shielded her eyes from the bright light. "At least, not anything that can't wait." She darted a meaningful glance at Abby.

As if reading her mind, Abby said, "Don't hold back on my

account. Is Mia right? Did something happen between you and Jayce?"

CeCe waved a hand at Mia, who lowered her blinding cell phone. With all eyes on her, heat swept across CeCe's face. But so did a giddy smile. "Actually, yes." She held up her left hand, wiggling her ring finger.

Her friends stared blankly.

"I don't get it," Sage confessed. "We already know about your fake engagement."

"Wait!" Mia cried, grabbing CeCe's hand for a closer look. "This is a different ring!"

CeCe's grin widened. Mia really did have a gift for observation.

"A different ring?" Abby asked, wrinkling her brow. "What does that mean?"

"It means," CeCe said slowly, her heart fluttering. "That Jayce proposed for real. And I accepted."

Their shocked gasps and squeals echoed around the room.

Mia jumped up and down like a little kid on a pogo stick. Abby and Nadia cheered.

CeCe turned to Sage, her dearest friend in the group, and the one who knew her best, hoping she'd be happy with the news.

Her friend gazed at her with joyful tears in her pale green eyes. "I'm so thrilled for you both!" She drew CeCe into her arms, and whispered, "I've been praying for this."

Her throat suddenly tight, CeCe returned her hug.

"When did it happen?" Sage asked, taking a step back.

"A few days ago," CeCe admitted sheepishly.

"And you've waited this long to tell us!" Mia cried. "For shame!"

"We didn't want to draw attention from Abby and Logan's big day."

"That's sweet, but definitely not necessary," Abby said with a bright, genuine smile. "Your good news only adds to the celebration."

"Plus, now we can have a double wedding," Mia teased.

"Fine by me!" Abby beamed.

CeCe laughed, appreciating their enthusiasm. "I don't think we're quite ready for that. We still have a lot to figure out. Like, where we're going to live."

"Can't you live in Blessings Bay?" Sage asked hopefully, as if the thought of her friend moving hadn't occurred to her until now. "Jayce could take his private jet back and forth from LA."

"He prefers to use the jet sparingly, since it uses so much fuel." When she thought of his recent trip to South America, she still couldn't believe the lengths he'd gone to on her behalf.

"He could just buy a smaller plane," Mia pointed out. "Maybe he could even get a pilot's license and fly himself."

"We've only been engaged for a few days," CeCe reminded her with another laugh. "We have time to figure it out."

While her friends continued to plan their future, her phone pinged.

CeCe retrieved it from the side pocket of her shorts.

A Google alert she'd set for Jayce's name popped on the screen.

At the ominous headline, her heart sank.

"Hollywood Heartthrob in Hot Water."

"What's wrong?" Abby asked in response to her stricken expression.

"I—I don't know." She clicked on the headline and a video filled the small screen. Her blood instantly chilled. "It's an interview with Jayce's agent, Gretchen." *Former* agent, she mentally corrected.

"What's she saying?" Sage asked, straining to hear.

"Hang on." Mia grabbed CeCe's phone and plugged it into the projector.

Gretchen loomed above them, large and formidable.

CeCe shuddered.

"I knew something was off the second Jayce mentioned his engagement," Gretchen told the excessively preened male interviewer who wore way too much hair gel. "But I never thought he'd lie to me. Or to his fans."

CeCe gaped in horror. *What did she say?*

"That's why I had to let him go as a client," Gretchen continued as if she'd been forced to bear a heavy burden. "Difficult as it was, I can't work for someone who would maliciously mislead his fans for some tasteless publicity stunt."

"That's a lie!" CeCe blurted, indignation rising in her chest like molten lava. "Jayce fired *her*."

"It's sad, really," Gretchen waxed on with a simpering expression. "I know his last film didn't perform as well at the box office, but to stoop so low." She shook her head in feigned disbelief. "I've already heard from several directors who refuse to work with him again. Frankly, after pulling this fake engagement scam, I doubt he'll be cast in any films at all, let alone in a starring role."

"That witch," Mia hissed, glaring daggers at the screen.

CeCe forced herself to inhale, too outraged to breathe without concerted effort. The nerve of that woman to blame the whole debacle on Jayce when the sham relationship was originally her idea!

"How did you uncover the truth?" Hair Gel asked.

"Quite easily," Gretchen claimed. "To be honest, I don't know how Jayce expected to get away with such an egregious lie. In a small town like Blessings Bay, secrets don't stay hidden for long."

"Who do you think told her?" Abby asked.

"I have no idea," Mia growled, gritting her teeth in her fury. "But if Jayce fired her, she wouldn't go down without a fight. I bet she used plenty of underhanded, dishonest tactics to dig up whatever dirt she could find."

"And hit pay dirt," Nadia muttered, her expression pained. "Poor Jayce."

Poor Jayce. Nadia's words reverberated inside CeCe's head, loud and punishing. With today's cancel culture, Jayce stood to lose everything. His status in Hollywood, his career, and his reputation. And what about his screenplay? Had he really come so far only to be blacklisted?

"Are you okay?" Sage placed a gentle hand on CeCe's shoulder.

CeCe's eyes stung as she stared at the screen, watching helplessly as Gretchen continued to defame Jayce's name. "No," she whispered, unable to meet her friend's gaze. The friend who had every right to say *I told you so.*

Lies tend to cause more problems than they solve—those had been Sage's exact words. And they couldn't be more true.

"I'm so sorry, CeCe." Sage wrapped an arm around her shoulders, offering support.

"You heard it here first, in a prerecorded exclusive interview from earlier this morning," Hair Gel boasted, displaying a little too much glee at Jayce's professional demise. "Was La La Land's leading man caught in a web of lies? What exactly does the Hollywood Huckster have to say for himself? Let's find out."

Suddenly, Jayce appeared on-screen.

CeCe stiffened.

"We reached out to the A-lister for a comment, and he agreed to appear via live stream from an undisclosed location with a special message for our viewers."

As Jayce addressed Hair Gel with more grace and civility than the man deserved, CeCe tried to place his whereabouts. He was supposed to be at Logan's bachelor party. They'd planned to attend a classic car show with a Four Tops tribute band, then barbecue on the beach. It was hard to decipher his exact location since he appeared to be video-calling the interviewer from his cell phone, but from the sliver of sunset in the background, she guessed they'd made it to the beach already.

"What I did was wrong," Jayce acknowledged, his voice steady and sincere.

CeCe's chest squeezed. It hurt to watch him in the hot seat, exposed for the world to judge and condemn, but she couldn't look away.

"I made a bad judgment call when I was trying to help a friend," he admitted. "But the motive behind my actions doesn't excuse them. I shouldn't have lied. And I deserve whatever repercussions come my way."

CeCe wanted to jump into the screen, to stand by his side. Every fiber in her being longed to defend him from the harshness of cancel culture. Yes, he'd lied. They both had. And she wouldn't argue that they'd done the right thing. But did he really need to lose everything as a result?

"I also owe my fans an apology," Jayce continued, his words heartfelt. "Especially my younger fans who look to me as a role model. I value honesty and integrity. And I didn't exhibit either quality when I chose to fabricate a fake engagement with my best friend. That's why I think it's important to come clean and confess the whole truth."

He paused, and CeCe held her breath. What was he going to say?

"When I told the world that I loved and planned to marry CeCe Dupree, I'd only told a partial lie. We weren't really engaged, but I've been in love with her most of my life."

"Finally! I've been saying that for years!" Mia shouted at the screen as if he could hear her.

CeCe blushed as the rest of her friends swooned over his sweet response. Had Jayce just declared his love for her on national TV?

"It took a fake engagement for me to finally confront my true feelings," Jayce confessed. "CeCe is the most incredible woman I've ever known. She's kind, compassionate, and can bake a killer coconut cake."

At the unexpected compliment, CeCe laughed along with her friends.

"She's fun, supportive, and isn't afraid to give me a kick in the pants when I need it. And trust me, I need it—a lot." Jayce grinned, and for a moment, CeCe felt as if he were speaking to her alone.

She smiled up at the screen even though he couldn't see her.

"She's been my best friend from the time I learned to tie my shoes," Jayce said. "And as long as she's in my life, worries like whether or not I'll have a career tomorrow don't seem quite as consequential."

CeCe's chest swelled with a surge of affection. And also pride that he'd taken ownership of his actions with such maturity. While she hoped and prayed their poor judgment wouldn't end his career, she admired the way he'd handled himself in the aftermath.

"If there's a takeaway from my situation," Jayce told the camera, "I think it's this: Often, it isn't enough to merely avoid dishonesty. Sometimes, the hardest, most rewarding thing you can do is to tell the whole truth. Even when you're afraid."

When Hair Gel thanked Jayce for the live-streaming exclusive, his tone softened from one of exaggerated accusation to borderline respect. Jayce politely ended his video call, leaving the man to dissect the conversation and disseminate his overinflated opinion, which CeCe didn't find all that interesting. She unplugged her phone from the projector.

"Wow," Nadia breathed. "That was quite the emotional ride."

"No kidding," Sage agreed. "But Jayce handled himself admirably."

"He was a total prince," Mia lauded. "And Mr. Spray Tan and Gretchen the Ghoul can kick rocks."

CeCe smiled. She could always count on Mia to speak her mind. "Is it okay if I step outside to call Jayce for a minute?"

"Of course!" Abby assured her. "Please tell Jayce we support him one hundred percent."

"And I won't work for anyone who won't hire him," Mia added, which warmed CeCe's heart. Considering Mia's foley skills were highly coveted in the industry, her threat would carry some weight.

She thanked them before slipping outside. Jayce answered on the first ring.

"You saw it," he said in lieu of hello.

"If you mean your impromptu interview, then yes, I did. Are you okay?"

"I'm fine. Better than fine, actually."

"I don't believe you." His entire career had just imploded. How could he be fine?

"I wouldn't lie to you. I'm a reformed fibber, remember?" he teased, adding in a more serious tone, "But honestly, I'm okay. Humbled, but okay."

"What about the movie roles you lost? What if Gretchen was telling the truth about speaking to the directors? How will it affect your screenplay? What if you're blacklisted and no one in Hollywood will work with you anymore?" The words spilled out of her, unrestrained with worry.

"All valid questions, even if I lost track of them," he chuckled softly. Instead of answering, he asked, "Where are you right now?"

"Standing outside the theater. Why?"

"I'm a few minutes away. I'll be right there."

"What about the bachelor party?"

"The guys will understand. I need to see you." With his last words, his voice lowered to a thick and throaty murmur.

"I'll wait here." She hung up the phone, suddenly flushed.

After a few minutes, he appeared in the lamplight, striding purposely toward her. Her throat went dry. *You're being ridiculous*, she chided herself. *It's just Jayce.*

Except, there was no such thing as *just Jayce* anymore. He was *her* Jayce. Her fiancé. The man she'd soon promise to have and to hold, until death do them part.

He didn't stop his stride until he'd scooped her into his arms. Holding her close, he whispered, "I can't believe how hard it is to be apart, even for a second."

She melted against him. "I know the feeling."

"Don't be mad." He pulled back to meet her gaze. "But I told the guys about us. I know we said we'd wait but—"

She interrupted him with a laugh. "Don't worry. I couldn't keep it a secret, either."

"Phew! I was afraid I'd spend the first few days of our engagement in the doghouse."

"Not on my account," she said, then immediately sobered. "But Jayce, I'm really concerned. Do you think it's as bad as Gretchen makes it sound?"

"Maybe. You never know with Hollywood. Some scandals are career breakers. Others are career makers. Only time will tell. But either way, I'm glad the truth is out there. And there's at least one person in the industry who's willing to work with me."

"Who?"

"Victor Delance. He called right before you did."

"He's the producer who wanted to read your script, right?" Her pulse quickened with hope.

"That's the guy."

"Don't leave me in suspense! What did he say?"

"The call lasted all of five seconds, but he said, and I quote: 'Kid, I like your style. And your script. Let's make a movie.'"

"Jayce! That's fantastic!" Her heart swelled with happiness. Maybe things would work out okay after all.

"Thanks. I owe it all to you."

"Don't be ridiculous. I'm not the one who wrote the screenplay."

"Sure, but I wouldn't have written it without your tough love."

Love. A few days ago, hearing that word on Jayce's lips would've carried an entirely different context. But now, she knew it extended far beyond the confines of friendship. And it would only deepen over time.

"So, what's the next step?" she asked before she got too lost in her daydreams about the future.

"He wants me to meet him at his office Monday morning to go over the details."

"Oh." Her euphoric mood instantly plummeted. "You're going back to LA?"

"I have to. There's a ton of stuff to sort out."

"Sure. You're a bigshot screenwriter now." She attempted a smile, desperate to be happy for him regardless of what it meant for their fledgling relationship. She knew life wouldn't be easy, despite their engagement. It wasn't as if a ring would fix their geographical complications.

"Not a bigshot yet, but thanks for the vote of confidence." He grinned. "I was referring to all the packing I have to do. Plus, deciding what to do with my place in LA and where I'm going to live next."

"Wait." Hope shot through her like a lightning bolt. "Does that mean—?" She didn't dare finish her thought.

"What do you say, Future Mrs. Hunt? Want to go house shopping with me?"

"Here? In Blessings Bay?" Her heart nearly burst from excitement.

"I can write from anywhere. And there's no place I'd rather be than right here, with you." He looped his arms around her waist. "So, is that a yes to the house shopping? Or will Spock and I have to check out places on our own?"

She slid her arms around his neck, a smile on her lips. "It's a yes, *mi dawlin*. A million times yes."

Her sultry accent had the desired effect.

He claimed her mouth with his beneath the glittering marquis lights.

Not a platonic peck. Not playing pretend.

A deep, passionate, toe-curling kiss.

The kind of kiss that let her know, without a doubt, they were definitely, undeniably, irrefutably way more than friends.

Chapter Thirty-Nine

ABBY

ABBY STOOD before the full-length mirror in her bedroom, in awe of her reflection. And a little dazed. Before Logan, she never imagined she'd wear a wedding dress again, let alone one so close to perfection.

For her first wedding, Donnie's mother had talked her into choosing an extravagant ballgown with a sweetheart neckline, corseted bodice, and a full, flouncy skirt that rivaled Cinderella's. While she'd looked beautiful, she hadn't felt like herself.

This time, she wore a vintage tea-length dress with a fit and flare cut in the most gorgeous white silk satin. She gave the skirt a little swish, loving the way the lightweight fabric swirled around her bare legs.

"You belong on the cover of a bridal magazine," Nadia gushed.

"Maybe an issue printed in 1954," Abby countered with a good-natured grin, although she appreciated the compliment.

"You look stunning, dear," Verna murmured from over her shoulder. In the reflection, her motherly gaze glistened with unshed tears.

"If I look half as good as you did on your wedding day, I'm

happy." Abby turned to embrace her. "Thank you," she whispered, determined not to cry and smudge the makeup Nadia had meticulously applied.

"I couldn't be more pleased to pass along my dress to you, the daughter of my heart." Verna's voice quivered, and before they both broke down in tears, she cracked a smile. "Besides, the only thing from my wedding that might still fit is my veil. And maybe my shoes."

Abby laughed, grateful for the levity. She'd opted to go without a veil, leaving her hair in soft waves around her shoulders. And she'd nixed her shoes, too. She wanted to feel the warm sand beneath her feet as she walked down the aisle, connecting her to the place she'd quickly called home.

"Okay," Nadia said thoughtfully as she studied her wedding day checklist. "We have something old." She gestured to the dress with her ballpoint pen, then flashed a sheepish smile, adding, "Sorry, Verna. No offense."

"None taken, my dear. Although, I prefer the term vintage, like a fine cheddar cheese that gets sharper with age."

Abby suppressed another laugh. Considering Verna's orange-tinted curls, the comparison couldn't be more fitting.

"You're definitely sharp as a tack," Nadia told her sincerely before returning to her list. "Okay, next we need something new."

"This lipstick is new." Abby admired the petal-pink hue that made her lips look a little fuller.

"I have something better." With a conspiratorial smile, Nadia handed her a small box wrapped in pale gold paper.

"What's this?" Abby untied the cream-colored bow.

"It's from Logan." Nadia's dark eyes twinkled.

Eagerly, Abby tore away the paper and lifted the lid. Inside, she found a shimmering mother-of-pearl hair comb. "It's beautiful," she breathed, mesmerized by the way light danced off its iridescent sheen.

A pretty notecard nestled beneath the comb. Abby slid it from the box and read the printed front.

A gift for the woman full of motherly love and wisdom, who is both nurturing and strong, and reflects light to those around her.

Just beneath the artfully printed script, Logan had hand-written a single word.

Ditto.

Abby smiled. Her almost-husband: a man of few words but unlimited affection. Her heart soared at the thought of marrying him in mere minutes, muffling the melancholy thoughts of Max lurking just beneath the surface.

Nadia swept a few strands of Abby's hair away from her face, skillfully securing them in place with the comb. "Perfect. Something old, something new. Now you need something borrowed."

Abby studied her reflection, noting her lack of adornment apart from the comb and simple stud earrings. "I don't have anything borrowed." Technically, the dress didn't count, since Verna had insisted she keep it.

"Hold that thought." With a mischievous glint in her eyes, Nadia reached into her purse and withdrew a rectangular wooden box with intricate engravings. "I'd like you to borrow these." She flipped open the lid, revealing two gold bracelets dotted with dainty pearls and tiny, delicate bells.

"Nadia, they're gorgeous! Thank you!" Abby eagerly slipped one on her wrist, but Nadia smiled and shook her head.

"They're anklets. It's tradition in India for the bride to wear them when she walks down the aisle. The gentle tinkling sound represents the joy she brings into the marriage."

"Oh, that's lovely." Verna moved closer to admire their exquisite, graceful design.

Abby met Nadia's gaze, her throat cinching with emotion. "These are yours, for your wedding someday, aren't they?"

"Yes, but I want you to wear them first."

"I can't. They're too special." Abby placed the anklet back inside the box and passed it to Nadia.

"Please. It would mean so much to me if you'd wear them." Nadia set it back in Abby's hands. "I admire you so much, Abs. Watching you this past year, everything you've overcome, the way you've chosen joy in the midst of heartache, the way you and Logan have worked through so much together." Her voice hitched, and she gathered a breath before adding softly, "I hope to follow in your footsteps on my wedding day. Sharing these anklets would remind me to walk down the aisle with the same love, grace, and strength that you've always shown."

Abby caressed the smooth, polished wood, humbled by Nadia's words. Did her friend really see those attributes in her? She didn't always feel strong or joyful, but maybe she exuded more strength and joy than she realized?

Moved by her graciousness, Abby embraced her friend, hugging her fiercely. "I'd be honored to wear them. Thank you."

Carefully dabbing around her damp eyes with her fingertip, Abby sat on the edge of her bed while Nadia fastened the anklets. When she'd finished, Abby stretched out her legs and wiggled her bare feet, delighted by the delicate twinkling of bells.

"Now all you need is something blue," Verna pointed out.

"I actually have that one covered." Abby headed for her nightstand, the melodious anklets pleasantly accompanying her every movement.

Her fingertips grazed the small trinket box where she kept

Sam's sliver of sea glass, and her chest squeezed. The heartache over Max's absence spread over her, sharp and piercing. She closed her eyes, focusing on each breath.

In and out. In and out.

They hadn't heard a word from Sam since they left, and the silence had become more deafening each day. Eventually, she'd had to face facts: Max wasn't coming to the wedding, and she needed to make peace with that.

She opened her eyes and lifted the lid of the trinket box. At least she could hold a piece of Max with her, tucked into her bodice. Not glamorous, by any means, but it was the only way she could hold the sea glass close to her heart.

Abby gasped. Where was it?

She quickly scanned the scant contents. Her wedding band and engagement ring from Donnie. The key to Logan's grandmother's recipe box. A few keepsakes from her childhood.

But no aqua stone.

A small sob lodged in her throat, stifling her ability to breathe. Max's absence hurt badly enough, but now she'd lost the sea glass, too?

"Knock knock." Logan's clear, grounding voice called from the other side of her bedroom door.

Her heart leaped. They weren't supposed to see each other before the ceremony, but at that moment, she wanted nothing more than to feel the comforting strength of his presence.

"May I come in?" he asked, cracking open the door a few inches.

Nadia and Verna looked at Abby, who nodded.

"We'll give you two a minute." Verna gestured for Nadia to follow her out the French doors leading to the back garden, leaving Abby alone.

"Come in." Abby turned, her pulse racing as the door eased open.

The instant Logan stepped across the threshold and caught sight of her in her wedding dress, he stopped short. A spark of awe and adoration lit his eyes, his gaze both tender and intense.

Warmth swept through her body. Her cheeks flushed. Beneath his raw, approving gaze, she'd never felt more beautiful.

"Wow, you look incredible," he said when he'd finally found his voice.

"Thank you. You don't look half bad yourself." In truth, she nearly melted to the floor. The casual suit in a deep denim hue displayed his lean runner's physique to perfection and enhanced the blue of his eyes. Paired with a white cotton button-up, sans tie and shoes, he exuded laid-back sex appeal. *I can't believe I get to marry this gorgeous man.*

"I really want to kiss you," he murmured in a husky rasp.

"I think it's against the rules," she teased, her own voice equally breathy.

"I'm in a rule-breaking mood today." He stepped toward her, and she surrendered to his strong arms.

His kiss lasted several blissful seconds, soothing the ache in her heart.

When they finally parted, he confessed, "I knew once you walked down the aisle and didn't see Max standing next to me, you'd miss him all over again. I didn't want that moment to be the first time we saw each other today. I hope that's okay."

"It's more than okay," she told him, touched by his intuitive, compassionate heart. "I wouldn't want it any other way."

"Good." He grinned, then added, "Plus, I wanted to give you this." He reached into his trouser pocket and withdrew a long gold chain.

Her gaze fixed on the slender pendant of aqua sea glass, and a gasp escaped her lips. "How did you—?"

She couldn't finish her thought, too enraptured by the beauty of the necklace. A gleaming gold coil wrapped around the pale blue stone like a gilded embrace, securing it to the chain.

"I knew you wanted to keep the sea glass close by today, so I asked Sage to make it into a necklace for you. The gold wire around the stone can be undone, in case you don't like it."

"In case I don't like it?" Abby echoed in an incredulous whisper. "Logan, I love it. It's stunning."

He smiled, pleased by her reaction. "May I?" He undid the clasp.

Abby spun to face the mirror, her pulse fluttering as Logan fastened the pendant around her neck. It hung at heart level. She placed her palm over the smooth stone, pressing it close to her chest before turning back around to face him. "Thank you."

He cradled her face in his strong, steady hand, gazing deeply into her eyes. "I love you, Abigail. And I can't wait to marry you."

With a playful smile, she swayed onto her tiptoes and whispered, "Ditto," before stealing a kiss.

Chapter Forty

ABBY

ABBY DESCENDED the wooden staircase leading from the promenade to the beach below, the tiny bells tinkling at her ankles. As her bare foot left the last step and sunk into the silky sand, her heart stilled.

Her loved ones rose from their bamboo chairs and stood, facing her, but her gaze swept past them, immediately fixed on the man standing beneath the driftwood archway. The sun set behind him, painting the entire sky gold.

She tightened her grip on her bouquet. *This is it.*

Logan met her gaze, speaking the depth of his love in a single searing glance. A swell of affection rose in her chest, shortening her breath into tiny flutters. It took all her self-control not to sprint down the aisle and fling herself into his arms.

Slow, deliberate steps, she reminded herself as the Blessings Beats began their acoustic rendition of "All My Love" by the Four Tops. While the band harmonized about giving all their love for as long as they lived, Abby took her first step toward forever with the man who held her whole heart.

She locked eyes with Logan, not veering her sightline for a

second, especially not to the empty spot beside him where Max should be standing.

Attuned to her emotions, Logan guided her with his loving gaze, so steady and sure. With each stride, the sea glass gently jostled, tapping in tune with her heartbeat.

Max will always be with you. She held to the truth so tightly, she conjured Max's presence in her mind. She could hear his sweet, familiar voice shouting, "Abby! Wait for me!

"Wait! I'm here! I made it!" His shouts carried above the music, playing tricks on her.

She gave a short, sharp shake of her head, trying to dispel the distracting illusion, but at the look of shock and sheer joy on Logan's face, her heart lurched.

Was it possible—?

Barely daring to breathe, she spun around.

The music halted.

Max scamped across the sand toward her, a vision of pure bliss in a mini suit matching Logan's—the one she'd packed for him with hopeful optimism.

She flung her arms wide, laughing through her tears as Max nearly toppled her over with the force of his hug.

Beaming up at her, he said, "Dad said we could come. But then our car broke down and we had to take the bus. It stopped a bunch of times, but we made it. Isn't that great?"

Carefully dabbing her eyes, she nodded. "Really great." The words escaped in a breathy gasp, so small and inadequate, yet all she could manage amid her overwhelming emotions.

"I told Dad I'm the best man, so I gotta be there because I'm supposed to stand at the front next to Logan while you guys say your vows and stuff. And I have to hold on to the ring for him or he might lose it and then you guys can't get married."

Abby suppressed another mirthful laugh. Was that how Logan had explained his role?

Max stood tall, full of pride in his huge responsibility. She wasn't about to burst his bubble. Smiling, she gestured toward Logan and said, "You'd better get over there and get the ring, then."

Max skipped down the aisle toward Logan, who scooped him into a bear hug, his happiness splashed across his face.

Abby blinked back a fresh wave of tears. Just when she'd learned to let Max go, God answered her prayers. His timing couldn't be more mysterious, yet also perfect.

She glanced over her shoulder.

Sam stood near the bottom of the steps, watching from a distance, his hands shoved into the pockets of a too-large tan suit.

Her heart softened. He didn't have to be here. He didn't have to bring Max all this way, on a crowded bus, no less. Yet, he did. And she couldn't be more grateful.

"I'll be right back," she told the pastor and all the waiting wedding guests.

She met Logan's gaze, and he nodded in understanding, encouraging her to go. After handing her bouquet to Piper in the back row, she crossed the sand toward Sam.

"Sorry we're late," he said the moment she'd reached him, the depth of contrition in his eyes communicating remorse for so much more than his tardiness.

"I'm just happy you're here," she said sincerely. "Thank you for bringing Max back."

"I should have done it sooner," Sam admitted, digging his toe in the sand.

She sensed he had more to say, so she waited for him to continue.

Finally, Sam spoke, staring at the sand. "Max asked me to

pray with him before bed every night, just like you used to. And do you know what he prayed for, every time, without fail?" He lifted his gaze, his expression pained. "He prayed that we could all be together."

Abby's chest squeezed. Until recently, she'd beseeched the Lord with the same request. But Max, with his childlike faith, never gave up hope. Not on his father's return. And now, not on them.

"The other night, I finally faced the ugly reality," Sam confessed. "The only thing standing in the way of Max's prayer was me. My fears. My insecurities." His deep brown eyes glinted with raw humility. "It's hard to admit this as a grown man, but the truth is, I felt threatened by you and Logan. I was scared to start over as a father. And when I looked at you two—at how much you loved Max, and how much he loved you—I was afraid I couldn't compete."

A surge of empathy blazed through her, burning the back of her throat. How many times had she felt the same way, desperate to be all Max needed, knowing she could never fill his father's void? She wished she'd known Sam's concerns sooner, so she could've quickly dispelled them. "Max loves you more than anything in the world. He never stopped believing you'd come back for him." Her voice trembled, but she pushed through, adding with earnest conviction, "We never replaced you in his heart. He simply made room for us, too."

"I know that now." He smiled, soft and sincere. "That's why I've decided to move back to Blessings Bay."

She inhaled a sharp, shuddering breath, certain she'd misheard. "Y-you're coming back? To stay in the bungalow?"

"Actually, I called Iris. She's agreed to rent me her cottage again. I still need to find work, but I trust God'll sort that out, in His timing."

Without thinking, Abby threw her arms around his thin

shoulders. "Thank you, thank you! This is the most wonderful news." She felt as if her heart might burst with happiness.

Sam stood stiffly for a moment, then relaxed, returning her hug.

When Abby finally stepped back, he flushed, smiling shyly. "I'm not very good with people, Mrs. Preston, er, Mathews," he corrected, as if he just realized her last name was about to change. "But I'd like to get better."

"How about calling me Abby, for starters?" She grinned.

"I think I can handle that. Abby," he said a bit awkwardly.

"Come with me." She grabbed his hand and tugged him toward the stalled ceremony.

"I don't want to intrude."

"Nonsense. You're family now." She situated Sam beside Piper before leaning over to retrieve her bouquet.

As she straightened, she noticed Sam's gaze land on the sea glass dangling around her neck. His eyes sparked with recognition, and the corner of his mouth lifted.

They shared a knowing smile before she resumed her position at the end of the aisle.

By now, the sun had dipped below the horizon line, leaving the sky a dusky blue with streaks of pinks and purple. Candlelight flickered in the tall glass votives lining her pathway as she floated toward the altar where Logan and Max stood side by side, just as she'd hoped and prayed they would.

Above the music and rhythmic rumble of ocean waves, she heard the faint tinkling of the bells around her ankles—the melody of her own making—reminding her that through it all, joy and love could abound.

As long as she made room in her heart.

Epilogue

FLUSHED AND BREATHLESS, Mia deserted the dance floor as the lively rendition of "Thriller" transitioned to the slower tempo of "Stand By Me" by Ben E. King.

Recouping from her flawless execution of Michael Jackson's iconic choreography, she sipped a cool glass of water, watching starry-eyed couples sway and shuffle their feet, lost in their own little worlds.

Surprisingly, the award for the most besotted dance partners went to Jayce's parents, Richard and Karen. Like two hormonal teens at prom, they couldn't keep their hands off each other. It would've been gross if it wasn't so sweet.

"That could be you out there," her mother said wistfully, sneaking up behind her with another slice of wedding cake.

Mia wrinkled her nose as Karen shamelessly cupped her husband's backside with both hands. *Ew.* "No thanks."

"You're almost thirty, sweetheart. Don't you want to settle down and start a family like all of your friends?" Her mother tried to sound nonchalant as she licked lime glaze off her fork, but this wasn't the first time they'd had this conversation. And, not unlike herself, her mother didn't have the gift of subtlety.

Mia counted the couples on the makeshift dance floor—a section of hard-packed sand with twinkling lights stretched overhead. Newlyweds, Abby and Logan. CeCe and Jayce. Sage and Flynn. Nadia and Evan. Sage's mom, Dawn, and the kooky but fascinating billionaire recluse, Edwin. Even her own mother had found love again with Evan's dad, Michael—aka Big Mike, as she'd called him since childhood.

Did she want to join the Couples Club? Maybe someday. But not badly enough to lower her standards. She'd date if and when the right guy came along. "I'll get married and start popping out grandkids as soon as I meet someone remotely interesting."

Her mother sighed. "You're too picky. And you're too hasty to judge. I'm sure you could find gobs of interesting men if you gave them a chance."

Mia sipped her water. She'd given plenty of men a chance. Even second chances. But they were either a colossal bore or a superficial creep. The last guy she'd dated actually told her she'd be hotter if she didn't dress so weirdly.

She glanced at her flared cocktail dress with 3D silk flowers covering the skirt and bodice. She felt like a fairy princess. Not the most conventional wedding attire, for sure. But it made her smile. And it made other people smile. Was that so wrong?

"Sorry, Mom. You set the bar too high when you married Dad." Her father had filled the world with fun, laughter, and creativity. Plus, as a toy engineer, he always had some new, exciting gadget to show her.

Her mother's features softened. "I suppose I did. And while there could never be another man quite like your father, it doesn't mean there aren't plenty of good men out there."

"BonBon, are you pestering Mia about her love life again?" Big Mike handed her mother a glass of champagne to go with her cake.

She loved the way he called her mother BonBon instead of Bonnie. It couldn't be more fitting, considering her profession as a confectioner.

"You know she's too busy making all the sound effects for Hollywood's biggest movies to worry about babysitting a boyfriend." Big Mike tossed her a wink, and Mia smiled.

She'd always shared a special bond with Evan's dad. When her father passed away right before freshman year of high school, he'd taken on a larger role in her life, teaching her important skills like how to change a tire, surf a ten-foot wave, and barbecue the perfect steak.

"Don't encourage her, Mike," her mother huffed. "I'd like grandkids before we're all in diapers at the same time."

Big Mike laughed, deep and boisterous. You could tell a lot about a person from their laugh. And Big Mike's laugh matched his big heart.

"As much as I love discussing your future need for Depends," Mia teased. "I'm being summoned." She gestured toward her group of friends who'd left the dance floor and stood off to the side, chatting. In truth, they hadn't even glanced in her direction, but she needed an excuse to escape.

Before her mother could protest, Big Mike came to her rescue by asking her mother to dance.

Mia mouthed *Thank you* before rushing over to her friends. "Save me. Weddings make my mom crazy. If I'm not careful, she'll have me betrothed to some boring banker obsessed with birdwatching by the end of the night."

"We can't have that," Sage said with a laugh. "We were just telling Sam we need someone else to captain the Bookshop. Flynn and I can't keep up with the sailing tours on our own."

"Especially since we're adding Moby Dick–themed whale-watching tours this winter," Flynn added. "With Sam's sailing experience, he'd be a great fit. We're hoping he accepts our offer." He looked at Sam. "What d'ya say? Are you interested in being back at the helm?"

Mia held her breath, eager to hear his response. After his shipwreck experience, his answer could go either way.

"I think I am," Sam admitted. "Despite what happened, I still feel at home on the water."

"That's what I was hoping you'd say. Welcome aboard!" Flynn shook his hand. "Stop by the pier tomorrow morning and we'll discuss details."

Mia beamed, thrilled by how well everything was working out for everyone. Sam had decided to stay in town, and now he had a place to live and a way to pay the bills. Jayce had also opted to move back. He'd finally landed his dream girl *and* his dream job.

Since Evan had returned home a while ago, she was the only one in their trio heading back to Los Angeles. And now that all her friends would be here, in Blessings Bay, LA held little appeal apart from her job.

"Oh, hey," Jayce interrupted her musings. "I forgot to tell you. I spoke to the owner of East Street Cinema about buying and reopening the theater."

"And?" Her heart skipped in anticipation.

"Sadly, he was against the idea."

"What? Why?"

"I don't know. He wouldn't say. He just said under no circumstances would he allow it to reopen as a movie theater. He was strangely adamant about it."

Her hopes deflated. "Does Old Man Owens still own the place?"

"Yep. For almost fifty years now."

"Darn. He'll be a tough nut to crack." Mia frowned. "He's always been such a grouch."

"Maybe because you call him Old Man Owens," Sage

teased.

Mia brushed off her joke, too engrossed in her thoughts. She couldn't lose the theater. She'd practically grown up there. And after her dad died, it had become her haven. In a way, it had saved her. She needed to return the favor. "There has to be a way to change his mind and reopen it."

"Good luck," Jayce said. "I offered him a price way above market value and he still refused. Besides, he already hired an architect to redesign the space."

"Redesign? Into what?" She couldn't bear the idea of the beautiful, historic theater becoming something basic and boring. It needed to be restored, not redesigned.

"I don't know. But the architect arrives in a few weeks. Too bad you're heading back home tomorrow or you could ask him."

Mia sipped her water, mulling over her options. She wasn't currently working on any projects. Plus, she could technically work from anywhere. Did she have to rush home? "I guess it wouldn't hurt to stick around awhile."

"Great." Jayce grinned. "If anyone can convince George Owens to change his mind, you can."

"Thanks for the vote of confidence." But in case she couldn't, she needed a plan B. She needed to win over the architect. "Who's in charge of the redesign?"

"Some hotshot from San Francisco. Henry Sutton. He's famous for repurposing old buildings into modern utilitarian structures. Historical societies hate him. So think again if you plan to recruit him to Team Reopen the Cinema."

"We'll see. You know I love a challenge." She flashed an impish grin.

Henry Sutton won't even know what hit him.

· · ·

CAN MIA SAVE THE CINEMA? FIND OUT IN *THE UNINTENTIONAL TEAHOUSE*.

Letter From the Author

Dear Friend,

I decided to include this letter at the end of the novel to avoid spoilers.

Strangely, certain aspects of this series have coincided with my personal life in ways I never could have predicted. Partway through writing the first book—after I'd created the character of Max—we met a young girl in foster care. After fervent prayer, we dove headfirst into becoming certified foster parents and wholeheartedly welcomed her into our family, hoping to adopt.

Like Abby, I experience a surreal surge of maternal love for this child, far deeper than I could've imagined after such a short time together. And, also like Abby, I felt the gut-wrenching heartache of saying goodbye to a child I believed would be mine forever.

I can't fully describe the grief and confusion I felt when our story didn't unfold the way I'd hoped or expected. There are still days I struggle, dwelling on the many what-ifs. However, I can genuinely and gratefully say that I trust in God's sovereignty and rest in His goodness. And, like Abby, I steadfastly believe that every moment with our foster daughter was worth each tear we shed... and those we continue to shed even now.

While I was able to write a happy ending for Abby, Logan, and Max, our family's story isn't over yet. We continue to pray, hope, and love our foster daughter, with unwavering faith that God is still at work in our lives and hers.

In a way, it's been cathartic to write Abby's story, to grow and heal together. That's one of the things I appreciate most about literature—we find ourselves among the pages. We find others, too, experiencing their triumphs and tears alongside them. And we each take something different away from the story—a nugget of truth that's all our own.

I'm immensely thankful for the blessing and privilege to write these stories. And I pray the Lord uses them to bless others, despite my imperfect writing.

As always, thank you so much for reading. And if you ever have the time, I would love to hear from you. You can reach me at hello@rachaelbloome.com, 2945 Hwy 49 S, Mariposa, CA 95338, or in my private Facebook group, Rachael Bloome's Secret Garden Book Club.

Blessings & Blooms,

Rachael Bloome

Acknowledgments

Phew. We made it! Writing and publishing this book coincided with the birth of our second child, so crossing the finish line feels extra miraculous.

With this book, I need to thank all the usual suspects—each of whom deserves extra credit for patiently working around my wonky schedule, especially since our little man decided to arrive ten days early.

The MVP award goes to my husband for his daily love, support, and encouragement. Our family—particularly our moms—also deserve gold medals.

My eternal gratitude belongs to my incredible publication team: my critique partners, Dawn and Elizabeth (amazing writers and human beings); Ana Grigoriu-Voicu with Books-Design, for creating the most gorgeous covers; Krista Dapkey with KD Proofreading, for graciously extending my deadline; and Beth Attwood, for fitting me into her schedule at the last minute. These ladies are a powerhouse of talent, and I couldn't do this without them.

Heartfelt thanks to my wonderful ARC Team, who read this story on the shortest timeframe yet. You ladies are such a blessing!

Continued thanks to the truly amazing readers in the Secret Garden Book Club on Facebook, and to every reader on my newsletter. Getting to know you has been the highlight of this job.

And lastly, to every reader who has ever picked up one of my books—thank you! You make this career not only possible, but worthwhile. I will be forever grateful.

About the Author

Rachael Bloome is a *USA Today* bestselling author of contemporary romance and women's fiction novels featuring hope, healing, and the unbreakable bonds of found family.

Rachael is a hope*ful* romantic joyfully living in her very own love story. She's passionate about her faith, family, friends, and her French press. When she's not writing, helping to run the family coffee roasting business, or getting together with friends, she's busy planning their next big adventure.

Learn more about Rachael and her uplifting love stories at www.rachaelbloome.com and connect via the following social media sites (you can even listen to free audiobooks on her YouTube channel!):

CeCe's Toto Cake Recipe

Before writing *The Unexpected Inn*, I'd never heard of Toto cake, but I'm so happy I stumbled upon the dessert while doing research. It reminds me more of a breakfast bread like coffee cake—not too sweet, but a subtle, scrumptious flavor. I hope you enjoy this unique twist on the traditional recipe.

INGREDIENTS

For the cake:

- 2 cups all-purpose flour
- 1 ½ cups shredded coconut, lightly toasted (see step 1)
- ¾ cup packed dark brown sugar
- ½ cup coconut sugar (or light brown sugar)
- 1 teaspoon baking powder
- ½ teaspoon baking soda
- ½ teaspoon salt
- 1 teaspoon ground nutmeg
- 1 teaspoon ground cinnamon
- ½ teaspoon allspice
- ½ cup unsalted butter, browned and cooled (see step 2)
- 2 large eggs, room temperature
- 1 teaspoon vanilla extract
- 1 cup coconut milk, well stirred

For the toasted coconut topping:

- ½ cup coconut flakes (or shredded)

- ¼ cup brown sugar

- 2 tablespoons melted butter

- Pinch of salt

For the lime glaze (optional):

- 1 cup powdered sugar

- 2–3 tablespoons fresh lime juice

- 1 teaspoon finely grated lime zest

- Pinch of salt

INSTRUCTIONS

1. Toast the coconut: Spread 1 ½ cups shredded coconut on a baking sheet. Toast at 325°F (160°C) for 6–8 minutes, stirring once, until lightly golden and fragrant. Set aside to cool.

2. Brown the butter: In a small saucepan, melt ½ cup butter over medium heat. Cook, stirring occasionally, until golden brown with a nutty aroma (5–7 minutes). Immediately transfer to a bowl to cool.

3. Preheat the oven: Set oven to 350°F (175°C). Grease an 8x8-inch square pan or 9-inch round pan with butter.

4. Mix dry ingredients: In a large bowl, whisk flour, toasted coconut, brown sugar, coconut sugar, baking powder, baking soda, salt, nutmeg, cinnamon, and allspice.

5. Combine wet ingredients: In another bowl, beat eggs, then whisk in cooled browned butter, and vanilla extract.

6. Combine all ingredients: Stir the wet mixture into the dry ingredients, alternating with coconut milk, until just combined. The batter will be thick.

7. Prepare the topping: In a small bowl, mix ½ cup shredded coconut (or flakes), brown sugar, melted butter, and a pinch of salt until sandy. Sprinkle evenly over the batter.

8. Bake: Pour batter into the prepared pan. Smooth the top, then sprinkle the topping evenly. Bake for 50–60 minutes, until golden brown and a toothpick inserted in the center comes out clean. If the topping browns too quickly, cover with tin foil for the final 10–20 minutes.

9. Cool & glaze (optional): Let cake cool in the pan for 10 minutes, then transfer to a wire rack.

For glaze: Whisk powdered sugar, lime juice, lime zest, and a pinch of salt until smooth. Drizzle over cooled cake, allowing it to seep into the crunchy topping.

Notes & Storing

• Stores well in an airtight container for up to 4 days; flavor improves the next day.

• I made this recipe with both conventional store-bought butter and a higher quality Amish butter. I found the flavor to be richer with the higher quality butter, but it can be made with any butter you choose.

Book Club Questions

1. Which character did you identify with the most? And why?

2. Which storyline did you find the most compelling? And why?

3. CeCe and her father suffer from a strained, distant relationship. Who do you think is most to blame? How could they have handled things differently?

4. At what point in the novel did you suspect Sam was Max's father? Did the details of his return play out the way you'd expected? If not, how did they differ?

5. In Jayce's screenplay, he writes that real love casts out fear. What does this statement mean to you?

6. CeCe ponders how far is too far to go for a friend. Has a friend ever asked for a favor that opposed your moral beliefs? How did you respond?

7. For years, Jayce didn't pursue a romantic relationship with CeCe in part to preserve their friendship. Do you think there are circumstances where his rationale is valid? Or is it always best to confess your true feelings for someone?

8. When their fake engagement is exposed, CeCe fears dire consequences for Jayce's career. What consequences, if any, do you think he deserved? In today's society, do you think he'd face backlash for his dishonesty?

9. Sage tells CeCe that lies tend to cause more problems than they solve. Do you believe her statement is true? Are there ever circumstances that justify lying? Or is honesty always the best policy?

10. Jayce wonders if more people regret the things they said or the things they didn't say. Which do you think is true?

11. Abby tells CeCe that healing isn't always about erasing the sadness, it's about learning to let the joy back in. Do you agree with this statement? Why or why not?

12. What themes did you notice in the novel?

As always, I look forward to hearing your thoughts on the story. You can email your responses (or ask your own questions) at hello@ rachaelbloome.com or post them in my private Facebook group, Rachael Bloome's Secret Garden Book Club.

Rachael Bloome

STORIES WITH HEART & HOPE

POPPY CREEK SERIES

The Clause in Christmas

The Truth in Tiramisu

The Secret in Sandcastles

The Meaning in Mistletoe

The Faith in Flowers

The Whisper in Wind

The Hope in Hot Chocolate

The Promise in Poppies

A Very Barrie Christmas

BLESSINGS BAY SERIES

Blessings on State Street

The Unexpected Inn

The Unbound Bookshop

The Uncomplicated Café

The Unintentional Teahouse

STANDALONE NOVELS

New York, New Year, New You

Printed in Dunstable, United Kingdom

67964235R00153